OGRE HUNT

OGRE HUNT
THE ORIGINS STORY OF MONSTERS™ BOOK ONE

MARTHA CARR
MICHAEL ANDERLE

This book is a work of fiction. All of the characters, organizations, and events portrayed in this novel are either products of the author's imagination or are used fictitiously. Sometimes both.

Copyright © 2023 LMBPN Publishing
Cover Art by Jake @ J Caleb Design
http://jcalebdesign.com / jcalebdesign@gmail.com
Cover copyright © LMBPN Publishing
A Michael Anderle Production

LMBPN Publishing supports the right to free expression and the value of copyright. The purpose of copyright is to encourage writers and artists to produce the creative works that enrich our culture.

The distribution of this book without permission is a theft of the author's intellectual property. If you would like permission to use material from the book (other than for review purposes), please contact support@lmbpn.com. Thank you for your support of the author's rights.

LMBPN Publishing
PMB 196, 2540 South Maryland Pkwy
Las Vegas, NV 89109

Version 1.01, February 2023
ebook ISBN: 979-8-88541-160-8
Print ISBN: 979-8-88878-120-3

THE OGRE HUNT TEAM

Thanks to our Beta Readers
Mary Morris, Malyssa Brannon, David Laughlin

Thanks to our JIT Readers

Christopher Gilliard
Wendy L. Bonell
Diane L. Smith
Peter Manis
Dave Hicks
Jeff Goode
Jackey Hankard-Brodie
Jan Hunnicutt
Dorothy Lloyd

Editor

SkyFyre Editing Team

CHAPTER ONE

Off the Coast of Newfoundland, 953 A.D.

Brother Amdi gritted his teeth against the violent rocking of the drekar longship. By all rights, he shouldn't have been here. His wrists were bound roughly behind his back, and his gut lurched in agony with every rise and fall of the cresting waves. Blood already stained his cassock through.

He didn't have much time. That was perfectly clear. His fellow monks had even less.

All Brother Amdi had to do was hold on a little longer. To wait for his chance to do what the entire monastery had been trying to achieve.

I am the only one to survive. The responsibility falls to me.

The longship's deck echoed with raucous laughter as the *thump* and drag of heavy weights scraped across the wood. Brother Amdi lifted his head. Two massive Vikings hauled the fallen, lifeless bodies of their two other prisoners toward the portside rail of the ship.

All these men were huge, battle-scarred, and heartily

provisioned for the homeward journey after plundering the monastery in Denmark. Most of them were tattooed. None seemed the least remorseful that two of their three captured monks had expired less than halfway through their journey.

Brother Amdi couldn't look away as the Vikings unceremoniously tossed the bodies overboard.

"No room for these ones in low storage, eh?" The Viking with a huge gut of solid muscle turned away from the rail and dusted off his hands, chuckling.

"Not unless you want to give up your own rations, Algeyr!"

Another round of blistering laughter rose from over two dozen men moving about the deck. Some trimmed the sails while others hauled great armloads of plundered loot into one massive pile toward the stern where Brother Amdi lay propped against the center mast.

"Trade your rations with the monk's," another man shouted.

The Viking who'd cracked the original heartless jest glanced at Brother Amdi and sniggered. "Not a fair trade. This one's more likely to meet his end before Drengr opens the next barrel."

More laughter followed, but the amusement died down as the crew steadfastly returned to their work. The ship was never willing to let anyone's attention slip for long.

They still had a long way to sail back to wherever they'd come from. Even with the drekar's long, slender build slicing across the waters of the Labrador Sea with staggering speed, now that the sails had been fully turned into the brisk winds.

Brother Amdi bowed his head, which wasn't difficult to do with his strength so quickly leaving him. He sent up a silent prayer for the souls of his brothers lost to the sea.

"Don't look so aggrieved, monk." The Viking who'd been ordered to stand watch over Brother Amdi since they'd set sail stood four feet from the monk and the pile of stolen treasure. He glanced at Brother Amdi with a raised eyebrow, then nodded out to sea. "Your men got what they wanted, after all."

"Oh?" Brother Amdi coughed, his gut raging with pain from the stroke of a Viking blade that had buried its teeth into his flesh. A dribble of blood escaped the corner of his mouth. It bubbled as he drew in a ragged breath. "What do you know of what they wanted?"

"To join your one god, eh? Or does meeting their end on a Viking ship prevent your people from reaching their final resting place?"

The monk had no reply to that. Perhaps Brother Langsom and Brother Thermund had come to believe in the Christian god through their work in the monastery. Many of the other monks had, merely by default. However, Brother Amdi knew the difference between centuries of studious devotion and the ultimate purpose for which his monastery had stood.

With great effort, he shifted his weight to the side and craned his neck to peer into the clear skies over the sea.

In the early evening of the day that would most likely be his last, the sun still hung high in the sky.

We are close to the peak now. The Summer Solstice is at its height, and here I am in the center of it all. Only a little longer...

He had to keep this Viking guard beside him interested.

Perhaps even willing to listen to a few stories, the most important of which would reveal itself as the only truth Brother Amdi had ever known. As long as he lived long enough to fulfill it.

"Your tribe is powerful," he muttered.

The guard shot him another sidelong glance. "What does a monk know of power?"

"Not much." Brother Amdi coughed again, and another gurgle of blood rattled through his chest. "My brothers never stood a chance. We both know this."

"None of you fought back."

"It is not...our way. Even if we had, your tribe would still have taken everything."

The Viking chuckled. "From a village of men who never learned how to fight? Of course."

"We are—" Brother Amdi grimaced at a flare of debilitating pain as he tried to readjust his position against the center mast. "We are artisans. Our strength lies in the recording of knowledge."

"Knowledge did not save you from the sword, monk."

"No. Yet history has a way of protecting us from past mistakes."

It had been a long shot, of course. Still, that one statement seemed to stoke the guard's interest. Brother Amdi nodded toward the haphazard sprawl of plunder around his feet.

"What mistakes would a monk not wish to repeat if he spends his life hiding away behind walls and scrolls?"

"Not my own." The monk sucked in a searing breath and risked a quick look at his overseer. The guard raised an eyebrow, and Brother Amdi took his chances with the

Viking's patience, hoping it would be long. "Have you heard the story of the elemental humans and their blood human rivals?"

The Viking snorted. "We take your treasures, monk. Not your stories."

"Ah, but when stories are all we have, those may be the greatest treasures yet."

A deep frown darkened the guard's brow, then he folded his arms and nodded. "I'll be the judge of that."

Good. He's interested. Please let me live long enough for the rest.

Brother Amdi grunted against his pain. "Long ago, two tribes from my homeland possessed powers that may have rivaled even the strength of Vikings. Elemental humans wielded control over earth, fire, water, and air. Blood humans were known to force new shapes onto the creatures of the land."

The Viking clicked his tongue. "Death delivers a different shape as well, monk."

"No, I do not mean death. This was the creation of monsters. Imagine a frog swelling and taking the form of a beastlike man."

A low chuckle escaped Brother Amdi's guard. "This power does not sound useful."

"Oh, it was. For sowing war." The monk spat a glob of blood onto the deck, though most of it dribbled down his chin to join the rest soaking his cassock. "These tribes battled for ages until the elementals had enough. They wished to end the devastation. In a moment of final retribution, they discovered how to do this."

The Viking gazed out across the sea. While he remained silent, Brother Amdi noticed the man's thoughtful frown.

He wants more. Give him more before he ends you.

"The most powerful of the elemental tribe gathered to stand against the matriarch of the blood humans. They imprisoned her in a silver coffin and buried her in the coldest waters of the sea. The Circle of Creation. Elemental magic was strong enough in this nexus of both tribes' power to keep the matriarch at bay, dreaming for ten thousand years. When that was finished, the elementals covered the world in ice and snow and deadly cold."

"To rule the world without their enemies, ah?"

"No." Brother Amdi leaned his head back against the mast and closed his eyes. "Such a surge of power to end the war killed most of the elemental tribe. The survivors fled south in diminished numbers, thinking their duty fulfilled in their attempt to save humans from the warring tribes. The age of ice brought peace to the land, but the blood humans have not forgotten the betrayal. Or their queen buried in the depth of the ocean's heart."

The Viking chuckled. "And you believe this history of mistakes?"

"Yes." The monk peeled open one heavy eyelid to glance at his captor. "My brothers and I come from the last few remaining blood humans."

"Ha!" The man slapped a hand against his thigh and pointed at his prisoner. "You tell a fine tale, monk. It will not save you."

He thinks it is a lie. They all do. As long as it keeps them dull until they witness the truth.

Brother Amdi glanced at the sky again, gauging how far

they'd come since setting sail and how much farther the drekar had to go until it reached the perfect place within the sea.

Not long.

His Viking guard squatted beside the pile of stolen treasure to rifle through the trinkets. He lifted a silver goblet and turned to smirk at the monk. "Such treasure kept by men who do not use it, eh?"

"We gathered and cared for some valuable items, yes." Brother Amdi slowly slid his gaze to a battered, worn scroll, rolled up and tied with twine. "The most precious of what you've taken today lies in that scroll."

With a gruff laugh, the guard unburied the aforementioned scroll from the piles. Rolls of cloth and a scatter of coins fell away as he lifted the parchment and shook it at the monk. "*This* is precious to you?"

"Not the physical scroll. The recorded knowledge within." The monk swallowed thickly. "See for yourself."

Smirking at the whole ordeal, the Viking jerked off the twine to unravel the scroll. "Your stories amuse me, monk. Perhaps this is the value of your people." His smirk faded when he fully unraveled the parchment and studied it with a deepening frown. "What is this?"

"The truth."

"This is nothing." The guard flicked a finger against the scroll, making Brother Amdi wince. "I had traveled half the world before I was twenty years on this earth, monk. I recognize languages you cannot fathom from where you've been hiding away inside stone walls. This is no language."

"It is." Brother Amdi nodded.

"Then tell me what it says." The man shuffled toward

the monk, still lowered into a crouch, and held the fully unrolled scroll before him. "If you have such knowledge, prove it."

For the first time since seeing the Viking tribe rip through the monastery with their impressive strength, their whistling swords, and their complete lack of fear, Brother Amdi cracked a small smile. It was only a flicker at the corner of his mouth, all he could manage beneath the pain consuming his body and the rattling in his chest that came with every breath. Yet it was genuine.

He glanced one more time at the sky and envisioned their location within the sea. It was then he felt the nexus of magic wash across the deck of the drekar, unnoticed by the warring Viking tribe stealing his people's treasures back to their home.

Now. Finally.

"As you wish." Brother Amdi took one final glance at the Viking's scowl, then turned his attention to the scroll.

Of course, it was no language the man or his tribe had ever seen before. The words had been lost to the human race for centuries, but Brother Amdi had spent his life studying and mastering the text. Like the others of the remaining blood human tribe before him.

His lips moved quickly as he read the incantation buried beneath millennia of history, waiting and hoping for the right moment to seize power once more.

As he read aloud, a cold, thick fog rolled across the waters like an oncoming storm. The light was blotted from the sky as the fog rose to the top of the highest sails, concealing the waters from these seafaring warriors journeying home.

Beyond the longship covered in mist, the Labrador Sea churned. Great, breaking bubbles rose to the surface, growing larger and rippling across the otherwise calm waves. The longship rocked violently above the watery chaos. Huge, thick vines of ancient seaweed rose from the ocean floor, unfurling across the tumultuous surface like a clenched fist slowly opening its many-fingered hand.

When Brother Amdi reached the end of the incantation, the waters stilled. The fog parted as swiftly as it had enclosed around the Viking drekar. The deck fell silent as over two dozen warriors gazed in awe and trepidation around them, wondering why the sea had acted this way for the first time in all their years of voyaging.

The Viking holding the scroll before the monk shuddered and tossed the parchment onto the pile of loot. "This weather makes as much sense as your story, monk."

Brother Amdi nodded as his energy seeped from him. "My people never learned to navigate the waters like yours. We had need, yes, but no power over the seas. However, we did learn the value of patience. Centuries of it."

The guard snorted and rose to his feet. "Your wounds have made you mad."

"Yet they have brought me here."

"Kapitan!" The cry rose from a Viking by the starboard rail. "Something in the water!"

Men left their stations to crowd around the one who'd shouted, trying to see what had caused the alert.

A long, slender rectangle of bright silver bobbed on the surface of the water, held up by a network of seaweed and vines spreading across the ocean as far as the eye could see.

The kapitan, a fiercely tattooed Viking with his head

shaved on either side of a thick braid and missing his left ear, stomped across the deck to have a look for himself. "It seems someone lost their spoils at sea."

The crew chuckled.

"Bring it in," the kapitan ordered. "See what has been so generously left for us."

CHAPTER TWO

The thump and slide of oars lowered into the water filled the air as the Viking crew chopped their way through the seaweed toward the floating silver box. Four men leaned precariously over the starboard rail at the bow and reached toward the box with fishing hooks on long wooden poles to drag the mound of seaweed toward them. The metal box thumped against the hull.

"Pull it up," the kapitan barked.

Men heaved and grunted as they struggled to lug the heavy treasure over the side of the longship. It landed with a *thud* and sent a warning tremble through the deck.

Brother Amdi had stopped paying attention to the Vikings. Instead, he stared at the sky, now awash with the golden-orange rays of sunset.

It is time.

A pained grin dripping with blood crossed his haggard features, followed by a deep, relieved sigh.

The guard who'd listened to the monk's story turned

and studied Brother Amdi with a frown. "You wish to meet your brothers and your god now, yes?"

The monk's eyes rolled back in his head. "The prophecy is at its end. My part is finished."

The guard scowled and cast longing glances at the silver box on the deck, knowing he would be punished if he left his post beside the dying monk. He sidled closer to Brother Amdi. "What did you say?"

"You and your tribe did your part," the monk mumbled. "You have brought me here to the Circle of Creation to fulfill the final piece of the prophecy. Now, I have done mine. Thank you."

The guard still couldn't take his gaze from the silver box in the center of the deck. "For what?"

"For hunting us down, Viking. It was the only way…"

Finally, the man looked down at the monk and noticed the vacant glaze in Brother Amdi's eyes, the pallor in the man's face, and the rapid rise and fall of his chest. "You look unwell, monk."

The guard, whose name was Rólfr, lowered into a squat. He reached toward the back of his belt to remove the satchel of herbs he kept on him at all times. "This may at least relieve the pain of your passing. Not all Vikings are heartless heathens. The exceptions may be few, but…"

Rólfr paused with a handful of pain-numbing herbs pinched between his fingers when he saw the monk's dead eyes staring up at the darkening sky.

The brain-addled man had finally died of his wounds. And by the gods, the monk had *thanked* him for taking him prisoner.

The Viking sighed and returned the herbs to the pouch,

strung it through his belt again, then reached out to gently close the monk's eyes. "I am sorry you met your end this way. Go in peace to whatever afterlife you seek."

"Get it open, men!" the kapitan roared.

The shimmering silver box somehow hadn't quite lost its sheen despite the last of the day's light fading from the sky. The four men prying open the lid finally got enough leverage to pop the seal of this watery treasure. A round of excited, curious cheers rose from the crew.

Once the lid slid off the top and clanged to the deck, a deathly silence washed over the longship.

Rólfr immediately stood. He turned from the dead monk and the monastery's claimed treasures. "What is it?"

He didn't have to ask the question, and none of the men had cause to answer. Rólfr could see for himself. It was perfectly clear why no one on board could bring themselves to speak.

That was no treasure in the silver box. At least, not the kind these Vikings had expected.

Inside, an olive-skinned woman lay on a bed of plain, undyed fabric. Her long, dark hair was arranged around her shoulders, neatly falling across the red tunic she wore. Of course, her eyes were closed. This had to be some type of funerary vessel, but Rólfr couldn't understand how the woman had been so perfectly preserved.

"They imprisoned her in a silver coffin and buried her in the coldest waters of the sea," the monk had said.

Rólfr swallowed thickly. He glanced at the incomprehensible scroll he'd tossed aside, then at the dead monk propped against the center mast, then at the darkening sky above them.

Ten thousand years. Impossible.

Another shudder trailed down his back. Rólfr was not the sort to give in to some weak artisan monk's superstitions. Or anyone's. He'd seen the world. He'd conquered so much with his tribe under his kapitan's command. All he'd known and seen with his own eyes proved the monk's tale had been merely that. A tale and nothing more.

Until the woman lying in the still-dripping silver box gasped.

The men standing around her stepped back, muttering disbelieving curses and shoving those behind them back toward the sides of the deck.

The woman's bright-green eyes flew open as her back arched. The motion forced the woman's chest up and out of the coffin as if she were being hauled by the front of her tunic. Her mouth gaped as far as it would go, and when she released the breath she'd sucked in, it came out as a bloodcurdling scream.

Rólfr recognized everything within the sound. This was no scream of terror or pain. The sound split through his head with only rage and the desire for vengeance. It was a sound he'd made before in his younger years. One he had heard from others of his tribe who'd lost more than they'd imagined possible.

Ten thousand years spent dreaming of revenge...

Rólfr's mouth dropped open in horror when wave after pulsing wave of shimmering, translucent energy burst from the screaming woman lying in that box. The force of each devastating ripple violently rocked the drekar on the still waters and the bed of seaweed on which the Viking crew had stranded themselves.

The rest of the crew backed farther away, but there was nowhere left to go other than to throw themselves overboard. None of them would admit to it, but they all wanted to.

They didn't have time.

Two of the closest men who'd helped pry the lid from that ancient coffin screamed and grunted, doubling over beneath the force of the magic spraying from the woman's millennia-long resting place. Sick, wet crunches split the air as they roared in agony. Their shoulders and backs popped and cracked in violent jerks before their bodies bulged against their leather vests and ripped clean through. One of them fell to the deck, writhing in agony, then instantly rose to all fours and let out a blood-chilling howl.

Because he was now more beast than man. A wolf on two legs, fur rippling across his previously bare chest and arms as four-inch claws extended from fingers curved in pain and rage.

Then the rest of the crew was ripped from their startled horror as they shifted into new shapes of their own.

The kapitan's flesh rippled and lost all its sun-kissed color, paling to a deathly white as his eyes glowed red and two wickedly sharp fangs sprouted from his upper jaw. With a monstrous hiss, he launched himself at the closest crewmember, whose shoulders bulged into hulking masses of gray-hued muscle studded with warts. They grappled with each other on the deck, snarling and bellowing.

All the monsters from Brother Amdi's tall tale were being created in front of Rólfr's eyes. Werewolves, vampires, ogres, goblins, trolls, and orcs.

The lookout who'd heralded the discovery of the

ancient coffin let out a piercing scream as his head split into six pieces. Each of them elongated, stretching out to complete the form of the six-headed Scylla before his wormlike body thumped across the deck, seeking blood and flesh to fill each of his mouths lined with razor-sharp teeth.

One Viking doubled in size, his newly sprouted hooves pawing at the deck as his head became that of a horned bull with glowing red eyes. His bovine nostrils spewed black smoke as he snorted and bellowed into the night sky. A minotaur on the deck of the drekar.

Another became a curving lump of humanoid shape made of clay. A golem came to life as it took on the dreams of the woman who'd created it. Each transformation sowed more chaos as the crewmembers took monstrous forms and entered the fray for no reason other than they'd been commanded to do so.

Rólfr stumbled sideways when dozens of angry hisses came from his right. A fellow Viking, now unrecognizable, snarled at him as dozens of snakes attached to the gorgon's head coiled to strike.

They were all changed. Every man aboard this ship had taken another form, and all traces of humanity had disappeared from their hearts.

The creation of monsters. Exactly as the monk said.

Rólfr's heart pounded furiously in his chest as he dove beneath the swing of an orc's meaty fist and hurtled through the chaos toward the silver coffin. He had to close it. He had to stop the mad, undead witch's magic before everything was overrun—

A final pulse of energy erupted from the coffin and

hurtled across the deck until it pounded through Rólfr's chest.

It stopped him dead in his tracks, ripping through his limbs and drowning all thought of who he'd been, who he was, and what made him not only Viking but human. The sound of his own bones breaking and rearranging inside him deafened him to the battle on deck. Agony ripped through his very pores, then Rólfr didn't think anything at all.

He was gone.

In his place stood a massive, snarling silverback alpha werewolf, eyes flashing between silver and red as he charged toward the coffin.

With a bellow, he lifted the lid from the deck and slammed it haphazardly back onto the coffin. It wasn't on straight, and the alpha found himself transfixed for a moment as one devastating claw rested on the lid. The blood witch's wide green eyes stared into his.

He growled and shoved the lid fully back into place. His claws screeched against the metal surface and left a trail of shredded marks in its wake. Then he hauled the sealed metal box toward the starboard rail. It took only the alpha's renewed and terrifying strength to get his claws beneath the box and fling it overboard.

The box hit the water with a *smack* and a hollow *thunk* before the island of ancient seaweed reclaimed the cursed tomb and dragged it beneath the waves once more.

The battle raged behind the silverback alpha, but he paid it no heed. Instead, he staggered to the prow as the longship caught the currents that would eventually pull it to shore.

As the moon of the Summer Solstice lit up the deadly waters of the Labrador Sea, the alpha threw his head back and let out a long, mournful, vengeful howl.

It almost rivaled the scream from the blood human matriarch.

Yet It was nothing compared to the centuries of punishment the alpha and what remained of his crew would endure beneath the curse no one but a dying, bloodied monk had seen coming.

CHAPTER THREE

<u>Cliffs of Moher, Ireland, Present Day</u>

Halsey Ambrosius clapped her hands together and tore down a funnel of howling wind from the clear night sky. Her elemental magic instantly responded to her command and launched itself toward the dozen werewolves racing across the open ground toward her.

The full moon reflected specks of yellow and silver in the monsters' eyes as they darted forward on all fours. They raced toward the two young fighters holding their ground between the farmland beyond and the edge of the cliffs.

Halsey's attack caught the closest werewolf in a hurtling spiral of buffeting wind and sent the beast flying backward. It crashed into one of its fellow monsters and sent them both tumbling away with snarling yelps.

Her cousin Brigham stood beside her with a smirk, his cowboy boots planted firmly in the sparse grasses along the cliff. "Now you're trying to show off."

Halsey glanced at him. "You're the one standing there

with a fireball in your hand. I'm just wondering when you're going to actually use—"

He launched the fireball at the closest werewolf streaking toward them. The flames hit the monster's shoulder, and it reeled backward. The attack only caught for a moment before the beast fell and rolled across the ground, inadvertently putting out the fire that would otherwise have consumed it. The scent of burning hair and slightly charred meat filled the air, and the werewolf snarled at the smoking wound on its fur-covered arm.

"Now you can stop wondering and keep fighting, huh?" Brigham flicked the lighter in his other hand and conjured the single flame into another churning ball of fire.

"I've *been* fighting. They keep coming."

Behind them, the ocean waves crashed against the rocks beneath the moon. The spray lifted high, peppering the air with saltwater and the smell of fishy brine. Halsey called on the foamy mist and drew the water from the ocean into another funneling spear to aim at the werewolves. Her cousin launched fireball after fireball, fueled by his constantly sparking lighter.

"They shouldn't," he observed through gritted teeth. "I thought they sent us out here to keep things under wraps. Not to fight off an army."

Their family, the Ambrosius Clan, had been responsible for keeping these monsters in line and out of human knowledge for generations. Despite their lineage in the monster militia and all the battles they'd engaged in around the world, something was different tonight.

With her watery attack finally powered up enough to use,

Halsey launched the churning spear of seawater at a werewolf covered in red fur. It struck the creature's neck, crushing his larynx, and the monster dropped. Instantly, his werewolf form faded and left a bruised, motionless man with an unruly red beard and tangled red hair lying naked on the cliff.

"Why now?"

The cousins skirted the edge of the cliff and noticed another contingent of wolves coming from the north.

Brigham *tsked*. "They're getting ballsy." He shot two more fireballs in quick succession. "What's next, huh? Ogres racing out of caves to smash up villages?"

His next flick of the lighter produced nothing but a tired spark. Out of fluid. Halsey rolled her eyes and pulled another spiraling windstorm from the sky. When it touched the ground where the werewolves converged, the monsters leapt aside to avoid the impact.

Brigham pocketed the empty lighter and reached out with both hands toward the spray of dirt and ripped-up grass from his cousin's last attack. His elemental magic worked as well on the earth and the power beneath it, although he preferred fire. He morphed the crushed ground into shards of thick, bullet-like projectiles and tossed them at the oncoming beasts.

"There better not be any ogres after this," Halsey added as she raced forward with her cousin to take the fight to the oncoming werewolf horde. It gave them more space to move without being cornered at the cliff's edge above the ocean's raging waters. "I need a vacation."

Her cousin laughed and sent a rippling wave of power through the ground toward the closest werewolves, sending them flying like bowling pins. "We're in Ireland, cuz. You don't reckon that counts as a vacation?"

She snorted and used the broken land Brigham had disrupted to pepper another werewolf running toward them as it split from the unlikely pack. When he leapt for the cousins, a massive boulder caught him in the chest. He crashed down with a yelp.

"I mean somewhere warm, Brigham." Halsey thrust her hand into the air and drew a low-hanging cloud toward her, morphing it into an icy spearhead that caught another werewolf through the thigh.

"Home's warm enough."

"It's not a vacation if I go back to Texas and stay there. The Clan'll think I've got too much time on my hands."

"You do if you take a vacation."

"Don't you think we've both earned one by now?"

"With all these werewolves spilling out of the shadows where they don't belong? Sure." Brigham pulled a new lighter from his pocket and flicked it to draw another fireball into his hand. "We ain't done 'til they're back where they came from."

The flames illuminated his face before he ignited the lighter a second time, doubled the size of his raging fireball, and sent a column of churning flames spiraling into the oncoming horde.

Halsey wiped the sweat from her brow despite the chill in the air and shook her head. "If Aunt Gracelyn heard you talking like that…"

"You can leave my mama out of this." Brigham chuckled and sparked the lighter again. "She's back home, snug as a bug."

I should be somewhere warm and by the ocean, with a drink in my hand and no monsters in sight. This is getting ridiculous.

As Halsey reached with her magic toward the energy of the ocean to draw more firepower, a blood-curdling howl filled the air.

The werewolves barreling toward them skidded to a halt on all fours. Every one of them turned their jagged noses to the air and looked over their shoulders for the source of the call.

"Aw, really?" Brigham heaved a dejected sigh. "Don't tell me there's more coming."

"Brigham, look." Having abandoned her pull on the seawater, Halsey pointed toward a mountain peak north of them, where a mist of fog had cleared.

The cousins had a clear view under the full moon of a massive alpha werewolf standing upright. His face lifted to the sky as he howled again and again.

With snarls and obedient yelps, the werewolves turned tail and raced back toward the single mountain peak.

"There." Brigham jammed the fresh lighter into his pocket and dusted off his hands. "Looks like we scared them off."

"Really?" Halsey narrowed her eyes at the massive alpha in the moonlight, directly where the rest were headed in their inexplicable retreat. "They were *called* back."

"Come on. You can't be serious. Werewolves aren't *called* to anything. They're mindless beasts."

"Yeah, but…" Halsey cocked her head as the lone alpha turned. Before he returned to all fours, she caught the glimmer of moonlight on the silver fur of his hunched back, then he was gone too. "Everything about this mission is strange."

"Cuz, if you don't already think monsters are strange enough, maybe you should take that vacation. Get your wits about you again."

She playfully socked him in the shoulder, and he chuckled.

They waited another minute to be sure the attack was over.

The werewolves had completely retreated.

Not because they realized they'd bitten off more than they could chew. Halsey frowned at the mountain. *That silverback alpha's been giving orders.*

"All right. That's over and done with." Brigham turned and pointed at the naked redheaded man sprawled on the grass. "Reckon we should clean up where we can, right?"

"Right." With another dubious glance at the moonlit flatland of sparse grasses along the cliffs and the illuminated mountaintop with no sign of movement or the silverback alpha, Halsey followed her cousin toward the body and the chewed-up ground, the only evidence of their fight here.

CHAPTER FOUR

Among many things the Ambrosius Clan's monster militia had drilled into them since they were children was the importance of not leaving any evidence behind. Naked dead men who'd met their end as werewolves in a battle with two elemental humans would absolutely cause the locals to question what had happened here tonight.

Or any of the other frequent and mildly exhausting nights when Halsey and Brigham had been sent out to various parts of the world over the last two months.

"You don't think there's something else going on here?" she asked as they approached the body.

"I think we did our job." Brigham studied the dead man, then gazed out over the cliff. "I also think it's a good thing we're on the water now, don't you?"

"What?"

"Care to help me with the old heave-ho?" He jerked his thumb over his shoulder toward the edge of the cliff.

Halsey sighed. "Fine."

She reached out, calling for the energy of the buried

roots beneath the salt-dried grasses. The ground trembled, and a dozen strong brown roots burst from the earth to obey the elemental magic summoning them.

Halsey concentrated as she directed the vines to wrap around the dead man's body, tying him up with nature's provided tools. Beside her, Brigham pulled more stones from the earth. The cousins' magic worked together to wrap up the evidence and weigh it down to ensure the dead werewolf didn't bob back up to the surface somewhere else along the coast.

More than anything, this was to keep the human world from asking questions. To keep them ignorant of the battles the Ambrosius Clan's family operatives waged with monsters in the darkness of night, when the creatures of human nightmares came out to wreak havoc.

When it was finished, they glanced at each other and shared a grim nod.

This wasn't the first time the cousins had carried a body between them, and it certainly wouldn't be the last.

It's about to get a lot more frequent if these monsters keep acting against their usual MO like this.

Halsey grabbed the redheaded man's still-warm ankles as her cousin took the wrists. She gave herself a moment to look at the dead man's throat crushed by her own magic.

I wish we didn't have to kill them just to get the others to turn back.

The cousins half-carried, half-slid the body across the grass toward the cliff. Brigham grunted, cleared his throat, and nodded. "On three."

They lifted the man and swung him side-to-side like a hammock.

"One. Two. *Three!*"

The werewolf's body sailed over the edge of the cliff and plummeted to the dark, churning waters below as another massive wave crashed against the deadly rocks. There was no sound of a body hitting the water over the roar of the ocean. Halsey and Brigham peered over the edge to be sure their handiwork had accomplished its job.

Halsey expected to see the body disappear. What she didn't expect was a massive carpet of seaweed floating on the surface of the water below, illuminated by the moonlight and stretching as far as she could see.

No, it wasn't only floating there.

The seaweed rippled like a giant creature in its own right, wrapping itself around the bound body to drag it under as if receiving a gift.

She frowned and scanned the water for signs of other monsters beneath the waves they might have to deal with. There were as many hiding in the depths of the sea as in the dark shadows of mountains, forests, and caves on land.

Below on the thin strip of sandy shoreline, about half a mile north of where they crouched on the cliff, something silver and metallic glinted beneath the full moon. "No."

"Yes." Brigham straightened and dusted off his jeans. "He's gone."

She hardly heard her cousin as she stared at the gleaming metal, half-hidden by strands of the same watery kelp that had carried the dead werewolf from view. "It's impossible."

"You feeling okay?" Her cousin looked at her with a raised eyebrow. "We both know this isn't the first time you—"

"I'm not talking about the body. I'm talking about *that*."

Brigham followed his cousin's pointing finger up the line of the cliff to the glint of metal beneath the night sky, and his eyes widened. "What is it?"

Halsey swallowed thickly and leapt to her feet. "Come on. We have to be sure."

"Of *what*? Hey, nobody's gonna find that body. Why are you so..." He sighed as his cousin raced along the side of the cliff, occasionally peering over the edge to gauge the distance. Brigham rolled his eyes and muttered, "Here we go," before sprinting after her.

The waves crashed against the cliffs with a deafening roar despite the bed of seaweed bobbing and stretching toward the strip of shoreline.

"Hey! If you found another monster, cuz, I reckon we should call it in—"

"Don't tell me you've already forgotten the legend," Halsey shouted over her shoulder.

"What legend?"

"The great war, Brigham. Come on. The elementals raging against the blood humans. The ancient ones who captured the blood human matriarch and buried her in a silver coffin in the ocean before covering the world in ice to hide our ways."

"Well, you call it a legend, but I tend to agree with the scientists. The Ice Age was a natural part of Earth's evolutionary—"

Halsey spun to face her cousin. Brigham stumbled to a halt as loose pebbles and a few larger stones skittered beneath his feet to topple over the edge of the cliff. "Oh, yeah? And what do the *scientists* say about people like us who can bend the elements to their will? What do they say about werewolves and gorgons? Trolls and vampires, huh?"

Brigham bit his lower lip and frowned. "Well, if human scientists knew anything *about* us..."

Halsey rolled her eyes, spun again, and continued her path along the cliff, searching for a safe way down to the shoreline. "You know what I'm talking about. Science doesn't explain the origin of monsters. The legend does."

"Halsey, no one even knows if the legend is true." Brigham hurried after her. "You know how history works. It's a bunch of stories passed down over hundreds of years. Even in *our* family. Sure, we have magic and fight monsters, but that doesn't mean what they told us as kids is the real deal. Anyone who was actually *there* before the Ice Age sure isn't around anymore to tell us what's real and what's a load of—"

"Found it." Halsey's wide eyes glimmered with a mix of hopeful expectation and apprehension. "Watch your step."

"Huh?"

She disappeared over the edge of the cliff and scrambled down the sloping decline as loose earth gave way to sand crumbling beneath her boots. Halsey could only focus on the silver box below her, which still shimmered despite the new fog rolling in from the sea and occasionally blotting out the full moon. She heard Brigham struggling down the slippery slope behind her, but she couldn't stop approaching the inexplicable treasure washed ashore.

Inexplicable only if the legend is a load of crap like Brigham thinks. But if it's true, if it all really happened...

Halsey caught her breath and slowly approached the

silver box. Her cousin joined her, and they stopped two feet from the silver coffin.

The lid had been pulled off and rested in the wet sand beside the empty tomb the Ambrosius cousins' ancestors had forged and buried in the ocean. A line of staggeringly long claw marks slashed across the top of the lid.

"Whoa." Brigham puffed out a breath and ran a hand through his hair. "Those look like werewolf claws to you?"

"Yeah…" Halsey took another step toward the coffin. Her eyes widened with horror as she gazed at the plain, undyed fabric lining the inside of the box. "This is it."

"An empty box?" Brigham kicked a patch of seaweed off his cowboy boot and snorted. "Halsey, this isn't—"

"What day is it?"

"Huh? Um…Tuesday."

"No, the day of the year." She turned toward her cousin, then glanced at the full moon hanging high in the sky. "It's the night of the—"

"Summer Solstice," Brigham whispered as realization dawned on his features. He slowly looked down at the empty coffin in the sand.

"Then it's true. All of it." Halsey swallowed. "The Mother of Monsters has returned."

"She left again in a hurry, wouldn't you say?" Brigham's uneasy chuckle fell flat.

Halsey gripped her cousin's forearm and turned to look him in the eye. "The war Meemaw told us about has already started. Right here. Right now."

He frowned. "Then we need to call home and tell everyone—"

Another piercing howl split the air. The cousins turned

toward the cliff and the sound echoing across the water with blood-chilling clarity.

High on that same peak, the silverback alpha lifted his grizzled face to howl at the moon suspended over the glistening waters of an unforgiving sea.

CHAPTER FIVE

<u>Lufton, Texas, Present Day</u>

Before the shiny black SUV came to a stop in front of the massive mansion on the outskirts of Lufton, Texas, Halsey Ambrosius had the rear passenger door open and was already hopping out. Her sneakers hit the pavement with a squeaking scuff, and she completely forgot to thank the driver and shut the door behind her.

The driver glanced out the front passenger window to see the twenty-three-year-old booking it toward the wide front steps of the house, then looked in the rearview mirror. "Rough mission?"

Still in the back seat, Halsey's cousin Brigham Ambrosius ran a hand through his auburn hair and sighed. "Something like that. Thanks for the lift, Connor. As always."

"Well, it *is* my job," the driver replied with a chuckle. "And my pleasure, as always. Don't worry about the luggage. I've got it."

"Thanks." Gritting his teeth, Brigham scooted across

the back seat to dart out of his cousin's still-open door. He closed it quickly without slamming it, then took off after her. "Halsey."

"We already talked about this," she called over her shoulder as she reached the front stoop at the top of the circular stairs.

"Uh...not really." He broke into a light jog and jumped the steps three at a time to join her. "You told me what *you* were gonna do, and I couldn't get a word in edgewise before you jumped out of a moving vehicle."

"The car was basically stopped." Halsey scoffed, grabbed the massive iron doorknocker shaped into a hammer and anvil, and slammed it three times against the thick wood. The knocker's clamorous echo bounced off the immaculately paved driveway and the two small marble fountains on either side of the stairs. She dropped the knocker as she sighed and glanced aside at Brigham. "You know we need to tell the Council about this. Like now."

"Sure." Brigham shrugged, stuffed his hands into his jeans pockets, and stared at the enormous door. "I'm not sure barging in like this and calling a meeting while we're still fresh from a mission is the best way to do it, though."

"You want me to take this potentially world-changing information and...what? Wait to see if something really terrible happens, so we'll have proof?"

"You know how the Council feels about doing anything without proof."

"I have all the proof we need right here." Shooting him a pert look, she patted the back pocket of her jeans where she kept her cell phone.

The sound of the SUV's trunk closing echoed across the

courtyard. Connor trudged toward them, carrying the cousins' small, practical luggage that got them through mission after mission.

Before the driver had gotten halfway up the stairs, Halsey's limited amount of patience ran out.

"This is ridiculous." She rolled her eyes and grabbed the front door's enormous iron handle. She had to squeeze with both hands to engage it. A low, hollow *thunk* rose from inside, and she shoved the door inward with her shoulder

Brigham's eyes widened at his cousin's complete disregard for safeguards and protocols. "Really? You can't even wait for Marilyn to answer the door?"

"We're not strangers, Brigham. Come on." Halsey stormed into the foyer, her voice echoing with clarity among the marble floors, immensely high ceilings, well-oiled wooden accents, long tables, and tall, arched windows lining both sides of the front door. "They know we're coming back. And no, I *don't* feel like waiting. This is important."

His shoulders sagged as he watched her take off across the foyer, then he stepped out of the way to let Connor through with their luggage. "You know what the Council's gonna say to that, right?" he called to Halsey.

"If I say yes, will it keep you from lecturing me the rest of the way there?"

Brigham ignored her sarcasm and hurried after her. Rather than the militia's debriefing room in the east wing, she was headed directly toward the back of the mansion. "Order, Hal. Protocol. Cold, hard evidence. *That's* what's important to them. Charging through the mansion like this without any of those isn't a recipe for being heard."

"They'll hear me." Halsey darted around an old suit of armor at the end of the narrow hallway behind the mansion's grand central staircase, then turned left to keep heading toward the back. "They don't have a choice."

"Not when you come home storming in like a crazy person…"

"We can't ignore what we saw out there, Brigham. There's no way to spin it as a trick of the light, our imaginations running wild, or taking one too many hits to the head."

Brigham frowned as he turned the corner after her. "*I* didn't take any hits to the head out there. Did you?"

"No. That's my point." The soles of her sneakers squeaked across the marble floors, but she wasn't slowing down. "We're completely in our right minds. You know it, I know it, and the Council knows it. Otherwise, they wouldn't have sent us out to Ireland in the first place."

"Yeah, and they're gonna end up seriously questioning that decision if you go through with this," he muttered, not sure whether he wanted her to hear or not.

Halsey didn't care either way. At this point, nothing would stop her from presenting the disturbing information they'd discovered more or less accidentally, including the Council itself. Which was exactly why she was handling it this way.

After another sharp right turn down the labyrinthine corridors in the back half of the mansion, she slowed as the double doors to the Council room came into view. When she was a little girl, those doors filled her with wonder and fascination. The thick, dark red wood had been oiled so meticulously for so many years that sometimes when the sunlight spilled through the hall skylights at the right angle, the doors looked like they'd been set on fire.

The finest silver detailing lined the doors from floor to ceiling, as if someone had painted vines, leaves, stars, moons, suns, mountains, and trees with the smallest paintbrush in existence. Few people in the world could claim as much skill and precision with metalworking as the Ambrosius Clan, and even fewer could have accurately pinpointed the source of their skills.

Being a family of alchemist elementals came with its perks, of course.

And its secrets.

Those doors still filled Halsey with wonder and fascination, but now it was tinged with frustrated urgency she couldn't ignore. *They'll believe me. They have to. This is why we're here, why we do what we do. If the Council can't see that...*

She pushed the thought aside and continued. The corridor felt long and ominous, even with daylight streaming in through the tilted windows, and she finally responded to her cousin to distract herself.

"We're the best team they have, Brigham. Nobody questions sending us out."

"Correction." He lifted a finger for emphasis as he followed her, even though he knew she wouldn't turn to look at him. "They haven't questioned sending us out *together* since the time I saved your ass from that troll three years ago."

Halsey laughed. "You didn't save me. I knew the troll

was under the bridge where it belonged. Which was why I climbed down after it."

"Yet you still needed your bigger, stronger, older cousin to fire off a few shots and pull you out of the river."

She stopped in front of the double doors and slowly turned with a smirk. "First of all, those shots weren't remotely necessary. Second, I *had* the troll. You're the one who got spooked by a little fire."

Brigham grinned, his hazel eyes the same color as hers wide and glinting in the sunlight spilling through the windows. Eye color was one of the few physical traits the cousins shared. "When it's not coming from me? You're damn right."

"And third..." Halsey faced the doors, rolled her shoulders back, and lifted her chin. "You're only two months older than me. Unless you have any points that hold up under even a *little* scrutiny, please stop trying to stall me."

She reached for the door handles crafted into thick, twisted vines ending in broad leaves wreathed in flames. Before her fingers closed around the cold silver, Brigham grabbed her upper arm with enough pressure to make her pause.

When she turned her head to meet his gaze, all traces of her cousin's good humor and carefree nature were gone. Brigham wore a concerned frown, though his eyes still glinted.

"Come on, Hal," he implored, his hand still clamped around her arm. "Let's think about this, huh? Get our story straight—"

"Our story *is* straight. You were right there with me. You saw the exact same thing."

"I'm not talking about the story of our mission. I mean the way we're gonna tell the Council, or even *if* it's a good idea to tell them right now. Hell, we can skip the debriefing room altogether. Go grab a few beers or something instead. Maybe take some time to settle into being back in the States. One less thing for them to blame when you can say you've had enough time to recover from the jetlag, right?"

Halsey raised an eyebrow and covered the back of his hand with her own. "This isn't jetlag, and you know it." She loosened his grip on her arm and brushed his hand away. "This is a serious issue. What we saw at the base of those cliffs could change *everything* about who we are, what we do, and what we're fighting for."

"Halsey..."

"I know you're only trying to protect me." She turned back toward the doors. "But the biggest danger to the Ambrosius Clan right now, maybe even the entire world, is *not* standing up and saying something about it."

Brigham grimaced as the heavy iron handles groaned beneath the weight of his cousin's hands.

Halsey shoved both doors, letting them swing open fully under their immense weight, and stepped inside. "You can stand next to me as my partner while I tell them, or you can stay here and watch from the sidelines. Either way, I'm not backing down from this."

Brigham wrinkled his nose as she confidently strode across the gigantic circular Council room toward the low, round table in the center. "Of course you're not backing down," he muttered, this time so she couldn't hear him. "That's not who you are, but they're not gonna see that as a good thing the way I do."

Halsey wasn't wrong, though. She and Brigham made one of the best monster militia teams the Ambrosius Clan had these days. They might have even been the best team in the history of their family's legacy if Halsey's "eccentricities" could be overlooked. When it came to the Council, though, they usually weren't.

Brigham looked over his shoulder, but of course, the hallway behind him was empty. That didn't make him feel any better.

"Damn it." He took off after his cousin, pausing only to nudge the double doors shut. He rushed across the Council room to reach her in time. "Wait a second to sound the alarm, huh?"

She turned away from the table with its depressed slot in the center and frowned at him. "Why?"

"Because you have seaweed in your hair." Brigham smirked as Halsey combed her fingers through her long, dark-brown hair that passed for black in the right lighting. She'd never find it like that. "It's in the back. No, not… Here." He grabbed the long piece of mostly dried plant matter from his cousin's dark locks and held it out.

Halsey's mouth popped open. "You let me spend the last thirteen hours with seaweed on the back of my head?"

He shrugged, let the seaweed dangle from his fingers, then called up a touch of magic to manipulate its structural makeup. The seaweed strand grew rigid, then crumbled to dust. "This is the first time you've slowed down enough for me to notice, cuz."

She shot him a deadpan stare. "We spent nine hours

together on an international flight and another two hours in traffic on the drive home. Not to mention everywhere we were before we left Dublin."

Brigham dusted the invisible remains of the destroyed seaweed off his hands and failed to look apologetic. "Hey, at least I noticed it before you called the entire Council here. They'd use it as one more reason not to take you seriously."

"My hero." Her flat tone made them both snigger.

"Let the unofficial record show that I'm still seriously against this," he mumbled.

"Noted. We're doing it anyway."

Halsey stepped beside the round table and stopped in front of a tall copper pole mounted in a heavy base. Anyone who didn't know the Ambrosius Clan or the real purpose of this room would have assumed it was merely a place to mount the Clan's banner. The flag drooping from the top of the pole depicted a silver blacksmith's hammer crossing a silver sunburst across a background of deep, rich brown. Yet it was only for show.

A family of alchemists who specialized in manipulating or changing the chemical structure of metals to suit their needs couldn't help designing everything with a dual purpose.

Halsey wrapped her hand around the copper pole and studied the intricate decorative work one of her long-dead elemental ancestors had crafted along the length of it.

'We're the best at what we do, and we look damn good doing it.' If the Council cared about adopting new mottos, that would be it. Still, a motto is gonna be the last thing on their minds when I tell them what we're facing now.

CHAPTER SIX

Halsey pressed her lips together, tightened her grip on the pole, and pulled it from the base with one swift jerk. The crisp *ring* of metal sliding against metal filled the massive Council room with a fading echo, and the tip of the pole glinted in the light spilling through the floor-to-ceiling windows in the back.

"There's still time to change your mind," Brigham grumbled as he stared at the rich brown fabric fluttering from the pole.

Halsey frowned in disapproval. "Pick a side, cuz."

Brigham scrunched his nose. "Can't I choose my *own* side?"

"No." Taking care not to bang the pole against her leg or the edge of the table, Halsey walked slowly toward the front and leaned forward. The slit in the table's center was lined with the same copper the pole was made from, which added to the effectiveness of the hidden mechanism her family was so proud of.

Why we can't adapt to the times and start using group texts is beyond me, but whatever.

The decision whether the Clan would adapt their current protocols to the modern world or drop outdated standard procedures was made by the Council anyway. Creating new rules from scratch based solely on the latest advancements had been out of the question for as long as Halsey could remember.

Today, she was about to change that, or at least attempt to.

I have to try. They have to listen. Otherwise...

The thought of what might be at stake if the Council refused to credit her report almost made her shiver. She swallowed the sensation, raised the pole in one hand, and jammed the intricately designed tip into the copper-coated slot.

Once again, the echo of sliding metal filled the Council room. This time, it was joined by a thick metallic *clunk*. Halsey gripped the pole with both hands now and put her shoulders into it as she turned the pole. The small, segmented hole in the table spun half an inch clockwise. Another heavy clunk filled the room, followed by a series of faster, lighter clicks that radiated away from the round table like rubber balls bouncing across the floor.

Only there weren't any rubber balls to be seen.

The mechanisms her ancestors had built hundreds of years ago beneath the floors of the Council moved swiftly and delicately the way they were designed. Gears turned over and over, catching on their neighbors and creating a ripple effect of spinning cogs and shifting machinery made to reach their destinations. Not necessarily in record time, but efficiently enough that the process couldn't be stopped once it had begun.

Most of that had to do with the machinery being built into the foundation of the room. None of it was visible from where Halsey and Brigham stood, but they heard everything with crystal clarity, and that was the point.

She might as well have dumped a bucketful of rubber balls onto the table and let them bounce. That was as much control as Halsey had over what happened next.

They'll see it like we did. When I tell them everything, when I show them, they won't be able to ignore what's happening.

In fact, she was so convinced the Ambrosius Council would see her reasoning, value her report, and launch into action after this meeting was over that Brigham's reaction confused her. She had no idea why her cousin stood there like a statue, grimacing as he stared at the colossal circular stained-glass window on the back wall of the room. The golden glow of the hour before sunset spilled through, illuminating the scene depicted there in nearly every color imaginable.

Halsey turned to study the window with him and wrinkled her nose.

It's not that *impressive. We're not here because of a story playing out in a bunch of colored glass...*

"Hey." She elbowed her cousin and leaned forward to be heard over the constant clicking and low rumbling of the activated machinery that sounded the alarm for an emergency Ambrosius Council meeting. Brigham raised his eyebrows and glanced sideways before returning his gaze to the window. "Do you think you could at least *look* like you want to be standing here with me?" she asked.

"I don't," he replied from the corner of his mouth. "I thought I made that clear when I followed you through the mansion and gave you a dozen different reasons to sit on this a little longer."

"Nobody's forcing you to stand here with me. I won't hold it against you if you go take a seat right now."

He shook his head a fraction of an inch. "You know I'm not gonna do that."

"Well, thanks." She turned toward him, examined his stance, and snorted. "Maybe go with less 'bound and gagged and forced into this' and more 'I've got my cousin's back 'cause we're partners,' huh?"

Brigham laughed, then drew his hands from his pockets and folded his arms instead. "Like this?"

"I mean, it *does* still give the impression that you're not happy about this—"

"I'm *not* happy about it, Hal."

"But at least now you look like you're standing in your own conviction. That's an improvement." She jokingly punched him in the shoulder a split second before the rumbling, clicking, and moving halted. The final nail in the coffin arrived in the form of a resounding *boom* like a judge's gavel coming down.

The silence filling the circular chamber was more startling than the noise. Now all they had to do was wait.

For Halsey, that was the worst part.

Brigham scanned the seven elevated Council seats spaced evenly around the perimeter of the room. He leaned toward Halsey and lowered his voice in the stark silence. "No matter what happens, try to stay calm, okay?"

She scowled. "I can do calm."

"I know you *can*. It's whether or not you *do*."

"If this is supposed to be a pep talk, cuz, you're failing miserably."

He clicked his tongue and slowly shook his head. "I don't want them to have any more ammo to use against you, all right? That's all. Especially after the last time you called a Council meeting—"

"Last time was totally different," she whispered harshly. Even after lowering her voice, her words still echoed harshly around the chamber. "Also, you promised you wouldn't bring it up again, especially during high-tension situations."

"Oh, you mean like when we're standing in the middle of the Council room waiting for the whole family to make an appearance and tell you *the same thing*?"

Halsey set her jaw and found that *she* was staring at the stained-glass window. "Sounds like you still haven't made up your mind about standing with me on this."

"Hey, I'm right here." Brigham spread his arms. "From where I'm standing, it's not the craziest thing in the world to be worried about you. Honestly, Hal, what you're about to tell them *does* sound nuts. You know that, right?"

She reached for her back pocket to reassure herself with the solid weight of her cell phone. "We have proof. When the shipment finally gets here, nobody will be able to tell me I'm blowing things out of proportion. They'll all see it for themselves."

"Okay. Yeah. Just…you know."

"What?" She spun toward him. "What do I know?"

Brigham lifted his hands in concession. "How you get when things…take a turn."

"Oh, yeah? How did I *get* when we stood at the edge of those cliffs, fighting back the biggest pack of werewolves either of us has ever seen? Bigger than anything *anyone* in this Clan has seen before? Did I end up embarrassing you then, too?"

"I'm not embarrassed."

"So this is what your *confidence* looks like." Halsey snorted. "Forgive me, but I'm finding it uninspired right now."

Brigham folded his arms again and shook his head.

When the expectant silence settled back over the Council room, Halsey regretted the way she'd spoken to her cousin. She knew he was on her side. Brigham had *always* been on her side. She was the only child of Aidan and Gilliam Ambrosius, so her cousin was also the closest thing Halsey had to a sibling.

He's only trying to look out for me. I get that. Except he's better at having my back out in the field than in this room.

Still, Halsey wasn't exactly cut out for politics and militia-wide leadership, either. She was a monster hunter, plain and simple. An operative in the monster militia that had been organized, owned, staffed, and controlled by Ambrosius Clan members for longer than anyone could remember. Their family and their purpose extended further back in history than even the oldest of the Clan's records preserved in the mansion's extensive library.

That didn't make her decision any less important. Right now, the entire Clan faced something a lot more dangerous than the monsters they'd been fighting, pushing back, and keeping out of normal-human discovery for generations. She was about to show them all.

As soon as the damn Council decided to answer the call and show up.

Halsey gritted her teeth and scanned the empty Council seats like her cousin had. She tilted her head, listening for the sound of more mechanisms activating within the walls of the mansion. After twenty seconds of absolutely nothing, she growled in frustration and spun toward the entrance to the Council room. That wasn't the problem, either. Brigham had closed the doors behind them. She should have realized he'd remembered. Calling a Council meeting didn't work if every detail of the room and its occupants wasn't perfectly in place.

"Where *are* they?"

Brigham shrugged and released a noncommittal hum.

"It shouldn't be taking this long." Halsey folded her arms and glanced around the enormous room that had made her feel small so many times in her past. She had no doubt she'd end up feeling that way again, standing in the center of the chamber while the seven presiding Councilors loomed over her from their raised seats. If they ever made it to the Council room in the first place.

Halsey's eyes widened as she realized how many things she hadn't thought to check before following her gut and pulling a big move like this. "What day is it?"

Brigham raised an eyebrow. "You asked me that yesterday."

"Day of the week, Brigham. What's the day of the week?"

"Uh…Thursday."

She bit her bottom lip and paced in front of the table. "Thursday. Okay, nothing happens on a Thursday."

"Except for *this*..."

"Nobody has a birthday in June." She stopped abruptly and spun toward her cousin. "You didn't get an email about an administrative day or anything, right?"

Despite his best intentions to look perfectly serious about their perfectly serious situation, Brigham smiled crookedly. "Administrative day? This isn't an elementary school, Hal."

Halsey rolled her eyes and resumed her pacing. "I'm only trying to make sure we didn't miss something important."

"*We* didn't miss anything. Remember? I'm here—"

"As moral support and to make sure I don't do anything stupid or hurt myself. *Not* because you agree with the urgency of what *we both saw in Ireland*. Yeah. I get it." As she kept pacing, she couldn't help looking up at the seven Council seats built into the walls eight feet off the floor.

Come on. I called a meeting. They have to answer. That's how we do things. Why else would they bother with a stupid pole-key in the middle of an empty room?

"They'll be here." Brigham set a hand on her shoulder before she could spin and stalk back in the opposite direction. "That's what all this is for. Maybe...take a breath or two. And don't hold them."

Halsey released the massive breath she had, in fact, been holding, then slumped her shoulders with another huge release of energy. "I feel like nobody's taking this seriously."

"Nobody thinks it's a joke, either." He patted her back with quick reassurance. "We have the track record to prove it, okay?" When Brigham glanced at his wristwatch, he snorted and almost choked trying to cover it up. "Besides, it's only been four minutes since you stuck the thing in the thing."

Halsey's nose crinkled. "That's it?"

"Takes a little time to get the message out there. It's not email."

"It should be."

"They'll be here, Hal."

The older Ambrosius cousin hadn't spoken a moment too soon. The loud, echoing *thunks* and *clicks* of the mansion's machinery swarmed back toward the Council room like a horde of mechanical insects closing in on their target.

I'm not a target. Halsey straightened her shoulders and clenched her fists at her sides, eyeing the Council seats to see which one of the seven would show up first. *I'm one of their best, and I'm taking action because we have a serious problem. That's what this is.*

The clinking and groaning was so loud now that further thought was impossible.

Brigham squeezed her shoulder once more, then dropped his hand and turned to the seats that were officially about to be filled.

Neither cousin was surprised when the center Council seat directly below the stained-glass mural burst into a ten-foot wall of fire that almost brushed against the ceiling.

Halsey swallowed and stared at the elevated chair. Beside her, Brigham chuckled softly and shook his head.

Of course Lawrence is the first one in. Please don't let everyone else take that long to get here.

CHAPTER SEVEN

As quickly as it erupted into flame, the center seat settled with a thick *whump* of air, and the flames snuffed out. In their place stood Lawrence, his long graying hair pulled back into a ponytail above his slate-gray suit. Halsey had grown up watching her oldest uncle wear the same exact outfit day in and day out. She would never admit to anyone how long it had taken her to realize the man most likely had a different identical suit for every day of the week.

As soon as the last bit of trailing smoke tendrils dissipated above his head, the Council chair on the far right of the curving line of them started to shift. Small, segmented pieces of the wall above it folded in on themselves and retracted. Trickles of water streamed from the resulting holes and grew into gushing waterfalls. Anyone else might have thought it was a busted pipe flooding through.

After a few seconds, the water spilling over the sides of the seat's platform and into a basin on the floor beneath it stilled. The streams of water started to move backward in shimmering cords, pulling against gravity until they coalesced into a churning, glimmering bubble of crystal-clear water that could have been pulled directly from the pristine waters of the Maldives.

A dark form materialized inside the sphere, then the magical hold on the water released all at once. The deluge cascaded in a crashing rush, though not a single drop spilled out of place or splashed onto the marble floors.

Where the sphere had been stood Beatrice, who had apparently been out in the river at the back of the estate's property. She'd answered the call in flipflops, a bikini, a sunhat, and dark sunglasses. At least the woman had shrugged a loose, flowing shawl over her shoulders so she wouldn't preside over the meeting underdressed.

Halsey was momentarily distracted from her purpose here by the fact that Beatrice had shown up not fully dressed. *Fifty-seven and Aunt Beatrice is still rocking the two-piece. I hope that's included in our family's genetic traits.*

Beatrice whipped her sunglasses off her face and glared at the cousins.

Halsey blinked and looked away from her aunt, reminded that this wasn't a fun family gathering by the river on a hot summer's day. Not that the Ambrosius Clan had those anyway.

Keep your head in the game, Hal. This is serious.

Two seats to the left of Lawrence's chair, the wall rumbled and shuddered. Segmented pieces fell away as they had at Beatrice's arrival, but instead of water, thick, lush green vines darted through the openings. The ends curled around the edge of the balcony, coiling tightly and eliciting wooden groans of protest before yet another figure was launched through the hole.

Florence was covered head to toe in dirt and bits of plant matter, with streaks of pollen across her khaki gardening uniform. The woman hadn't taken the time to remove her gardening gloves or even set down the trowel she'd been using before she'd heard the call. When she brushed her forearm across her mouth and chin, she managed to wipe off the dirt while also leaving a fresh streak along her cheek. She didn't look happy to have her Thursday evening disturbed by an emergency meeting, either.

After that, the other four Council seats filled up quickly. Halsey's second cousin Wallace emerged beside Florence with his arms full of rolled-up scrolls, looking thoroughly confused. His sister Blanch, who was in her early fifties but looked ten years older after nonstop missions without vacations or real breaks for thirty-five years, walked up the staircase built into the wall behind her seat. When she took her place in front of her chair, the woman's right hand went to the enormous knife she always wore strapped to her hip. Halsey suspected the woman didn't even take it off to sleep.

After that came Brigham's mom, Gracelyn. Of all the Ambrosius Council members, Halsey's aunt looked the most normal. She didn't care about making a grand entrance with the use of her elemental magic like the others. That didn't mean she looked any less pissed off about being summoned here without warning.

From the corner of her eye, Halsey noticed Brigham

dipping his head and trying to avoid his mom's scrutinizing gaze.

Way to show solidarity, cuz. You're twenty-four. It's not like she can ground you and send you to your room.

That would have been suitable advice to give herself as well. No sooner had Gracelyn appeared on her seat's platform than the seventh and final member of the Ambrosius Council emerged from the curved wall of the Council room.

While it lacked the pomp and circumstance of the other Councilors' entrances, this one still had a few more frills than Gracelyn's. Thin, delicate lines of silver, copper, and black iron emerged from the segmented wall like water poured into geometrically carved trenches. The lines zigzagged up, down, and sideways, moving at ninety-degree angles to their destinations a split second before another mechanized piece of the wall gave way.

When the brilliant streaks of metal, an alchemist's pride and joy, reached the edges of the platform, a heavy *thunk* rose from inside the wall, followed by the sputtering *click* of thousands of tiny, intricate mechanisms whirring into motion. Like an escalator prematurely designed in the Middle Ages, panel after panel of moving wood and glinting metal churned inside the hole.

Then the top of the final Councilor's dark-haired head came into view, and his boots thumped louder than the old-world machinery. He stalked toward the edge of the platform to stand behind the shimmering lines of metal he'd activated to precede his arrival.

This seventh member was Aidan Ambrosius. Built like a bear and might even have been in a fight with one or two real bears if the stories were to be believed. There was some contention among the Clan operatives over how it had happened. Whether by bear attack, a fight with one of his sisters, or at the hand of any number of monsters he'd fought and occasionally killed over the long course of his career. To this day, Aidan still hadn't verified anything to the younger generation of Ambrosius elementals.

Whatever had done it, the man had lost his right eye at a relatively young age. He was rarely seen without the well-oiled, gleaming rich brown eyepatch the same color as his short but unruly hair. The shade almost perfectly matched the background of the Clan banner.

In addition, two claw marks scarred the right side of his face above his tangled brown beard. Even with such severe battle scars and what many would call an unfortunate disability, Aidan was still the Ambrosius Clan's fiercest militia operative to date.

By an unfortunate stroke of luck, Aidan took the chair directly beside Lawrence's seat. The head of the Council, with his long ponytail, shimmering suits, and undeniable love for manipulating fire, was a force to be reckoned with. Yet as Halsey regarded them both from her place behind the round table, there was no denying that Lawrence looked small and frail compared to Aidan.

If I ever needed a good reason not to join the Council, that's it right there. Put the two of us side by side, and no one would ever believe I'm his daughter.

When she was eleven, Halsey went through a phase of questioning it herself. It lasted until she'd finished her initial militia training and realized how naturally elemental magic and monster hunting came to her, courtesy of Aidan

Ambrosius' genes. Plus, the man had the uncanny ability to make her suspect he could read her mind.

Like right now.

Aidan clasped his hands in front of him, tilted his head, and fixed his dark, glittering gaze on his daughter and nephew. He might have been missing an eye, but his bushy eyebrows still worked. They drew together into a dark, disapproving frown that cast more worry lines across his face than Halsey had seen in a long time.

Nobody likes disappointing their dad. I get it. He won't be disappointed. I think.

Now that the seven Councilors had finally gathered in one place, the gravity of what she was about to share sank in. She started to rethink the solidity of her plan. She'd been so certain the Council would be entranced by the tale of their discovery she'd failed to anticipate the obstacle of their foul moods at having been pulled from…whatever they'd been doing.

Okay, this might be harder than I thought. But this is why we have the emergency alarm. This is why these protocols exist. So they can hop down off their high horses, or I can knock 'em off when they see what we're dealing with.

The Council room fell silent again. Though it felt like everyone but Brigham stared at Halsey, they were waiting for the Council leader to open the emergency meeting he hadn't called. Halsey watched her Uncle Lawrence instead of trying to get a read on the others' current moods.

Lawrence's graying ponytail slithered over one shoulder as he dipped his head to look at the team of militia operatives standing in the center of the room. That was what Halsey and Brigham were now. The fact that everyone here was also related by blood, elemental magic, and the Ambrosius family legacy was beside the point.

The Ambrosius Clan Council ran a tight military ship. They were undiscovered by and therefore unaffiliated with any other military or government agency on the planet, yes. However, this was still the Clan's monster militia, Halsey and her cousin were soldiers, and she'd broken rank by calling them here before anyone even knew they'd returned from their latest mission.

Halsey met her uncle's gaze and held it, waiting for him to give her the floor. She failed to recognize he'd already given it to her by staring in that unnerving, unblinking way of his.

"Well." Lawrence's soft but no less firm voice echoed around the chamber. "Judging by your vapid stares and the fact that neither of you appears to have anything to say, I hope you have a good reason for activating this whole thing. If somebody doesn't start talking in the next five seconds…"

"We're sorry for calling you in on such short notice," Halsey blurted, stepping slightly forward as if the force of her words had shoved her from behind. "We have new top-priority information and thought the Council would want to hear about it first thing. Before we did anything else."

She felt Brigham's gaze on the side of her face but didn't dare turn to look at him. Not when she was still riding the line between looking confident and flailing in a stew of what-ifs.

Gracelyn tilted her head and scanned her son. "I thought you two were in Ireland. Werewolves, wasn't it?"

"We were." Halsey nodded. "And yes. However, the

'pack of werewolves inciting fear with the locals' wasn't an accurate description of our primary target."

Beatrice narrowed her eyes and tapped the tip of her sunglasses' stem against the corner of her mouth. "You didn't find the werewolves?"

"No, we found them." Halsey frowned at her aunt, who generally didn't say anything unless she was about to launch an intense verbal attack against whoever or whatever she disagreed with at the time. "The count was off, though. If I hadn't been there myself, I would've said three or four packs happened to run into each other. We did see it, though. It was one pack coming after us, and their alpha—"

"I won't say a werewolf pack that size isn't unusual," Wallace interrupted, squinting from beneath thin brown eyebrows as he peered at the cousins. "Yet this is information that should be covered in your mission debrief, Halsey. Not in an emergency Council meeting."

The gazes of the Council members only seemed to get darker and more irritated after that statement, and Halsey wanted to shrink beneath the weight of their disapproval. "I understand."

Brigham stepped up beside her, elbowed her side, then leaned in to whisper, "Get to the point, Hal. The sooner, the better."

"Right. Yeah." She cleared her throat and drew a deep breath before belting her next sentence louder than was appropriate, but it was the only way she knew to sound more confident to the Council and herself. "Brigham and I successfully completed our mission, and we're happy to provide the details of that in our debriefing. When we get there. That's not why we called this meeting—"

"What's with all this *we* crap?" Brigham murmured. If the Councilors heard it, nobody gave any indication they'd picked up on the private aside.

Halsey shot him an exasperated glare before focusing on the Council hovering over them. "It's not why *I* called this meeting."

Great. Now I've made this about me and my inability to keep my own partner in my corner. Happy now, cuz?

After a moment of silence that seemed to last forever, Lawrence heaved a massive sigh and blinked so slowly he seemed to roll his eyes. "Now would be the time to tell us why you *did* call this meeting, Halsey."

"Because of what we saw *after* we completed our mission," she blurted. "I thought it was big enough to deserve the Council's full attention as soon as we got back."

Only Florence looked remotely intrigued by that until Halsey realized her aunt had widened her eyes at the gunked-up dirt beneath her fingernails instead of her niece's "important discovery."

I've already lost their interest, haven't I?

"We were on the Cliffs of Moher," Halsey continued, pushing herself past the apathy coming at her from all sides. "We managed to fight back the…unusually large werewolf pack, though I'm pretty sure their alpha called them to retreat—"

"The *box*," Brigham whispered on the verge of a shout. "Get to the *box*."

Silverback alphas calling three dozen werewolves away *from a fight can wait, I guess. That's probably a side effect of the main problem, anyway.*

Halsey nodded, reached into her back pocket, and slid her fingers around her phone. "After we...disposed of the evidence, like we do, we saw something at the base of the cliffs. Washed up on the narrow shoreline, half on the beach and half floating on this weird, thick bed of seaweed."

"Are we getting to the point anytime soon?" Beatrice intoned, waving her sunglasses around as she regarded the other Councilors. "I was in the middle of enjoying my day, and it doesn't sound like this was worth being called away from it—"

"It was a coffin!" Halsey shouted. Flustered by the failure of the Council and her superiors, her own *family*, to drum up enough patience to let her finish her report, she took too long to pull up the pictures she'd taken fifteen hours ago. "A silver coffin. Only a rectangular box, really, but it was big enough to hold a body."

"Oh, well, if it's body-*sized*..." Beatrice snorted and dropped into her seat before folding one bare, tan leg over the other. Her dangling foot bounced up and down, placing her flip-flop in danger of flying off at any second. "Then we'd better take a closer look."

"That's enough," Lawrence warned. His look got Beatrice to stop talking, but Lawrence didn't appear any more interested than he had ten seconds ago.

"The lid was only halfway removed," Halsey continued as she finally found the right grouping of photos. "Like it had already been opened but not, you know, taken apart. Maybe even opened from the inside."

"I still don't understand what you're trying to get at here," Gracelyn cut in and shook her head. "We don't pay attention to someone else's trash. Even if it does wash up on the beach during a Clan mission."

"That's not why this is such a big deal." Halsey held up her phone, then realized how ridiculous it was. The others were way too far to see anything on the tiny screen, and the Council room hadn't been outfitted with a projector for blowing up images captured with modern-day technology.

The Councilors squinted and peered over the edges of their elevated platforms, but no one could see a thing.

Beside her, Brigham closed his eyes and blew out a long, heavy sigh.

Aidan clicked his tongue and flicked his hand toward his daughter's upheld phone. A gust of wind spiraled down from his Council seat. Before she could react, the miniature cyclone whipped the phone from her grasp, and the device spun and tumbled as her dad called the wind back. He snatched the phone from the center of the magic, and the slight howling that had filled the Council room cut off abruptly.

He caught her gaze for a brief moment, his one good eye brimming with such cold, emotionless calculation that Halsey couldn't imagine the discomfort of being scrutinized with *both* her dad's eyes at the same time. Fortunately, she hadn't been born in time to know what that was like.

Aidan glanced at her phone with no expression.

At first, she thought her appeal to the Council's sense of duty was already dead in the water. Yet as her dad flipped through the series of photos she'd taken on the Irish Cliffs of Moher, a renewed spark of hope fluttered in her chest.

That means at least he's interested, which means we did find something. Now they have to drop everything they think they know about family legends and magical history to see this for what it is. Even if they believe me, they are not *going to like it.*

CHAPTER EIGHT

Aidan Ambrosius took so long with Halsey's cell phone and her proof of emergency that the anticipatory silence filling the Council room started to make her skin itch. She knew that wasn't physiologically possible, but knowing didn't make the sensation any less uncomfortable.

Her Aunt Gracelyn cleared her throat and nodded at her father. "Aidan, if you're gonna stand there flipping through a photo shoot, at least humor the rest of us with a little narration."

With his expression as unchanging as ever, Aidan kept scrolling and didn't look up. "Halsey can handle that."

"What?" Halsey froze again. She hadn't expected any of the Council members to *invite* her to keep talking, let alone her own father. She settled her gaze on her phone and nodded. "Right. Silver coffin. On a bed of seaweed. We got a look at the inside, and it was a bunch of plain, undyed fabric. Probably homespun, if I had to guess—"

"This Clan isn't in the habit of *guessing*," Florence cut in. "Neither is this Council."

"I know that." Halsey frowned in frustration. Aunt Florence always focused on her gardening more than anything else, and now she was interrupting with a comment on the least important part of this. "I'm not trying to lead this meeting with a bunch of conjecture—"

"That's exactly what this is," Lawrence insisted.

Halsey didn't dare fix the Council head with the same disapproving frown she'd given his sister. "We have proof."

"Let her get to the rest of it," her dad grumbled as he swiped through the phone.

She looked at him and grimaced. *I didn't take that many pictures on the beach...* She glanced at Brigham with a silent question. At this point, she'd already started the conversation. They were neck-deep in this meeting, and her cousin's only option was to continue supporting her. He nodded for her to continue.

"It's not only the coffin," Halsey continued. "Like I said, the lid was still there, pushed aside. What you can see in the pictures is a massive scratch across the top. Claw marks. I'm not guessing about this part. They're definitely werewolf claws."

"That makes sense," Blanch's flat voice rang across the Council room. "You were out there *for* the werewolves, weren't you?"

"Yeah, but none of them got to the beach. They chased us to the cliffs, and we fought them back from there. Before the alpha called them back..." Saying it out loud made her remember how insane the whole mission had been. Droves of werewolves chasing them, all far more aggressive than usual and willing to throw themselves at two effective elementals for an unknown purpose. The silverback alpha she'd glimpsed howling in the moonlight. The way the werewolves had retreated not in fear of Halsey and Brigham Ambrosius but in response to that lone, bone-chilling howl.

It was an insane mission, and trying to describe it right now makes me *sound insane. I get it.*

"So you found a treasure on the beach," Gracelyn added as she spread her arms. "I don't see how that warrants calling us here when you could have entered your photos into evidence during your debrief."

"It's not *a treasure*," Halsey snapped. Both her aunt and her father frowned a warning in response. She sighed and pulled her emotions under control because that was the only way the Council would listen to her. "It's everything put together."

She counted on her fingers as she laid out the pieces of the puzzle she and Brigham had put together last night at the base of those cliffs. Or at least *she* had put them together, and her cousin had refrained from confirming or denying her hunch. That was where Brigham liked to stay. Nice and comfy on the middle ground.

"The last two months of missions have brought up a host of strange behavior in the monsters we've engaged. Small changes, sure, and not nearly as odd as droves of werewolves chasing two elementals toward the beach. Or all of them *retreating* when they were called. It's about that, the silverback alpha, the coffin, the empty cloth, and the claw marks. You all know what yesterday was, don't you?"

The entire Council responded with a collective hum that didn't mean anything as they listened with dubious frowns or emotionless stares.

"Wednesday," Aidan replied as he scrolled through her photos one more time, then drew back his enormously muscular arm and tossed the phone to Lawrence.

"Um…yeah." Halsey stared at her uncle as he checked the evidence, his concerned frown unchanging. "That's not what I'm talking about, though. Yesterday was—"

Lawrence tossed her phone to the next Councilor, making it nearly impossible for her to focus on what she was trying to say. Now all her aunts, uncles, and second cousins were looking at her phone and *hopefully* the photos she intended for them to see.

"It was the Summer Solstice," she blurted, collecting her thoughts as her phone was tossed again. "And all this…" Toss. "All this happened under a full moon. So if you—"

The loud clap of Florence catching her phone rang out, and Halsey grimaced at the clump of dirt spilling from her aunt's hands to smear all over the device. "The lighting in these is excellent," Florence commented.

"Thanks." Halsey frowned. *That* was her automatic response? Beside her, Brigham sniggered. When she glowered at him, he shrugged and shook his head. *This is all one giant game for him, too, huh? Not helping, cuz.* "The lighting isn't the point, though. I'm talking about the legends, okay? The great war."

"Which was not fought last night on the Cliffs of Moher," Lawrence opined with sarcasm in his voice. It wasn't much, but it got a good chuckle from several Councilors.

Halsey clenched her fists at her sides, lifted her chin, and tried to look like the careless comments and constant interruptions weren't getting to her. "I realize when it was fought, but the great war wasn't completely won, was it? The elementals only imprisoned the Blood Matriarch. In a silver coffin they buried at the bottom of the ocean, in the Circle of Creation. We don't know anything about what happened after that, but we *do* know the monsters weren't wiped out with all the blood humans and most of the elementals the way they were supposed to be. Which means the war isn't over. It…took a long break."

"A very long break," Gracelyn mused. Halsey expected to see more amusement on her aunt's face, but instead, she found concern and a deepening frown. "Two-point-four million years, to be exact."

"I understand." Halsey cleared her throat. "I'm saying now that we have the longest list of evidential facts we've ever had about the war, the Blood Matriarch and what happened to her, and monsters. If the last two months of weird stuff on the job wasn't enough, *this* is the icing on the cake." She pointed at her phone, which was now in Wallace's hands.

He looked away from the screen, peered down at her, and chuckled. "Now we're talking about cake?"

Seriously? It's like they held a private meeting before they showed up here and agreed to deny everything I'm telling them without even knowing what I was gonna say first.

Lawrence raised a hand. "I realize this is difficult, Halsey." His voice boomed across the Council room with such force that the light chuckles and sniggers died under the wordless command for silence. "Standing in front of the Council to eloquently and succinctly state your case has always been a challenge for you."

"What?"

He continued, ignoring her surprise and confusion. "However, now that you've gotten the initial explosion of ideas out of the way, I'm sure I speak for all of us when I say *get to the point.*"

The end of her uncle's sentence echoed through the room with finality, as if he were calling the meeting to a close instead of ordering her to move on with the discussion.

Initial explosion of ideas? Sure. Let's see how well he *would handle it if everyone interrupted him and laughed and picked apart literally everything he said because it wasn't perfect.*

Even in her irritation, Halsey knew that would never happen. Lawrence was a born leader among the Ambrosius Clan, always well-spoken and articulate. Everyone on the Council was, in one way or another. Even her one-eyed bear of a father, who looked like he would rather crush another man's skull in his hand than sit around and talk militia policy and protocol.

Swallowing her anger, Halsey raised her head and nodded. "My point is, I think we're about to see even more changes in the monsters the Ambrosius Clan is sworn to hold at bay. My point is that I think we're on the edge of war again. My *point* is that nobody wants to put together the facts on their own because you'd be forced to consider that the Mother of Monsters is back—"

"The Blood Matriarch?" Beatrice laughed, and the others broke into condescending chuckles. "You can't honestly expect us to believe this."

"Why not? Because none of *you* want to believe it's possible?"

"It's *not* possible," Wallace declared with a smirk. "The

great war's final battle was fought in the Circle of Creation, and the elementals won. You've made it clear you already know that. The legends are only that, girl. There *is* no Mother of Monsters coming back to fight us and take her revenge for our ancestors *burying her at sea*." The oldest Ambrosius Councilor in the room snorted. "That's a fairy-tale for children, and taking it seriously is nothing but a waste of our time and resources. There is no Matriarch. There is no centuries-long sleep in the coldest depths of the ocean. There's no reason for any of us to be here right now."

Florence peered over the edge of her platform and kicked two small clods of dirt off her boots and over the side. She raised an eyebrow, nodded at the two young operatives, and sniggered. "Unless this is another one of your practical jokes, Brigham."

Halsey's cousin whipped his head toward their aunt, and his eyes grew wide before he chuckled self-consciously. "Right." When Halsey elbowed him roughly in the side, Brigham cleared his throat and shook his head. "No, actually. Not this time."

The room fell silent before the Councilors broke into scattered laughter and their own backhanded comments.

"You say that, but you look awfully suspicious…"

"It wouldn't be the first time he's cooked up a grand scheme like this to get a few good laughs."

"Shame that he's pulling Halsey into it, though. Does *she* know it's a joke?"

"Maybe that's part of it."

Halsey squeezed her fists again and tried to wait for the chatter to die down, but every word of doubt and carefree denial felt like another needle pricking her skin. Finally, she couldn't take it anymore.

"Everybody shut up and *listen* to what I'm telling you!" she shouted. Her voice echoed with as much clarity and finality as any other around the room. This time, she drew the response she wanted, and now she couldn't stop. "It's not a joke! I know what I saw. Brigham knows, too, only he won't make up his mind one way or the other about it. Which, honestly, isn't anywhere near as stupid as this entire Council writing off everything I've said. This is massive. It changes everything we know about what elementals are for and why the Ambrosius Clan fights the way we fight. If we're not prepared—"

"This isn't the first time someone's tried to warn us about being prepared," Lawrence proclaimed. "Those warnings were baseless, and we all know what happened to the elemental who tried to convince us the world as we knew it was coming to an end."

Halsey swallowed and directed a blistering glare at her uncle. *He'd really go that low? Meemaw was out of the game way before she started to lose it. I'm not crazy, and that's not fair.*

Lawrence continued. "Now, to be clear, I'm not saying you're headed down the same path. This fantasy of yours needs to stop, though. Here and now, before we—"

"Fantasy?" she shrieked. "You're kidding, right? While you sit up there on your fancy pedestal? When was the last time *you* were out in the field, Lawrence? When was the last time you fought monsters and paid attention to more than how many you could bash over the head in ten minutes?"

Her uncle's frown intensified. Beyond that, he didn't

look insulted by her outburst. It appeared he'd already decided not to give a shit, and that made her angrier.

"This is real," Halsey shouted. "I have *proof*—"

"Stop." Her dad's low, rumbling bark blasted through the circular chamber, and her eyes clenched shut. Aidan stepped toward the edge of his shimmering, geometric-lined platform. He nodded at Wallace, who still held Halsey's phone, and her second cousin tossed the device toward the center of the room.

Fortunately, Brigham was quick enough to snatch the phone from the air before it hit either the round table or Halsey's shoulder. He held it out toward her, but she wasn't paying attention.

Halsey's entire awareness centered on her dad's dark scowl, or at least what she imagined was a scowl. It was almost impossible to make out his expression under all that beard. Yet if Aidan had spoken up like that, he had something important to say. She hoped it wasn't to disregard everything she'd been duty-bound to tell the Council as soon as possible.

The man waited an eternity before he dipped his head and fixed his daughter with his one good eye. "You're an excellent monster hunter, Halsey. You and Brigham make an outstanding team, and this Council would do well to remember that."

"Thank you," she mumbled, daring to hope that her dad might take her side on this.

"That said, I see more holes in this theory of yours than I'm comfortable with. Your claim is no small issue for the Ambrosius Clan."

"I know." She nodded before his full statement sank in. "Wait, what holes?"

Aidan shook his head. "Your so-called proof, for one. Images on a phone aren't the most reliable source."

"You think I made this up?"

"I'm saying it's not enough."

"Modern images can be doctored for any intended purposes," Blanch joined in. "Anyone can do it. It's not that hard."

Halsey gaped in disbelief. "Why would I *doctor* those pictures?"

"I'm not saying you did. Only that it's possible." Blanch shrugged. "We would need to have someone thoroughly inspect them to be sure they're legitimate. Right now, that would expend more resources than I personally think this charade deserves."

"Charade." Halsey looked at the faces staring down from their elevated platforms and laughed bitterly. "Fine. Good thing I know what to expect from all of you because the photos are only the beginning."

Half the Council tilted their heads or frowned, curious enough not to cut her off again but not engaged enough to prompt further explanation. The other half stared blankly at the center of the room. Still, Halsey would wield her final piece of evidence because it was all she had left.

Brigham picked up on what she was about to say. He laid a hand on her shoulder and murmured in her ear, "We should wait on that one."

"Why?" She jerked her head toward him, so their faces were inches apart. "They already have it."

"Yeah, but *we* don't, Hal. I hate how much this makes

me sound as old as Wallace." Brigham jerked his head toward their older cousin, currently cleaning his glasses on the hem of his button-down shirt. "You're kinda putting the cart before the horse right now."

"Are you telling me the only other option is to shoot the horse and smash the cart to smithereens?"

"What? No." His eyes bugged out as he removed his hand. "Now you're being gruesome."

"No, I'm trying to get them to listen." Halsey rolled her eyes, turned away from her cousin, and patted her jeans pocket before remembering she'd already removed her phone.

"Here." Brigham handed it over. "For whatever you're planning next."

She snatched the device from his hand, then grimaced. "Thanks."

CHAPTER NINE

"Would you two like us to give you the room?" Beatrice called as she brushed her long blonde hair over one shoulder. Her entire beach-time ensemble looked ridiculous in the Council room, but the way her sunhat flopped over her face when she moved took it to a whole new level. "It feels like you're having your own private meeting *and* wasting our time in the process."

Halsey scrolled through her contacts and muttered, "Right, 'cause it's only okay for *Councilors* to waste time with all the crosstalk…"

"What was that?"

"Just a second," she called louder.

Brigham snorted and folded his arms.

"What is it now?" Lawrence asked dryly. "If you don't have anything else significant—"

"Oh, I do. Trust me." After finding the number she wanted, Halsey stabbed a finger to the screen to initiate the call, then put it on speaker and held her phone out for everyone to hear. "After this, you'll have something to look forward to when you realize I'm not full of shit."

Her cousin choked, then grimaced as he cleared his throat.

Language unbefitting an Ambrosius Clan operative wasn't something the Council generally let fly, but Halsey was already at the end of her rope. At this point, she didn't care as long as her family agreed to take her seriously. And they would.

The acoustics of the Council room captured every ring coming from her phone with perfect clarity. After the fourth ring, the line clicked, and a man's tired, hesitant voice echoed through the room. "Hello?"

"Hey, Patrick. It's Hal."

"Hey, Hal. Um…listen. I was about to call you."

"Good. Then we're still on the same page." She didn't stop to consider why the head of their recovery team, sent to Ireland to recover a specific piece of controversial evidence, sounded like he had bad news. She could only keep pushing because now she was fueled by the need to show the Council there was nothing wrong with her mind or her ability to do her job. "I wanted to check in with you on the status of our Ireland recovery."

As she said it, Halsey looked at the looming Councilors. Her dad's good eye widened while the shiny leather eyepatch lifted over the other. Beatrice rolled her eyes. Lawrence and Gracelyn looked intrigued, at least.

She soon realized Patrick's pause on the line was a lot longer than it should have been. "Patrick? You still there?"

"Yep." The man cleared his throat, then exhaled a sigh.

"Guess we are on the same page 'cause that's what I was gonna talk to you about."

"Okay..." Her satisfied smile faded.

"I told you we had a few other things to pick up in the area before we got all our shipping containers on the next freighter out of Dublin. That all went fine, but when we regrouped with the rest of the shipment to go over the manifest, your, uh... Well, that box you had us pick up off the beach..."

Halsey swallowed the lump in her throat. "What happened to the box, Patrick?"

"It's gone."

"*What?*"

"Listen, I've already had my guys scouring the entire warehouse down here. Nothing on the docks. Nothing in the security footage. We had that thing locked up tight, but it's like... I mean, if I'm being honest, it's like one of your own people blew in and snatched it right out from under us."

Brigham sucked in a breath through his teeth and dropped his head. The Council was all staring at Halsey. While that wasn't a new sensation, it had been years since the combined gazes of all seven Ambrosius Councilors made her entire body flush hot.

You've gotta be kidding me right now.

"Patrick." She continued, lowering her voice as if she were talking with the phone against her ear instead of having this humiliating public conversation. "I need you to find that item."

"I'm doing the best I can out here, Hal. Really. I've cut half my crew to track the thing down, but we don't even know where to start looking. The thing simply disappeared. Listen, if by some weird stroke of luck, we manage to find it, you'll be the first person I call. We can't hold back the whole shipment, though. It's not only your stuff on *our* manifesto, let alone the whole damn freighter—"

"No, I get it. I'm not asking you to delay the operation out there. Just…if you find it…"

"I got you on speed dial." Patrick sighed, and she envisioned the fully human man in his late forties running a hand through the blond hair he kept so short it almost made him look bald. "I'm sorry, Hal. I can promise you it won't happen again."

"Yeah, I believe you. Stay safe out there."

"You too—"

Whether or not Patrick intended to say anything else, Halsey couldn't bring herself to let him finish. She stabbed the red button to end the call, then stared at the device, momentarily unable to move.

These guys are the best recovery team we have. Patrick's guys don't screw around, and it's not easy to lose a giant silver casket that has to weigh a ton. Who the hell could steal it without anyone noticing?

The Council room fell silent again, then Lawrence cleared his throat. "Sounds like you might be focusing on the wrong problems."

"It's not Patrick's fault," she blurted. "Or his team's. They're the best at what they do, and if somebody stole the coffin—"

"Then you don't have any of the proof you were so adamant would convince us of your…story."

"It's not a story." All the fire had flushed out of her after that phone call, and she hated the way she was looking up at her family now. Whatever her expression looked like on the outside, it *felt* like desperation. "You all heard Patrick. They *had* the silver coffin. They were going to bring it back on the next shipment and drop it off here for all of you to see."

"In that case, it's pretty convenient someone swooped in and took it off his hands," Blanch noted with a shrug. "Don't you think?"

"No." Halsey scowled at the woman. "That's literally the most inconvenient part of all this."

"You and Patrick McCannon are close, aren't you?" Gracelyn asked.

Halsey shrugged. "As close as any militia operator gets with the head of their recovery team."

"So, it wouldn't be out of the question for Patrick to do whatever you asked him."

"What?" Another glance at Brigham said her cousin had no idea what was happening now or why his own mom was interrogating Halsey like this. "The only thing I ever ask Patrick to do is his job. That's it."

"Sure." Gracelyn nodded sagely. "Recover a shiny box off an Irish beach, safeguard it in one of his international warehouses before shipping it to the U.S. and your Clan's headquarters…"

"Lie for you over the phone when the emergency meeting *you* called doesn't go your way," Beatrice added with a heavy dose of sarcasm.

Halsey wanted to smack her aunt with the pools of water hanging around after the woman's elaborate entrance. In this room, though, the only battles allowed to be fought were with words. "Seriously, Beatrice? You think I'd ask one of our best teams to lie for me like that? That I'd call a meeting *first thing* after getting back from an international mission, only to jerk you guys around?"

"Well, that's part of the problem, isn't it?" Gracelyn suggested. "You're fresh from a mission, Halsey. Tired, maybe still slightly in battle mode, and with nowhere near enough time to recover from jetlag. Which, by the way, gets even the best of us."

For whatever reason, the other Councilors found that particularly funny, though they only reacted with sniggers and low chuckles hidden behind hands.

Gracelyn continued. "That's why we have immediate debriefings, isn't it? To give our operatives a chance to review their missions objectively, to settle physically and mentally into being back home again, and to avoid hasty decision-making. You decided it was better to circumvent the entire system because you think an old box washed up on the beach is the Blood Matriarch returned?" Halsey's aunt smiled tightly, which only aggravated Halsey more. "If this entire Council wasn't already aware of your tendencies to over-exaggerate at times—"

"I'm not over-exaggerating," Halsey protested. "I'm not even *regular* exaggerating."

"—it would be easy to assume you're going through some difficult mental...transitions that might be better served with a temporary change of duties."

"What?" Halsey's eyes bulged. When she looked at Brigham in disbelief, her cousin seemed equally shocked by his mom's words. She faced the Council again. This wasn't turning out how she'd wanted or even expected, and unfortunately, those were two different things. "I don't need a change of duties, and I'm not having some mental-health crisis, okay?"

When no one responded to her desperate, slightly unhinged statement, Halsey knew she'd lost this round with the Council and her family. She only didn't know whether they were capable of following through with Aunt Gracelyn's sentiment regarding the "temporary change of duties."

"You can understand how concerning this is," Lawrence stated.

"No." She shook her head and regarded her uncle with pleading eyes. "Lawrence. Come on."

"It's not the first time you've come to us with something that's not the same caliber of importance you were convinced it was." The Council head looked slowly to the left and right, meeting the gazes of the six other Councilors who seemed to be thinking the same thing.

None of them can think for themselves. Halsey turned her pleading gaze to her dad, but Aidan returned it with apathy. *Even my own dad. The guy who could break every neck in this room if he wanted. Now he's helping them go after mine.*

"Aidan put it perfectly," Lawrence contended. "You're one of our best, Halsey. Yet even the best of us need room to breathe sometimes."

"That's not what I need," she muttered, but no one paid attention to her anymore. Lawrence saying this only confirmed that the entire Council had made up its mind. From this point on, it was a matter of following protocol and "making it official."

"I'd like to propose to the Council a temporary hiatus

for Halsey Ambrosius," Lawrence declared. "For the duration of thirty days, for rest and recuperation after the impeccable work and dedication she's put into militia affairs in recent months. Followed by a personal and professional evaluation and adjudication as to whether she's fit to return to active duty at the end of the thirty-day period."

Halsey's shoulders sagged. She felt like she was floating up through her body toward the twenty-foot ceiling. *You've gotta be kidding me.*

"All in favor?" her uncle asked.

Five Council hands went up almost immediately. Aidan Ambrosius looked like he wanted to either rip somebody to shreds or storm back through the hole in the wall behind him. It only took another five seconds for her own dad to vote with the Council and against her. No one was willing to be honest and call it a probationary period instead of a prolonged vacation.

"That settles it." Lawrence clapped his hands together, then spread them wide. "Thirty days' leave from active missions. When it's time for you to report back for that evaluation, Halsey, we'll let you know."

Sure. If monsters haven't taken over the world by then and we're not all dead.

She knew that was stretching the realm of possibility, even for an Ambrosius elemental who hunted monsters for a living. Or at least she *used* to know. For the next thirty days, Halsey Ambrosius would effectively be unemployed.

Her father dipped his head toward her, looking apologetic but not willing to take back his decision. "This is for the best," he said gently. "It's how we stay proactive. All of us. The last thing we want is for history to repeat itself in this kind of situation. These thirty days will be good for you. We know you'll use them wisely."

The last part sounded like an apology, but Halsey wasn't listening to the end of her dad's short speech. The beginning and the middle had caught her attention like a spear through the heart, and she couldn't let it go.

This is how we stay proactive? By pretending everything this family thought about Mom is coming true for me *because I'm paying attention? Or by disguising the whole thing as a reason to walk all over Meemaw some more?*

She scoffed and shook her head. This had been a side mission of her own that hadn't come from the Ambrosius Clan Council. A side mission she'd failed in an epic way. This only meant her problems would be worse after her thirty-day probation because she wasn't imagining anything.

Her family didn't want to envision a world where they didn't have all the answers anymore.

"Please tell me that's the end of it," Beatrice grumbled as she returned her dark sunglasses over her eyes. "I've missed out on half an hour of sunlight at this point, and I'd like to make use of the other half-hour that's left. *If* you don't mind…"

"I'm pretty sure nobody cares," Brigham muttered.

Under any other circumstances, Halsey would have laughed. The most she could muster now was a muffled snort as Beatrice glared at Brigham, and even that sound fell flat.

Lawrence gazed vacantly at his youngest sister with a hint of disgust, and Beatrice stared right back in a silent sibling challenge the likes of which Halsey would never understand as an only child. The Council head shrugged it off before gesturing at his niece and nephew. "I'm calling this meeting to an end, and you two are dismissed."

Brigham shot finger guns at his uncle and winked. "Thanks."

Halsey scanned him. Her cousin's sheepish smile sealed the deal on the mess today had become. She spun and stalked toward the Council room's intricately carved double doors.

"Consider this another warning, Brigham," Gracelyn called after him. "If we find out *any* of this was another of your jokes, you can bet your ass you're paying your cousin back for her lost mission time."

The young operative faced his mom and spread his arms as he walked backward across the room. "Thanks, Mom. After all this time, it's awesome to know you still have so much faith in me."

"Uh-huh." Gracelyn's gaze flicked toward Aidan, but Halsey's father had nothing to add. He rarely did.

The rumbling *boom* of the doors opening from the inside echoed around the room. Halsey groaned as she pried them apart. She couldn't wait to get the hell out of there and put as much distance as possible between herself and the family who'd let her down.

CHAPTER TEN

As the massive doors started to swing shut, the low murmur of the Council's voices followed Halsey down the long hallway at the back of the mansion. Brigham yelped as he slipped through behind her. Two seconds later, another resounding *thud* sounded as the doors closed. The voices from the room snuffed out, and Brigham shouted over his pounding footsteps. "Hal! Wait up!"

"Wait up?" She threw a condescending look at him but slowed in her furious march. "What are we, ten?"

"Ha. I wish."

Halsey's uncertain frown went unnoticed because Brigham was focused on catching up to her so he could speak his mind.

He reached her and announced, "So. That was…different."

"If you're defining 'different' as 'a complete humiliating failure,' then yeah. Sure was."

"Aw, come on, Hal. It wasn't *that* bad."

"Says the guy who gets a slap on the wrist for being

everybody's favorite *funny guy*. You weren't suspended for a month."

"Suspended?" Brigham chuckled and waved the thought aside. "Nah, cuz. You got the royal treatment."

Halsey's deadpan stare pinned him. "I love you, but sometimes the way your mind works terrifies me. That's only from *half* the stuff that comes out of your mouth."

"A real compliment, coming from you."

"Meaning what?"

"Meaning I love you too." Brigham grinned widely and slung an arm around his cousin's shoulders, making her stumble. He turned with her around the corner of yet another interesting corridor. "Listen. You had a shitty meeting. I know. Everybody has at least one, and you've had at least *four* I can think of off the top of my head…"

Halsey's groan was half frustration and half botched attempt not to laugh. She couldn't stay irritated with her mission partner and best friend. She shrugged out from under his arm and shoved him playfully away. "You're not helping."

"Yes, I am. You gotta listen to the whole spiel before it makes sense, though."

"Fine." She gestured brusquely down the hallway and dipped her head in a sarcastic bow. "Spiel away."

Brigham sniggered. "First of all, you scared the shit out of them. I could tell because while you were freaking out about them playing Keep Away with your phone, *I* was watching their faces."

"I wasn't freaking out—"

"Bup-bup-bup." He raised an index finger in front of her lips, making her reel back in surprise. "Spiel."

Halsey cranked an eyebrow and said nothing as she waited for her cousin to back out of her personal space. *They think I'm nuts. It's like the whole Clan has it out for me, except the Ambrosius who acts like he's already insane.*

The thought brought a brilliant grin to her lips, which satisfied Brigham enough to start walking again. He clasped his hands behind his back and strolled beside her, peering at the delicate crown molding that lined both sides of the ceiling. He looked so much like their Uncle Lawrence that Halsey burst out laughing when he asked, "Now, where was I?"

"Scaring the shit out of our family."

"Yeah. That's right." He thrust the same index finger into the air and nodded. "That was item number one, meaning you got their attention."

"In all the wrong ways, but okay." They turned another corner, unconsciously following the route to the debriefing room in the east wing that habit and routine had cemented in their minds.

"All right, maybe it wasn't your top priority. However, getting their attention was *one* of the priorities. You definitely did that." Brigham frowned and started searching his pockets, front and back. When he didn't find what he was looking for, he shook his head and kept walking. "Second, you sure as hell proved our silver mystery box wasn't a fun Photoshop project on your phone."

"Oh, you mean the one that was stolen less than two hours ago without our *best* recovery team noticing a thing? *That* box?"

"Fine." He rolled his eyes. "Our *missing* silver mystery box. Same thing."

"Brigham, I know you're trying to make me feel better, but the only thing I proved in there is that I can't keep track of my own *crazy theories*. We were supposed to have that coffin here in Texas by the end of the month. Now we won't have it at all."

"Well, yeah, that does bring up a few minor complications." Her cousin found some extra pep in his step when Halsey snorted. "For real, though. Forget the weird shit that came outta my mom's mouth in there. The Council knows you don't run around bribing our support teams to get them to lie for you."

"Beatrice is the one who voiced *that* suspicion out loud."

"Yeah, but Gracelyn gave her the ammo. That's *her* fault. Everybody knows Beatrice jumps on judging people like a starving succubus jumps on a soul."

This time, Halsey broke out in full-blown laughter that echoed through the hallway. "True."

"I ignore everything Beatrice says anyway. None of it means anything." Brigham shrugged. "When you do *that*, it's a hell of a lot easier to see what happened in there. The Council knows that weird-ass casket exists. They've seen the pictures, *and* they know it was valuable enough that someone risked breaking into an Ambrosius Clan warehouse to get their hands on it. Which, again, scares the shit out of them."

"Why couldn't they *say* that?" Halsey's smile died again. Now that they were talking about it, she couldn't ignore that the Council had laughed in her face about a real threat and written the whole thing off as the "mental strain" of being an Ambrosius elemental. Which had nothing to do with it.

"I don't know." Brigham shrugged. "They get a kick out of being assholes?"

Neither cousin found their regular humor amusing. It only made today feel more defeating.

Halsey continued. "Seriously, though. How hard would it be to say, 'Thanks for bringing this to our attention, Halsey. Your pitifully small amount of evidence doesn't have us convinced, but it's enough to look into it. We'll have to get back to you on this one. Keep up the good work.'"

Brigham sniggered as they turned another corner. "Maybe 'cause it's a hell of a mouthful with an actual verbal admission that they don't have all the answers. We already know that. They only want to keep pretending we don't."

Halsey snorted, appalled yet not surprised that the Council would go to such lengths to make her feel like she'd stepped out of line. "It's not only me seeing through all their crap, then."

"Duh. Of course it's not only you. I'd bet my whole set of collectible lighters that *they* see through their own crap. Your dad most of all, which is weird because of…you know. The whole one-eye thing."

"Wow."

"Oh, come on." Brigham spread his arms as he struggled to come to his own defense. "That's not a crappy thing to say. You never even *knew* him with two eyes."

She laughed. "I would love to watch you say that to his face."

"You mean straight-up talk to Aidan Ambrosius about his missing eye? Ha. Yeah, you know what? Next time I lose the will to live, I'll give it a shot."

"See, *that's* what I have a serious problem with."

Brigham frowned and tilted his head. "My will to live?"

When Halsey glanced sideways at him, he didn't appear to be joking. She felt compelled to explain herself. "No. The fact that absolutely no one in this family would be caught dead saying anything bad about *Aidan Ambrosius* behind his back. Yet if one of their youngest, best, most *eccentric* operatives does anything outside their perfect box, it's open season. I'm not talking about myself, by the way."

"Yep." Brigham crinkled his nose and peered at the ceiling as they walked as if he could play out the memory of their meeting in a projection across the smooth, finished drywall. "I know. I was waitin' for you to bring up Meemaw."

"Talk about hypocrisy." With an incredulous snort, Halsey ran her hands through her hair and wished she had something better to do with them. She drove her voice up an extra octave in an impression of one of the Councilors. "'Oh, she's brought something strange and out of our comfort zone to our attention? You know what that means. Cecelia Ambrosius all over again. This is how we stay *proactive*. We don't want history *repeating* itself. Dear *god*, not another crazy Ambrosius woman!'"

Brigham laughed as they entered another hallway, empty like the others at this time of night. "I can see how they might think *you've* lost your mind…"

She smiled crookedly and pounded his shoulder slightly harder than necessary. "Jerk."

"Hey. Ow." Brigham grinned as he rubbed the offended body part, though it didn't hurt. "I have no idea why they still think Meemaw's cuckoo for Cocoa Puffs. I've always seen her as a sweet old lady with milk and chocolate chip cookies ready every time you walk through the front door."

Halsey turned her head and stared in disbelief. Brigham pressed his lips together so hard to keep from laughing that his face turned an alarming shade of crimson.

"I'm gonna pretend you didn't say any of that."

"Yeah, good idea."

They stopped short when a side door opened with the barest hint of squealing hinges. Two of the house staff barreled out the door, pushing a meal cart between them. The first man hustled past, walking backward and tugging the cart's handle, but the second man caught sight of Halsey and Brigham standing there with knowing smiles. His face lit up with the same familiarity. "You're back."

"Back from *what*, you old coot?"

"Not *you*, Jonesy. These two troublemakers."

Jonesy blinked, stopped pulling the cart, then looked over his shoulder and grinned at the cousins. "Well, damn. That was fast."

"It felt forever," Halsey replied, trying not to laugh at the abrupt change in their demeanor. "Is Cavanaugh still in debriefing, or did we miss our window?"

"The question is, does he ever *leave* debriefing?" Jonesy grinned and shook his head. "I'd wager probably not."

"Well, better late than buried in paperwork, right?" She nodded for Brigham to continue with her down the hall, but her cousin was focused on the meal cart. "Hey, Tom. Think you could spare a little somethin'-somethin'?"

The man pushing the cart grinned and reached under the ivory tablecloth covering the cart's lower shelf. He whipped his hand out and offered Brigham a small brown paper bag with the top neatly rolled up.

Halsey snorted. *Like one grown man sending another off to school with his lunch.* "You didn't even know we were back yet," she mused.

Brigham's mouth popped open as he accepted the snack. "How does that matter *at all?*"

Tom rearranged the hem of the cloth and nodded at her. "Damn near forty years working in this house, girl. If I've learned anything, it's to be prepared for everything."

Jonesy echoed the sentiment with a quick nod and a playful wink, and Halsey laughed. "Y'all git on now to where you oughta be."

"Yeah, you too." Brigham raised the paper bag toward the long-time employees without realizing his response might have been considered less than appropriate. Luckily, Jonesy and Tom weren't the types to take offense to a younger man's habit of not thinking before he spoke.

With Brigham's focus on his food, Halsey grabbed his sleeve and easily hauled him down the corridor with her. "You realize you basically told them to get back to work, right?"

Brigham snatched half of an egg-salad sandwich out of the bag and crammed the whole thing into his mouth. "An' wa' oo'ee gink we oo-ee?"

She stared directly ahead and tried to ignore the fuzzy image of her face-stuffing cousin in her periphery. "Chew your food, dude."

Four seconds later, Brigham's massive swallow rang out down the hallway before he smacked his lips and belched. "And what do you think *we're* doing, huh? Going back to work. Come on, cuz. If there's one person on this entire estate who *isn't* working, I'll…wear a piñata for a week."

"How about you *are* the piñata and make it two weeks?"

After tilting his head in consideration, Brigham stuck out his hand to shake. Halsey glanced at his outstretched fingers covered in deviled egg and mayonnaise and shook her head.

"Shit. My bad." Her cousin sucked the sandwich filling off his fingers instead as they turned the final corner at the end of the mansion's east wing.

Halfway down on the right was the debriefing room. Halsey stared at the door with wide eyes and tried not to grimace at the sound of Brigham noisily sucking his fingers. "Not better."

"Fine. Your loss on an epic bet." He reached for the door with his dirty sandwich hand. Fortunately, the funnier, more logical, and insanely messier Ambrosius cousin remembered at the last minute to use his forearm instead. "Keep looking on the bright side, okay?"

The door creaked open under his weight as he walked backward, and Halsey raised an eyebrow. "What's that, exactly?"

"Looks like you're finally getting that vacation you wanted."

"Ha. Yeah. I don't think a thirty-day suspension comes with frequent flier miles and a round-trip ticket out of Texas, though." They stepped into the enormous debriefing room designed to handle multiple militia teams at once, and Halsey puffed out a breath.

I guess it could be worse. I might be able to drive the whole estate so insane that they force me back into active duty early.

CHAPTER ELEVEN

Not long into her thirty-day suspension, Halsey decided she wouldn't make it through the entire month without either breaking the rules again or losing her mind. It wasn't the solitude or the potential for boredom that got to her. She and Brigham had gone weeks, occasionally months, without receiving orders for a new monster-hunting mission. During her first year as an operative, she'd only had three missions, and the wait between those had been bearable.

What got to her now was knowing she would have no missions, no job, and no purpose for a full thirty days. Awareness of the exact start and end date of her disciplinary sabbatical sucked all the joy and excitement out of waiting. The Ambrosius family would claim that reasonable expectations and things going according to plan formed the best possible outcome. Yet for Halsey, knowing what to expect was mentally excruciating.

Even a visit from her militia partner who was not

suspended from missions didn't pull her out of her funk. Brigham sure tried, though.

The first time he came, he'd thoughtfully brought along a case of beer and a box of pizza that was still hot and filled Halsey's house with the smell of fresh-baked dough, melting cheese, and sizzling pepperoni. Even then, Halsey didn't turn away from her ruminating thoughts and the activities she'd taken up to keep herself busy. In short, she was brooding.

Brigham didn't seem to mind, or maybe he didn't notice. After he'd already opened her front door, he gave it another quick, polite bang with his elbow before shuffling inside with his arms full of dinner. "Hal?"

The front half of her house was empty and silent until a sharp, thin whistle and the ensuing *thunk* of metal on wood rose from the back of the cottage house nestled alone among the rolling hills outside Lufkin. To anyone who didn't know the property, Halsey Ambrosius' home certainly looked like a quaint little cottage painted eggshell blue with navy trim and a green front door. Most people knew nothing about where she lived.

Her cousin was not included in that long list of people.

Chuckling softly, he kicked the door shut and made his way past first the low half-wall of the kitchen counter to the left of the entryway, then the deep purple couch and matching loveseat of the enormous living room taking up the back third of the house. The whistle and thump rose again from beyond the back wall, louder this time.

"You know I can hear you back there, right?" he yelled through another chuckle. "Hal. Seriously. You can't have it both ways."

"Why not?" she called from the other side of the sliding door set on tracks in the back wall, followed by another whistle and thump. "Looks like that's what *you're* doing."

That entire stretch of wall had once been glass to offer an incredible view of the back of the property. That view had changed significantly over the last few decades when the Ambrosius cousins discovered the place and goaded each other into testing their elemental magic in an abandoned cottage nobody seemed to want. Since then, the glass had been replaced with a thick wooden door found more often in barns than "respectable homes." Whatever those were.

"That's where you're wrong, cuz." Brigham stopped beside the sliding door, his arms still full of pizza box and cold beers. "You know how I know?"

Whistle. Thunk.

Halsey sighed. "You're gonna tell me anyway."

"I'm gonna tell you anyway. Reason number one." He cleared his throat as another *thunk* rose from the other side of the door. "I'm standing here with dinner, and you're too busy to let me in where all the fun's happening."

Now the whistling and thunking had stopped, only to be replaced by the wrenching creak and groan of more wood being splintered and pulled apart. Halsey's footsteps crossed the next room from left to right before she called out, "Let yourself in."

"I brought pizza and beer." Grinning, Brigham leaned closer to the door and listened for his cousin's movement. When he heard nothing, he clicked his tongue, rolled his eyes, and straightened again. "Okay. If that's how you wanna play it, fine. Don't say I didn't try to pull you out of this stupid funk I don't even understand."

With a long, slow exhale, he eyed the brushed-nickel door handle and imagined the one on the other side. He reached out with his magic to feel the plethora of available energy. It wasn't necessary, but lifting two fingers away from the edge of the pizza box and flicking them helped channel his magical connection with the green, growing things outside.

The results took longer than expected, but eventually, the creaking, snapping, and groaning of several long, thick brown vines peeling away from their resting places on the other side of the door snuck into the cottage's living room. The door slid aside with a low rumble of wheels across the iron track, and Brigham's grin returned as he stepped into what they jokingly called the add-on sunroom.

"Okay, Hal. I'm using magic to open doors in *your* house. Happy now? Halsey? Are you trying to—whoa!" He reeled backward as a small but no-less-deadly throwing ax hurtled mere inches from his face, whistling as it spun end over end. It hit the lefthand wall of the back room with a heavy *thunk* and didn't quiver once the blade lodged into the thick wood.

Brigham readjusted his grip on the pizza and beer, then whipped his head to the right to find his cousin. "Are you *kidding* me right now?"

Halsey shrugged, tossed another throwing ax straight up before catching it mid-spin, then muttered, "*You* walked into *my* house. Gotta watch where you're going."

"Where I'm—" Brigham bit his tongue when the second ax spun across the room and buried its gleaming blade into the hunk of dead, aged tree trunk in the corner of the room. "Come *on*!"

Halsey frowned, hefted the third ax in the set, then took aim and let loose. After another whistle and thunk, all three weapons were buried in the exposed inner bark of the tree. The outer bark had been chipped away years ago, which made sense. They'd used the thing as target practice for years.

Brigham scowled and tilted his head to study the results of his cousin's weapon-throwing practice. He raised his eyebrows and laughed breathily. "If those axes were any closer together, they'd be on top of each other. Plus, you wouldn't have any more axes..."

Halsey glanced sidelong at him, then sighed and stormed across the room toward the dead trunk. "Why are you here, Brigham?"

"Uh...well, it's *not* to get my head chopped off by my cousin's flying axes."

"Huh."

He snorted and scanned one of his favorite rooms in existence. The walls were made of ancient willow and oak trees, the roof a cross-work lattice of supple branches and thick boughs. All the major gaps in the ceiling had filled with creeping kudzu and flowering vines, but not a single manmade material had gone into creating this room. Plenty of sunlight still streamed through the small spaces between the foliage and kept the place well-lit. An enchanted fountain close to the center of the room kept the airflow constantly moving and cooled things down.

Though Halsey had figured out how to work water and air magic together for an effective fountain cooler, she hadn't told her cousin the secret to managing it. That didn't stop Brigham from asking every six months or so.

He better not ask me about it today. I am so not in the mood.

As she reached for the closest ax by a fraction of an inch, her cousin laughed.

"Huh. That's all you have to say?"

"What else do you wanna hear? That I regret my decision to bring up the Mother of Monsters with the Council? That I've learned my lesson, and I'm ready to come back to work? That now I see the value of this beyond-stupid suspension and realize I was an idiot to bring it up?" She gripped the ax handle and wrenched the blade free with a splintering rip that made Brigham grimace. "You wanna know if I'm *rehabilitated* enough?"

He burst out laughing. Even when Halsey tossed the ax in her hand again, it wasn't enough of a threat to stop him.

"Come on, Hal." Brigham glanced around the naturally and magically created greenhouse. "It's only been three days."

"Yeah. Three days of torture." When her cousin laughed again, she snatched the second ax and ripped it out, sending splinters of dry wood to shower the plant life and the tops of her sneakers. "It's not funny."

"It's hilarious." He crossed the room toward the patio furniture they'd set up eons ago beside the cooling fountain and set the pizza and beer down. "As far as disciplinary action goes, a month of mandatory leave is a slap on the wrist."

"No, what *you* got was a slap on the wrist." Halsey wrenched the final ax free, then shoved it into her left hand with the others. Her left hand needed to strengthen its grip. "You still get to go on missions."

"With who? My partner's on vacation."

She cocked her head and plucked a single throwing ax with her free hand. "Call it a vacation one more time."

Brigham grinned, stepped away from the table, and gestured with both hands. "I brought lunch..."

Halsey considered launching the ax anyway. When the scent of hot pizza finally hit, her stomach squirmed and released a sad, empty squelch. "Totally not fair."

"Yeah, you're telling *me*. I come bearing gifts, and you bring vengeance and a swift death to the party."

"Seriously. If you came here to distract me from my outrageously disproportionate *punishment*, you're doing a terrible job."

Brigham kept smiling at her. "Well, you haven't tasted the pizza yet."

Halsey snorted, put her axes on a nice, round stump behind her, and headed to join her cousin. "You get why this is so awful, right?"

"It's still hot." He opened the box, and the scent of bread and cheese and marinara intensified.

"Thirty days, Brigham. They grounded me for *thirty days*. What am I supposed to do for that long?"

The pop and hiss of the first beer bottle opening overpowered the constant burbling of the cooling fountain before he handed it to her. "These are ice-cold. Had 'em in the freezer for like an hour before I came over."

Halsey absently took the beer, then knocked it back for a long guzzle. A quick burp made her cousin laugh, but she hardly noticed. Now that Brigham was here, she had somebody to vent to again. It felt a hell of a lot better than practicing with her throwing axes in involuntary solitude.

Brigham waggled his eyebrows. "Good, right?"

With a massive sigh, she dropped onto a white metal chair at the matching patio table. The set had seen enough Ambrosius Clan action that at least half of the white paint had chipped away to reveal the dull gray metal beneath. "All their talk about being proactive and not wanting history to repeat itself... It's like they're *trying* to make me crazy so they can say, 'See? Told you you're nuts. Forget about the damn coffin, Halsey.'"

"You *have* spent the last three days locked up in your own house, destroying our clubhouse with a set of axes I haven't seen you use since we were...what? Sixteen?"

After swallowing another enormous chug of beer, Halsey slowly turned her head and raised an eyebrow. "You think that makes me look crazy?"

"Eh..." Brigham cracked open another beer for himself, then dropped into the chair beside hers. "Depends on who's looking. *I* know why you're doing it, but for everyone else, I'd put the ax-throwing right up there with that time Wallace made himself a camel-piss bath."

She almost choked on her beer but managed to swallow before it ended up all over the box of pizza. "Wasn't that supposed to be a remedy for gorgon bites?"

"I think so." Brigham scratched his head with one hand and brought the beer bottle to his lips with the other. "Still not sure it worked for him, though."

"Yeah... The ax-throwing's working for me."

"See?" Brigham's grin returned as he raised his beer and nodded. "It could always be worse."

Halsey fixed him with a deadpan stare. "I'm not toasting to that."

"I'll do it for both of us." His next sip drained half the bottle, which he slammed down on the table before reaching for the pizza box. "You're gonna have to feed yourself, though."

Halsey leaned over the table to get closer to the box, inhaled deeply, then let it out through tight lips, puffing out her cheeks. "That smells way better than anything in my freezer."

"You really haven't left the house."

"For what?"

"Seriously, Hal? For *food*. Fresh air. Life. You know, normal stuff."

"Oh, you mean normal for elementals? The ones who *don't* get punished for paying attention to the signs and having inquisitive minds plus something to offer beyond being the perfect elemental soldier?"

Brigham stared blankly at the open pizza box and the barely visible steam rising off the surface of melted cheese and almost-burnt pepperoni. "Okay. You're milking this whole spurned-operative thing dry, cuz. Again, it's only been three days.

"True." With a shrug, Halsey reached for the pizza, then paused. "Wait, you ordered a pizza?"

"What?" Her cousin scoffed, launched forward in his chair, and tore away the first slice for himself. "Come on. I'm good, but I'm not *that* good."

"It says delivery on the box."

"Uh-huh."

Halsey reached for the pizza again, eyeing her cousin

sidelong in case this turned out to be another of his practical jokes. She wasn't in the mood. Simply sitting down with her militia partner and best friend was as much as she could handle right now. "That's not an explanation."

"Okay, fine. You got me." Brigham bit into his slice and briefly closed his eyes. "Wow. That's way better than I expected."

"What did you do to the pizza?"

"Nothing." After shoveling two more bites into his mouth, he washed it down with beer and wiped his mouth with his forearm. "At least nothing that wasn't supposed to be done to it."

"Brigham."

"I found a bunch of brand-new delivery boxes in the main kitchen, okay?" He licked the grease off his lips and gazed conspiratorially around the room, searching over his shoulder like they were in a crowded restaurant where dozens of other people might overhear. "I think Jonesy's been stockpiling them for the last few months."

With her first bite of pizza halfway to her mouth, Halsey laughed abruptly, then turned a suspicious scowl on the box. "Please tell me it's a stockpile of *empty* boxes."

"Well, yeah. That'd be gross otherwise."

She shook her head and couldn't bring herself to eat the slice of pizza that smelled amazing. "I'm missing something."

"It's because of Rupert." Brigham licked his fingers, then grabbed another slice. "You know, 'cause he's always trying to order delivery. Or telling the staff to pick him up a pizza from that place downtown he's in love with."

"Marco's?"

"Yeah, yeah. That one." Brigham shrugged. "I only found the boxes a month or two ago. Now that I think about it, though, this must've been going on longer. I haven't heard Rupert complain lately about his food taking so long to get there."

Halsey held up her pizza slice and inspected the underside, trying to anticipate what her cousin was saying about the lunch that now smelled *too* delicious. "So, the staff has a pile of empty boxes, and Rupert's been getting his Friday-night pizzas. Not from delivery."

"Right."

"Then where the heck did this come from?"

"Oh!" With a vigorous nod, Brigham shoved another half a slice into his mouth, then repeatedly stabbed a finger at the open box until he'd finished chewing. "The freezer."

"Wait, you brought me a frozen pizza in a fresh delivery box?"

"Which you still haven't tried, by the way. Yeah, I noticed."

Halsey stared, then threw her head back and roared with laughter. Brigham smirked while he chewed on another slice.

"Rupert doesn't know the difference?" Halsey finally asked.

"Hey, my brother's a lot of things." Brigham grabbed two more beers from the case and casually popped them open while he talked. "Best mechanic we have. The guy can fight off a pack of gremlins for twenty hours straight and never run outta steam. Plus, he's predictable as hell. Friday-night pizzas, six o'clock. He's too dumb to tell the difference."

"I can't believe we're having this conversation."

"Yeah, but you're smiling."

To keep herself from cracking up again or snaking a few vines around her cousin's mouth to shut him up, Halsey ate a massive bite of pizza and couldn't tell the difference either. She wouldn't tell *him* that, though.

CHAPTER TWELVE

They ate the entire pizza together and talked about anything but Halsey's probationary leave, their emergency Council meeting gone wrong, missions, Ireland, shiny silver coffins on the beach, or the legendary Mother of Monsters. The conversation lasted a few hours before they'd run through everything else that could have been said, then the greenhouse filled with another heavy silence.

Halsey stared at the label of her half-full beer bottle and darted glances at her cousin. Ever the optimist, Brigham wasn't ready to talk about the one thing weighing them both down. He'd spent the last five minutes slumped in the patio chair with his legs outstretched and his favorite lighter in hand. Now that they'd stopped talking, the only sound outside the cooling fountain was the clang and scratch of Brigham opening the lighter, igniting a flame, and whipping the metal lid shut. Every time a new flicker of fire rose, he pulled the flame with his other hand and molded it into a new shape.

A Ferrari. A martini glass. One of Halsey's throwing

axes. An overgrown willow tree. A vapid-looking, wart-covered troll head.

Each time he whipped the lighter shut, he tossed his newest fiery creation into the cooling fountain to avoid unintentional damage to their childhood hideout with his elemental magic preference.

Halsey wasn't worried about it. Brigham had a much better handle on fire than, say, the creeping vines he'd used to open the sliding door. It did bother her that her mission partner took after their Uncle Lawrence as far as magical preferences were concerned.

Another thing I used to love watching. Now it only makes me think of Lawrence's stupid, stuck-up entrance and what a massive mistake he'd made by brushing me under the rug.

The next fiery sculpture Brigham crafted was too close to home. A snarling werewolf stood upright on its hind legs, claws extended. It was impossible *not* to recognize what it was. He'd brought up their next topic of conversation, though he'd been trying so hard not to.

"Whoops." With a self-conscious chuckle, he released the shape of the flames and chucked the churning fireball into the fountain after the others. "Gotta practice that one more. It's obviously not ready."

"Okay, listen—"

"It's all good, cuz. Really. You know what? I'll stop." He shifted in his chair, stuck the lighter back in his pocket, then flashed what was supposed to be a normal, carefree grin. "Probably almost outta lighter fluid, too, you know?"

"Huh." Halsey set her beer down and folded her arms. "Is that why you look like you sat on a cactus?"

"On a… Ha. What?"

"You've been here for hours, man. We might as well get it out of the way now."

"I don't know what you're talking about." He shook his head, snatched his last beer, and drank. Even more beer couldn't mask his grimace of discomfort. After Brigham placed the empty bottle on the table, his only options were to stare blankly across the greenhouse or give in. He faced his cousin, eyes wide, then groaned and slumped in his chair. "Damn it, Hal."

"We need to talk about it," she insisted. "*Really* talk. When my thirty days to sit and think are up, we're gonna have the same problem on our hands. That coffin's still out there."

"We don't even know what it *is*."

"We *do* have an unidentified silver coffin that washed up on the beach, was picked up and transported by our best recovery team, and was almost immediately stolen from a ridiculously secure facility in a different country." Halsey pointed at her cousin. "That *is* proof. The whole Council heard my call with Patrick, which means they can't deny we found something valuable enough for someone to successfully steal from us."

"True." Brigham shrugged, then shook his head. "I can't believe my mom tried to pit Patrick against you."

"Well, it was Beatrice who said out loud what everybody else was already thinking."

"It sounded even dumber comin' outta *her* mouth." They laughed, and Brigham leaned sideways against an armrest, so he faced her directly. At his sympathetic frown, Halsey looked both reassured and irritated by *anyone* pitying her or her circumstances.

Brigham didn't pity her, though. He only knew her well enough to guess what was going through her head. "No one takes her dumb shit seriously, Hal. Everybody knows you would never compromise a mission or our employees like that. Patrick straight-up wouldn't lie for anyone. Not even you."

"Right." Halsey exhaled, propped her elbow on the table, then slumped her chin into her open hand. "Still, it's not about what we all know Patrick would or wouldn't do. Even if she was annoying enough to say it out loud, Beatrice isn't the only Council member who's been expecting me to walk in my mom's footsteps since the second I was born. Now they're trying to make me sound like Meemaw."

Brigham's smile had disappeared, leaving no hint of his usual joking nature. All he did was shake his head and hold her gaze. "You are *not* crazy, Hal."

"*I* know that." She took a break from the intensity of her cousin's gaze and gazed around the greenhouse again. They'd used this room as a safehouse for games, jokes, and complaining about life as a young Ambrosius elemental since they were eleven. She squinted at Brigham. "You didn't believe me either when we found the casket."

He straightened and spread his arms. "Hey. I'm a realist. Logic and reason are more useful to me than finding a few coincidences, throwing them together, and calling it Legend Soup."

Halsey chuckled. "Legend Soup?"

"Yeah. You think that casket's been lying on the bottom of the ocean for over a thousand years. That it came up on the Summer Solstice under a full moon, and the Blood Matriarch washed up, awoke, and pulled herself out of the cozy silver box. On the other hand, I look at it like this." He counted out each of his points on his fingers. "Summer Solstice. Full moon. Way more werewolves than should ever be together in one place, acting super weird in Ireland. One giant alpha, like nothing we've seen anywhere in the world, *appeared* to call them all back at the last second.

"You happened to catch sight of a weird silver coffin on a bed of seaweed. The claw marks on that lid could have come from any of the dozens of werewolves on the cliffs that night. And yeah, somebody managed to steal the thing. That's weird, but it doesn't prove the Mother of Monsters floated back up from the seabed, let herself out, and is walking around out there being all revenge-y and…I don't know. Making more monsters."

Halsey licked her lips as she tried to figure out how she wanted to respond. "First of all, the Blood Matriarch is real."

"Sure. Also, most likely dead."

"That's where your attitude about this whole thing hits a brick wall, cuz." She flashed a tight smile before adding, "We're dealing with *magic* and *monsters* here. In our line of work, logic and reason are sitting at the kiddie table. That's how this works."

"Aw, come on." Brigham laughed her comment aside. "It doesn't matter how weird, supernatural, or mostly impossible it is. We're professionals. Maybe logic and reason mean different things to us versus the rest of the world, but we still know how to gauge what's happening. Even in *our* world, things work a certain way and follow certain rules. That's all I'm saying."

"Two months ago, that would've made sense. Except things *aren't* working a certain way anymore."

"What?"

Halsey widened her eyes, then swept a hand around the greenhouse. "That's when our missions got weird, Brigham. That's when monsters started to act funnier than normal, and we had to start compensating for it. Nothing as weird as almost a hundred werewolves throwing themselves at us like lemmings off a cliff, though."

Brigham wrinkled his brow. "We're going through a phase right now, that's all."

"Yeah, and it's called massive change!" She hadn't meant to shout, but she was so tired of everybody else writing off her concerns that she couldn't bear receiving the same treatment from her partner.

It's not his fault they took me off the job for a month. Still, there's no way he doesn't see what's happening out there and how it's all connected.

Ever the level-headed half of their team, Brigham smirked at her. "I'm glad you left those axes on the other side of the room."

Halsey closed her eyes, tried and failed not to laugh, then met her cousin's occasionally macabre humor. "Yeah, I'm thinking I should start carrying at least *one* all the time." They shared a chuckle that calmed her down enough to continue making her point. "You were there with me on that beach. You saw what I saw. You know the monsters aren't following their own rules the way they used to. You can't write *that* off as Legend Soup. Which is a stupid name for it, by the way."

He snapped his fingers and pointed at her. "Yeah, but it stuck."

"We have no idea what's going on out there. Coffin or no coffin, Mother of Monsters or some other weird thing from inside that box, we can't keep looking at the world like it's all another mission and the militia can handle it like we always have. The entire Council failed to hear that point."

"Oh, I know." Brigham sagely nodded as he grabbed an empty beer bottle and spun it on the surface of the table. "I'm with you all the way on that one. I guess, putting all legends and controversy and possible conspiracies aside, we need to focus on who stole the silver coffin."

"Right." Halsey snorted. "Actually, that was gonna be my next point. I'm glad we're back on the same page."

"Great, so you can leave the axes on the other side of the room while I'm here."

"Very funny."

Now that they'd agreed on where to direct their focus, the cousins sat in thoughtful silence for another five minutes. Brigham produced his lighter for another round of creative fire-shaping. This time the shapes were simple, three-dimensional forms. Triangle, square, sphere, key, beer bottle.

Halsey put up with his meditative habit. It meant her cousin was looking for solutions instead of trying not to talk about the figurative, or possibly literal, monster rearing its ugly head in front of the Ambrosius Clan. Once again, the constant burble of the cooling fountain mixed with the intermittent *clink-scrape-clink* rhythm of

Brigham's lighter became the background noise. He finally sighed in concession. "It could've been another clan."

She frowned and looked up from the spot on the table she'd been staring at for the last fifteen minutes. "You think we should start questioning the Havalons?"

He shrugged. "Or the Grendier Clan."

"Yeah, that'll go over well. 'Of course we questioned another elemental family, Lawrence. Who else would have enough guts and magic to steal from us? No, we didn't find the coffin, but an entire clan thinks the *whole* Ambrosius family's insane now, so go, team.'"

Brigham laughed and pumped a fist in solidarity. "I could print up a bunch of shirts that say, 'I stand with Meemaw.'"

"Hey, that's perfect. *So* helpful in getting them to take us seriously."

"We don't have to barge into another Clan's headquarters, ranting about coffins and Blood Matriarchs and the stars aligning for the end of the world." Brigham laughed at her exasperated glare. "Come on, Hal. We're all professionals. The Clans have different ways of doing things, sure. However, if we approach it like an actual investigation instead of a conspiracy theory, they *will* take us seriously."

"I get your point. Really." Halsey sat back and folded her arms, crinkling her nose in thought. "That doesn't feel right, though. Another elemental family *stealing* from us? Without a word or leaving a single clue behind? Come on. We both know the Havalons *and* the Grendiers would be way too proud not to gloat about pulling that off."

Her cousin sniggered. "True. They've been behind in their numbers for the last…what? Three decades?"

"Right, so if other elementals took the coffin, we would've heard something by now. At least Lawrence would have, and I don't think that man knows *how* to lie."

"He's lying to himself about that dumbass suit."

Halsey tried to cover a laugh before meeting her cousin's gaze. "You should talk to him about that."

"Yeah, no thanks. I'd rather ask him about the other Clans."

She drew a deep breath. Now that they'd broken the tension, the ideas kept flooding in the way they normally did when Halsey wasn't suspended from missions for trying to help her family. "I honestly don't think it was another elemental family, though."

"Oh, yeah?" Brigham ran a hand through his hair, then batted his eyelashes and grinned. "Do enlighten the rest of us concerning your suspicions, young operative."

Halsey barely registered his sarcasm or the semi-subtle way he'd already started blowing off her next idea. The more she considered the possibilities, the more this specific one made sense. "It could've been blood humans. A small group of them, most likely. If a single one was strong enough to try stealing from *us*…"

"Ha. Yeah, that's a good one." Her cousin leaned back and kicked his legs out. "Hey, I got one. Maybe it was the Mother of Monsters herself! She popped out of that casket, came back to find it missing, then magicked herself in and out of our facility without a trace. Because, you know, she's the Mother of Monsters."

"See, I can tell you're joking."

His vapid stare confirmed that of course he was joking.

Halsey tapped her fingers on the armrest and shook her head. "I'm not, though."

"Seriously?" Brigham snorted. "You want me to entertain that scenario like it's actually possible? Come on, Hal. The blood humans were wiped out during the great war. Otherwise, we'd be fighting them along with the monsters. They're gone."

"Obviously not."

He stared at her for what felt like a really long time, then his smile disappeared. "Okay. Explain to me how that's obvious."

"Wow. I didn't realize I needed to school you with a history lesson about magic and monsters and our own *family*…"

"Yeah, yeah. Whatever. Pretend I'm clueless and coming into this for the first time."

Halsey clicked her tongue and shook her head, but a small smile flickered across her lips. "Okay. Blood humans and shapeshifting magic against elementals and our magic. Since the beginning of time or whatever."

"Ooh." Brigham propped his chin in a hand and widened his eyes at her. "I'm learning so much already."

"Shut up. Blood humans got out of control, the elementals had to put a stop to it, and the great war was fought. If we're gauging the victory of that war on which side had the most soldiers left at the end, that would be us, obviously. We didn't *really* win, though. We couldn't kill the Blood Matriarch, so we had to stop her some other way."

Brigham thrust a fist in the air and shouted in a deep announcer's voice, "When our powers combine, we *are* the ones who chucked her coffin in the middle of the ocean!"

Halsey blinked and cocked her head. "Are you done?"

"We both are. That's the end of the story, Hal. The elementals sealed her away in the Circle of Creation, and the magic it took to get the job done wiped most of us out before kicking off the last Ice Age. We came south, lived regular human lives that happened to have magic sprinkled in, and that's that. No more blood humans."

"You see where your logic is seriously skewed on this, though, right?" When her cousin shrugged, Halsey fought to keep from yelling the rest at him. *If he's as into logic and reason as he says, how the hell does he not see the way history works?* She exhaled, calmed her own frustration, and continued. "Okay, look. The elementals sealed the Mother of Monsters up tight and got her off their hands to protect the world. They *thought* they got rid of the blood humans altogether, but that's impossible."

"Why? Because it fits your hunch that she's back?"

"No, Brigham. Because there are still monsters!" She laughed bitterly and sat up straighter. "Seriously. Remember the stories Meemaw used to tell us when we were kids? Any monsters left after the great war would've been wiped out by the Ice Age *our* family started. Something had to happen to get them back in the world, right? The Ambrosius Clan hasn't been fighting monsters all the way back *to* the Ice Age. Only since the tenth century or something."

"Huh." He stroked his chin and looked like he was considering it until he replied, "Maybe it took 'em that long to thaw out again."

"For the love of—seriously?"

"It's possible."

"No, it's not."

Halsey couldn't decide whether to laugh in his face or throttle him until he started thinking clearly again. Either option would have been effective in its own way. Instead, she decided to keep explaining what she'd assumed he already knew. It was also possible that Brigham knew what she was trying to say and enjoyed squeezing it out of her anyway, but she wouldn't stop now.

"Think about the story, okay? When monsters came back into the world, it was *only* because the Blood Matriarch was freed. Maybe for a short amount of time, but it was long enough for her magic to run wild and create a bunch of new and different forms. She's already been out of that casket once."

"Uh-huh. So, who put her back in?"

"I don't know. Maybe more elementals. That's not the point." Halsey grabbed the beer bottle in front of her, then remembered it was empty and set it down with a sigh. "The point is, she got out. The only kind of person who could have called the Blood Matriarch's prison from the bottom of the ocean and let her out is a blood human. Therefore, they still exist."

Brigham released a whining hum and shook his head. "Again, cuz. That's taking all the pieces that kinda look like they fit and smashing it all together into—"

"Don't say Legend Soup, dude." She pointed a warning finger at him. "Just don't."

"Well, at least you get the point."

"You're not getting mine."

"Hal, listen." He grabbed his armrests, scooted sideways from the table, and turned toward her. "There are a dozen different ways monsters could've made it back into the world, okay? Any one of them is as possible as the next. But taking Meemaw's bedtime stories and calling them history? That's asking for a wild blood human chase."

"Maybe." Halsey folded her arms. "Maybe that's what we need right now. Because monsters are doing seriously weird things, and somebody stole from us. Those things used to be impossible too, so maybe it's time we paid attention to the bedtime stories instead of writing them off. Maybe we need to listen to Meemaw."

They stared at each other, then Brigham chuckled and shrugged. "Okay. So that's an option. The thief was either another elemental or a blood human with a low chance of existing right now. Or hey, maybe it was a regular human. Somebody clueless about magic and monsters and everything in between, and they wanted to get their hands on a nice shiny box to sell for a fortune."

"Oh, jeez." She rolled her eyes and puffed out her cheeks. "I don't even wanna think about the problems we'd have on our hands if that's the case. You know how normal humans blow everything out of proportion if they get so much as a whiff of supernatural evidence. *One* glowing strand of chimera hair in the wrong hands…"

"Hey, some of 'em are on the right track." He shrugged. "You know what I don't get, though? How the hell they see a tiny bit of magic and take it in the opposite direction. I mean, lately it's all been UFOs or government conspiracies or whatever other shit doesn't make any sense."

Halsey raised an eyebrow and bobbed her head from side to side. "What do you think? Do we need to start looking for a regular civilian dumb enough to steal from us?"

He frowned and examined her. "That's not funny. How the hell would we do *that*?"

"I don't know. Maybe Patrick'll get back to me with more useless information that nobody would think is evidence except for me." She tapped her temple and winked. "Because *I* have an open mind."

"No, you know what you have?" Brigham nodded at the table. "An empty beer and a cousin who isn't ready to throw in the towel on drinking tonight. Excuse me while I get us more." He shifted to pull his phone out, and Halsey snorted.

"We can't get pizza deliveries all the way out here. What makes you think anyone's gonna bring in a booze order from the city?"

"Oh, they don't have to." He started a call and lifted the phone to his ear. "Jonesy likes me a hell of a lot more than Rupert, and I know the man keeps extra alcohol with his stack of extra pizza boxes."

CHAPTER THIRTEEN

Two days later, Halsey got a text from Brigham instead of an in-person visit, which hardly ever happened. The message did nothing to improve her outlook on the next twenty-five days of her suspension.

> **Can't hang out this weekend. They sent me to Kansas this morning for banshees. With Owen. Kill me now.**

While Brigham was more concerned with being sent out with yet another Ambrosius cousin as his temporary partner, Halsey had a hard time getting over the Council's decision to send him out at all. Without her.

If they think taking me out of the game and sending him off with our worst monster hunter is gonna keep us from being partners when my thirty days are up, they've got another one coming.

Still, she couldn't bring herself to reply to his text. Mostly because there wasn't anything to say to a situation like that. She didn't want Brigham to think she was angry with him, which was hard to avoid over text.

She tried to busy herself cleaning up around the house, sharpening her throwing axes, and cleaning her grandfather's old bolt-action rifle. Percival McAllister hadn't been an elemental, though the man's life had been as far from a regular civilian human as one could get.

The way Halsey's grandmother told the stories when she felt like talking about her late life partner, her grandfather had been as fierce in the field as any Ambrosius elemental. He'd refused to stay home and "let the magical people do all the work." His rifle was as close as Halsey could get to him. Even then, it didn't carry the same reassurance or sense of purpose as usual when she sat to disassemble and clean the weapon.

What was the point of taking such care with any of her weapons or anti-monster paraphernalia when active missions needed completing, and she was stuck in here?

For the rest of that week, she focused on minor improvements to the greenhouse. She wove the loose vines into a thicker curtain of foliage to block the worst of the direct sunlight during the midsummer heat. A few raised tree roots created extra built-in seating. She carved a face into the dead tree trunk she used for target practice that looked remarkably like her Uncle Lawrence. Still, there was only so much to do around an old cottage, even one with a magical add-on greenhouse. There were even fewer ways to keep Halsey from growing bored, restless, stir-crazy, and eventually pissed off all over again.

During the second week, she decided to quit waiting for the end of her suspension period before getting back to work. Technically, being on leave meant she could go wherever she wanted and spend her time however she saw fit. As long as it wasn't an active militia mission.

She'd been complaining about needing a vacation for the last several weeks before her emergency meeting. Now she couldn't stomach the idea of kicking back and doing nothing when the Ambrosius Clan, and all other elemental families, faced a serious problem. If they couldn't do their job protecting humans from the truth of monsters this world wasn't ready to face, they might even be looking at another great war. That wasn't even the worst-case scenario.

There was no use dwelling on the possibilities, so Halsey decided the best way to spend the rest of her mandatory leave time was doing what her family refused to. She'd investigate the legends and histories on her own.

Fortunately, the Ambrosius Clan believed in properly documenting nearly every piece of their family history. This included every elemental born to the Clan and each member's track record of monster hunting and militia service. Halsey wasn't sure how far back their meticulously maintained records went. Yet if there was any chance of discovering how they were supposed to handle a threat like the Mother of Monsters returning, she figured she'd find it there.

Seeing as they're so worried about 'repeating the mistakes of the past.' This is how we keep from doing that. History.

She had no idea how much history there was to sift through or how long it would take to find what she wanted. Hopefully, no longer than two weeks because then she'd be back in action.

On the day she decided to start her search, Halsey

showered, ate a bowl of cereal, and read the news on her phone. Even when she wasn't suspended from work, that had become one of her daily habits. One never knew when they'd find a hint of monsters running amok in the news reports of strange activity, mysterious break-ins, or grand larceny of unexpected objects where the authorities had zero leads. Most of the time, it could be attributed to a doppelganger or ghoul, though human civilians were often as good at making bad choices and thwarting authorities as monsters were.

This morning, the strangest thing Halsey read had nothing to do with monsters. At first.

As she read about the strange weather patterns repeatedly striking the northwestern coast of Africa in the middle of the summer, something in the back of her mind prompted her to pull up a continental map and look at where this was happening.

"Seriously. In the scheme of things, Africa is a straight drop down from Ireland. If this is a Mother of Monsters thing, she sure is taking her time from continent to continent."

Of course, that was still pure conjecture. The news outlets wouldn't cover strange weather patterns and natural phenomena following a newly freed, several-millennia-old Blood Matriarch. Yet Halsey couldn't shed the nagging suspicion that something about this weather was important. Specifically, the vast amounts of thick fog, churning waters, and stormy skies popping up along the African coast that lasted no longer than ten minutes before perfect summer days returned.

What are all those fog and storm clouds leaving behind that nobody's noticing?

That unanswered question, on top of all the others she'd been carrying for weeks, finally got her out of her cottage and on her way across the property toward the massive estate house. In all honesty, it was the last place Halsey wanted to be right now, but the only place that might offer useful information about the history of elemental warriors and the monsters they hunted.

As she pulled the cottage's front door shut, her phone buzzed in the back pocket of her shorts. She pulled it out without stopping to think about what to expect.

She hadn't expected a text from Brigham.

Would you consider nesting with birds and freezing everything around it but the tree normal behavior for a wyvern?

Frowning at her phone, Halsey walked down the trail leading away from the cottage, not built but worn down over the years by various family members walking it.

I can't tell if he's asking me for advice or making another joke.

You mean your partner doesn't have an answer?

After she sent the message, she realized it sounded more irritated than she'd intended, even though Brigham hardly took offense to much of anything. As far as she knew.

His reply was immediate and instantly soothed her worries about sending the wrong vibes over a text.

Come on, Hal. I only have one partner. Owen's just the idiot they sent me out with on this next mission, and he's almost as bad as Rupert. Dude has no clue what he's doing. Help a cousin out, huh?

She snorted and looked up from her phone long enough to make sure she was headed in the right direction as she typed out a vague yet helpful bit of advice.

No. Wyverns roosting with anything isn't normal. Don't tell that to The Burger, or he'll try to tackle those things with his bare hands.

Seeing it written out made her laugh as she walked at a slow, easy pace across the rolling hills of the Ambrosius Clan's one-hundred-and-eighty-acre property. She knew the path by heart, but it still filled her with a level of appreciation she wasn't getting from the Council or from work. Seeing as she wasn't technically working right now.

We've been right here in Lufkin, Texas, for the last four hundred years. Fighting monsters with this place as our home base. How am I still surprised by how damn hot it gets out here?

Halsey swiped the back of a hand across her forehead, which was already starting to drip with sweat from the Texas summer heat and humidity. Her ancestors had picked one of the best areas in the state to build the hub of all Ambrosius family activity. Back then, it had probably been much easier for the Council to establish a stronghold here, where there was so much more space compared to the numbers of regular humans.

At least, that was how Halsey liked to imagine it. The fact that her family's property spanned this much acreage across a large greenbelt and the surrounding countryside meant they were as comfortable as anyone was likely to get in midsummer Texas. They'd had to place a lot more enchantments over the last hundred and fifty years to ensure civilian humans didn't stumble across millennia-old elemental secrets. There were quite a lot more people in Texas these days.

By the time the back end of the enormous Ambrosius Clan mansion came into view at the bottom of the gently sloping hill, Halsey was kicking herself for not bringing a change of clothes. Her T-shirt clung to her torso, sweat dripped down her legs, and she wiped her forehead every five seconds to keep sweat from trickling into her eyes.

No. I would not have picked Lufkin in the middle of the summer as my next vacation spot. When all this is over, I'm going to Tahiti or wherever else has the lowest number of monsters to interrupt me. And I'm going alone.

The back doors to the estate house weren't nearly as grand or opulent as the front, and they didn't make as much noise when she tugged one open and slipped inside. The instant wave of cool, dry air hitting her face was an immense relief, and she stood there in the back hallway of the west wing with her eyes closed to let the feeling sink in.

When you can manipulate the air temperature without paying a cent for central AC, why not keep the entire building at a frigid sixty-eight degrees?

The thought made her snort. She opened her eyes and

looked around the narrow, relatively dark, purely functional hallway. Most of the west wing had been added onto the original layout over the last seventy years to accommodate the Ambrosius Clan's growing number of family members *and* household staff. One thing that hadn't changed about this part of the mansion was the Clan's enormous library, which held the same location since her ancestors had built this place.

The last time Halsey had the desire or the time to visit the Ambrosius Library was almost too long ago to remember. So much had happened since she'd gone from monster hunter in training to full-fledged militia operative. Remembering this brought a barrage of memories crashing through her mind. She grimaced as she stood there alone without a single staff member in sight.

You're not seventeen anymore, Halsey. You have as much right to the library as everyone else in this family, so use it.

Thinking it was one thing. Settling the knot in her gut at the idea of what she might have to ignore or endure when she stepped foot in the library was altogether different.

CHAPTER FOURTEEN

Though she knew exactly where she was going, when Halsey reached the double doors leading into the Ambrosius Library, she thought for a split second that she'd gotten herself lost. They looked so much like the intricately carved and filigreed Council room doors. The urgency and frustration she'd felt before storming inside to call an emergency meeting two weeks ago came rushing back full force.

She gritted her teeth, stared at the library's entrance, and forced herself to find the differences.

For instance, where the Council room's doors had carvings of leaves and vines, the library doors depicted a surprisingly accurate copy of the night sky over the northern hemisphere, complete with the proper constellations. Interspersed among the carved silver stars were thin lines of various metals forming patterns that made her think of her dad.

This could be his work, and I've never even thought to ask him about it.

There were also a few etchings of various scientific equations and illustrative figures from Classical-period philosophical works. Halsey snorted over the stark differences she hadn't noticed at first.

Sure. Logic, reason, and the scientific method. All part of meticulous record-keeping for everyone and everything in a long, glorious, magical *bloodline. I'd love to know how many other people in this family see the contradictions built into our protocols.*

The thought of Beatrice trying to complete a complicated math equation or Lawrence attempting a modern performance of their family's centuries-old ballads made Halsey laugh. That gave her the will to bite the bullet and walk through those doors. The library wasn't the Council room, after all. She was twenty-three, not seventeen. Two weeks ago, the Council had agreed she was one of their best operatives, even though they'd suspended her anyway.

What was there to worry about?

With a crooked smile, Halsey grabbed an iron handle crafted into a rolled scroll tied with ribbon. The shape of it felt both foreign and oddly familiar, and she drew a deep breath as she tightened her grip.

Feels like I'm back in school, trying to prove myself worthy all over again. Except I'm a hell of a lot more experienced this time.

The door smoothly opened when she tugged on the iron-scroll handle. Someone clearly felt it important to keep the library door hinges well-oiled and in top condition, while the doors to the Council room always carried a certain heaviness of neglect. Halsey shook her head and forced herself to pay attention to what was in front of her.

You're here for a reason, and it's not to think about how much you screwed up with the Council. Find the damn history lesson you know is hidden in here somewhere, then move on.

The ponderous wooden door whispered shut behind her, and she glanced around the library's vestibule. Now, the feeling of having stepped back into monster-hunting school was impossible to ignore.

The Ambrosius Clan Library was so massive it could have contained a more-than-comfortable single-family home. If that family were familiar with magic and didn't run screaming when they saw what was inside.

A massive statue of one of Halsey's great-great-great-great-ancestors took up the center of the front anteroom. Euphemia Ambrosius in all her glory, with a quiver of arrows strapped to her back as she wielded a longbow in one hand and clenched a monster's severed head in the other. The detail was gruesome, and Halsey examined the thing with a satisfied smirk before she pointed at Euphemia's defiant expression. "Life goals right there, Emmy. I bet they didn't appreciate the changes you made until you were gone. That's what happens to heroes and fire starters, right? Only recognized when you're dead and—"

"Halsey Ambrosius." The sharp, nippy voice she'd strived for years to forget echoed across the anteroom. "I find your unfailingly morose attitude appalling in the presence of such greatness."

She spun to face her Great-Uncle Charlemagne, Greta's older brother, and tried on the tightest smile she could muster. "Charlie! It's been a while—"

"Once *again*," Charlemagne barked as he shuffled across

the pristine hardwood floors, his cane clicking softly beside him now that he'd finally covered the tip of it with felt cushioning, "I was given the name Charlemagne by my mother, your great-grandmother Edna. I will not suffer the mangling of it, no matter how cute you may think it is."

Halsey pressed her lips together and swallowed, unable to take her eyes off the man in his mid-eighties with a hunch so steep he was practically at a ninety-degree angle. *Yep. He's still a stickler for the rules, and he still sounds like a barking Chihuahua.*

Her great-uncle traversed the vestibule and stopped a mere two inches away. He squinted behind his thick, frameless glasses and craned his neck to peer at her face. "What the hell are you doing here?"

It took everything she had not to laugh. Instead, she cleared her throat and gestured toward the statue of Euphemia. "Thought I'd pop by to brush up on some family history. You know, while I've got the time."

"You mean until you've whiled away your suspension." Charlemagne raised one bushy eyebrow, his nostrils flaring as his face pinched.

"Yeah. Something like that." Halsey stared into his glassy eyes. They'd once been the same brilliant blue as his sister's but had faded into a dull, colorless gray. *Awesome. Sounds like everybody and their great-uncle heard about Aidan's only kid getting a thirty-day timeout for absolutely nothing. Probably should've expected that.*

After thirty seconds of staring, she broke the silence to escape those beady gray eyes and constant scowl. "I'm gonna go look through a few things. I promise I won't bother you."

With another smile as tight as the first one, Halsey backed away and started to skirt the statue of Euphemia. "You know what? You won't even know I'm here."

Charlemagne's left eye twitched. "I doubt that."

"Okay, thanks!" she called over her shoulder, pretending not to hear the same gruff disapproval she'd gotten nearly every day during her seven years of training. *He's old, and he's family. What else am I supposed to do?*

"For your information," Charlemagne yelped as Halsey disappeared behind the enormous stone figure, "this statue was commissioned and completed well before Euphemia's death in 1847. Her greatness was unequivocally recognized during her lifetime. The statue was merely *erected* after her death."

"Really?" Though she couldn't see her great-uncle anymore with a huge sculpture between them, she assumed they were the only two people in the library. Everyone else had something better to do. However, his last-ditch effort to prove how little she knew only made her more curious. "Why'd they wait 'til after she died to put it up?"

Charlemagne cleared his throat. "Because she hated it. And she wielded that much respect."

The remnants of his last statement hung in the vestibule. Halsey frowned playfully at her great-great-great-great-something's stone backside, which did look like the sculptor had spent considerable time getting the details down. Perhaps, in the case of Euphemia Ambrosius' rear end, accentuating them. *So, they decided to stop respecting you when you died, huh? Same thing, I guess, only in reverse. I would've liked to ask* you *a few questions about the Mother of Monsters...*

She delivered a sharp salute to her powerful, well-respected Ambrosius ancestor, then turned on her heels and jogged up a half-flight of steps. The stairs led to the partially raised section of the library that housed handwritten accounts of Ambrosius Clan members and their accomplishments, spanning as far back in history as the oldest parchments they could preserve.

Most of that was accomplished through a complicated, highly effective weaving of protective enchantments in both the air and the moisture levels surrounding the oldest records. The family records were organized chronologically, so the farther she walked toward the back of the section, the colder it got. Halsey split her attention between wrapping her arms around herself to keep warm in her damp, sweaty clothes and trying to ignore the low temperatures so she could handle the centuries-old documents.

By the time she found family records from around the middle of the tenth century, the approximate date of the Blood Matriarch's short-lived return, her teeth chattered, and she couldn't feel her toes. She carefully unrolled the oldest of the documents and tried to sift through the old languages of elemental magic, which she'd mastered only to graduate from her training and never really needed again. Yet the oldest and coldest documents from her family's past gave her nothing.

No mentions of monsters popping up out of the blue. No accounts of surviving blood humans or brief run-ins with the Blood Matriarch while she'd been allegedly freed.

The only thing that sparked interest was the sudden change around the year 960 A.D. Either the original records keeper had taken on an entirely new tone in marking down the course of events back then, or a different Ambrosius elemental had been chosen to continue the tradition.

It was hard to tell the cause of such a drastic change in historical voice, but it wasn't out of the question to assume it had to do with the abrupt, unexplained switch in the type of information being recorded. The details switched from *'So-and-so helped a small, local village break through their severe and debilitating drought'* to *'We fought off a pack of small goblins no taller than a dog.'*

"This is ridiculous," Halsey muttered as she returned one meticulous record full of useless information before pulling another from the magically climate-controlled shelf. "If you're trying to keep records of every little thing, how hard is it to add a note? 'Oh, yeah. By the way, monsters are here now. According to legend, it was our job to fight these weird creatures off *before* the war, so now we think we'll follow the pattern and take up the mantle again.'"

If she was honest, she would have said there was a record missing from the scrupulous timeline. It wasn't impossible, but that would mean the missing information had either been lost, destroyed, or stolen. None of those options inspired confidence in her family's ability to protect their prized historical records or themselves.

The last thing we need is something else stolen from us.

Still, the more she searched through the records for any hint about what had changed, the more it felt like a missing piece of the historical puzzle was actually a big deal.

It took her another half-hour of pretending to read scrolls and old tomes before she'd worked up the courage, and the patience, to ask Charlemagne if he knew what happened to this glaring chunk of missing time. As she circled the far side of the library on the second level for a bird's-eye view, her phone buzzed in her pocket. Halsey choked on a laugh when she saw yet another text from Brigham, who still didn't have it together on his current mission.

Hey, Hal. You busy?

Halsey shook her head in amusement and tapped out a quick reply.

Just trying to pick apart some Legend Soup. Don't worry, it's not mine. Somebody else made it.

When her cousin responded almost immediately, she figured he was using voice-to-text. Probably in the middle of a fight with the wyverns he'd been ordered to get under control. The image of Brigham in Kansas, battling wyverns with his lighter in one hand, his phone waving around in the other, and their six-foot-ten cousin Owen huffing alongside made her want to ask for a picture.

Screw the soup, cuz. I mean, not literally. Obviously. But I could use a few suggestions right now. These wyverns are kicking our asses, and I'm pretty sure

Owen forgot to eat breakfast today. He's basically running on empty and not even trying to meet my expectations. Any idea how to get these things to quit trying to hatch somebody else's eggs before they burn this whole ranch to the ground?

Halsey frowned at her phone and tried to imagine wyverns doing anything other than guarding their tiny caves and terrifying children on camping trips with bursts of green fire. It was easier to imagine Brigham freaking out because Owen was a magical meathead who could take orders but couldn't think for himself.

Yeah, he's my partner. I'm the one who should be out there with him, not The Burger.

She decided to make a deal with him because he was also her cousin. Sometimes, family extorted each other when necessary.

Hang tight. I'm thinking.

CHAPTER FIFTEEN

Instead of stalking through the library to find crabby old Great-Uncle Charlie, Halsey raced across the second-story walkway lining the entire library, took the closest staircase two at a time to the ground floor, then barreled past the "Clan Militia Rules and Regulations" section to head for "Monsters—Species, Sub-Species, and General Characteristics."

The Ambrosius Library wasn't like a regular public library with tons of different topics and genres. No separating fact from fiction or knowing what one was getting themselves into by picking a specific genre over another. In Halsey's world, reality *was* fantastical, even if it wasn't the most exciting.

Never thought I'd be running through the library for someone else's mission. That's Ethel's job. They should let her start working early.

Then again, if Florence's youngest daughter Ethel was sixteen or seventeen instead of eight, the Council might have considered giving Halsey's youngest cousin a job like that. The girl was always in the library—except today, oddly enough. She always had a quick, smart reply anytime one of her older cousins tried to stump her with a question about elemental magic, monsters, or both.

Yeah, sure. Good work, Halsey. Wishing an eight-year-old was here instead of sucking it up and doing the legwork yourself.

That made her snort. Fortunately, the sound didn't make its way into the main area of the library because now she'd reached the Monsters section. The circular room inside the library could have been used for oratory performances, with rows of benched seating around the perimeter and the stage sunk eight feet in the center of the room. Now, those seats had been transformed into a circular bookshelf. To find what she was looking for, Halsey had to get to the center of the stage and make her own performance.

With absolutely no audience.

When her sneakers hit the sunken center of the room, the Monsters section came to life. More or less.

Like the trap doors and hidden mechanisms of the Council room, this special treasury of elemental knowledge and expertise passed down through generations started to move. Segments of wood and plaster twisted and spun like the room was a giant lid someone was trying to twist off. Thin, gleaming lines of perfect metalworking craftsmanship coiled between each level of circular bookshelves.

Each sub-section of information lit up with magical color-coding, displaying holograms of individual monster types in the air three inches above the appropriate shelves. One for vampires, one for trolls, one for ogres, one each for homunculi of various types—red, blue, purple, orange, green. Several of the enchanted creature faces snarled at Halsey as she spun slowly and searched for the one she wanted.

The wyvern shelf came into view, marked by a narrow, hissing, dragon-like face in neon pink light. She darted toward the section, dodging several moving shelves in the process. Even after growing up in this mansion and spending almost her entire adolescence in this library, she still had no idea how to turn off the magical turntable of Monster Facts.

A yelp escaped her as she barely avoided being whisked away by the chattering three-headed chimera section. She pivoted briefly to watch them spin away, then turned back to the section on wyverns. Published works, handwritten volumes, and well-preserved three-ring binders contained everything one could want to know about tiny dragons with only two legs stuffed the shelves. All around her, the room rumbled and shifted and spun like a giant roulette wheel.

It took a second to find the notebook she'd been looking for. She had to check the front covers of several spiralbound books, none of which provided the title of the DIY volume on the spine. She felt like she'd hit the jackpot when she pulled out the correct one.

"All right, here we go. *The Intricate and Often Overlooked Mating Habits of the Modern Wyvern in North America* by Florence Ambrosius. That's not a mouthful or anything." Halsey settled the notebook in one hand and flipped through it with the other as the Monsters section kept spinning around her. *She is* not *going to hear about this, or she'll never stop talking about her* writing process. *I think I'm the only person in the family who even knows she wrote the darn thing.*

As she flipped through her aunt's delicately handwritten collection of field notes and analysis graciously donated to the Ambrosius Clan library, her phone buzzed again. Then again. She almost chucked it across the room before remembering she was here because her cousin had reached out an annoying number of times.

She looked at her phone. Either the estate's cell service was lagging, or Brigham Ambrosius was officially freaking out.

Any time, Hal…

Okay, I know I can be overly casual about things sometimes. This is not one of those things. You said hang tight, but I don't have a whole lot left to hang onto.

Damn it, Halsey, help me out! We're getting killed out here! Yeah, that's figurative for now, but I don't know how much longer 'til it's literal! HELLO?

She ignored his panicked urgency and focused on what she could actually control. Which happened to be her access to the only information that could help him at this point.

Then she found it. The page detailing the tiny, mundane, seemingly useless facts about wyverns that no one in the Ambrosius Clan or any other elemental family would find worth writing down except Florence. Halsey had a feeling this was exactly what her cousins in the field needed.

After she'd figured it out, she tossed the notebook back onto the wyvern shelf before it spun away, then focused on delivering career-saving, and possibly lifesaving, information.

> **Okay, try this. Wyverns like to line their nests with smooth rocks and pebbles they think are the "most beautiful." Find the ugliest, dullest, most jagged rocks you can get and dump them at the tree. Or you can throw them at the nests. That should work. You can chase them off when they're airborne or give them a nice tornado on their way out. That's a thing in Kansas.**

> **If you want help with the next item on the list of weird monsters you can't figure out, you'll have to convince the Council that I'm fit to go back out in the field. That's the price of my genius.**

Halsey didn't expect an immediate reply from him. Brigham was no doubt out there right now, putting her unexpected helpful advice to good use. At this point, Owen was probably a lot more helpful than he'd been during their entire mission. He had directions to follow now and could put his brawn to work.

She also didn't expect the constantly spinning motion of the Monsters section to stop so abruptly. The absence of movement and momentum knocked her off balance. She reeled on the step, her arms flailing. Fortunately, she got her feet under her before she fell upward into the priceless volumes or downward into the center of the arena. The slightest pressure there would have started the spinning all over again.

She steadied herself against the closest shelf, which she assumed was filled with gargoyle information, judging by the closest title, *Wings of Stone.* She squinted and scanned the circular room. *Huh. Didn't know the Monster section had a spin-time limit.*

"That's it!"

"Shit." She rolled her eyes and slowly removed her hand from the shelf.

"I want you out of here." The muffled thump of Charlemagne's cane preceded the man's physical appearance. "Just because you can't *keep your head in the game* doesn't mean you have the right to storm in here and wreak havoc on the Clan records."

"Wait, what?" She finally realized her great-uncle was entering the room from behind her. When she turned, he was leaning dangerously far over the edge of the top row, scowling and swinging his cane at her. "Who said anything about wreaking havoc?"

"I did!" He kept swinging his cane. Spit flew from his mouth, and a hint of color rose in his otherwise grayed-with-age cheeks. "Two delicately kept scrolls in the First Era section have melted, Halsey. *Melted*! Did I not make it clear to you that those were to always stay put?"

"You mean...six years ago before I graduated and became an actual adult? With full access to the library—"

His piercing wail would have been fitting at a wake. Charlemagne jabbed the end of his cane toward the wyvern shelf. "And tossing titles willy-nilly all over the place however you please! Do you have *any* idea how long it took your aunt to compile that data on wyverns? Do you? I ought to have you permanently banned!"

"Well, don't do *that*." Unsure whether to laugh at the man's raging emotions or slink around him to avoid a potential smack from the cane, Halsey glanced at the offending notebook that hadn't been returned properly. "I'll go put it back on the—"

"You will not!" Charlemagne swung his cane with a *crack* against the edge of the highest step, then thumped the tip into the floor. "Out."

"Okay, okay. I'm sorry about the books, Charlemagne. Honestly. That notebook was incredibly helpful, and I'm not trying to ruin anything in the library."

"Well, your intentions haven't done much to keep you on the right path lately, have they?" His scowl deepened until the regular features of his face disappeared. "I don't want to see you in here again until I hear personally that the Council has deemed you fit for *real* work. Probably not even then."

"All right. I'm leaving." Fighting back a chuckle, Halsey lifted her hands in surrender and sidled along the middle level. "If I still need to find something, you know, for research purposes, can I at least put in a personal request for—"

"Out! Now!"

She slowed down only when she reached the exit. Then she had to climb three more levels of circular shelf-lined walkways until she reached the top. Her great-uncle didn't once remove his squinting gaze from her, even when she mounted the last stair and stepped cautiously onto the highest level beside him. He shuffled to face her, scrutinizing her every move as she retreated backward from the Monsters section.

Like I'm the bad guy here. Come on. There shouldn't even be a bad guy in a library.

Something else he'd said rolled through her mind without any obvious explanation, and she blurted, "When you say two scrolls *melted*, do you mean literally, or like they—"

Charlemagne growled and cracked his cane against the edge of the step before brandishing it at her like a sword. "So help me, girl…"

"Understood. Uh, enjoy the rest of your day."

Though she had almost nothing to show for her time spent searching the history, Halsey's only option now was to get the hell out of the library.

CHAPTER SIXTEEN

The library had been a dead end, but that didn't mean Halsey was out of resources. There was still one place she could look for answers, the only place in the world right now where Halsey wouldn't get turned away.

Greta Ambrosius knew what being shut down felt like.

Halsey said goodbye to the refreshing, magical air conditioning and once again braved the sweltering summer heat for a hike across the property.

Ambrosius Clan elementals were split between living somewhere on the family property and opting for autonomy and independence as civilians elsewhere in the state of Texas. Older generations like Greta, Charlemagne, Wallace, and Blanch had remained in the estate house since before Halsey was born. Her dad's generation was split, too, though every standing Council member was required to live on the estate for the duration of their terms. For the most part, those only ended with their deaths.

On the rare occasions she considered it, that sounded

like the worst possible way for an elemental monster hunter to spend the rest of their life.

Then, of course, there was Halsey's generation. Greta's grandchildren, Charlemagne's grandchildren, and a handful of Halsey's cousins removed so many times she couldn't keep track of how they were related. Clifford was the oldest, though he hardly came around the mansion anymore. Or if he did, he was phenomenally successful at avoiding public appearances. Halsey thought he was married, but she wasn't sure.

The last time she'd bothered to count, there were twenty-seven Ambrosius elementals in her generation, ranging from Clifford at thirty-two to Ethel, who'd just turned eight. The girl was still a few years from being old enough to start her training. She lived with her parents *off* the Clan property, south of Lufton. Most of the others who were old enough to decide, like Brigham, had moved into the city too. That made Halsey a rarity among her generation for picking a small, otherwise unmarked plot of land within the acres owned by the Clan.

For the longest time, she'd told herself she'd only stayed for *her* cottage. That no matter how fervently she'd scoured the available homes in Texas, she wouldn't have found one that felt like home. Over the last five years, though, she'd discovered a lot more about herself by living here than she'd expected.

One of the biggest surprises, which she wouldn't admit even if Brigham tortured it out of her, was that she had a softer spot for her family than she let on.

Though her childhood had been tumultuous, the good

moments kept her going. The happy moments. All the weekends, evenings, and summers spent with her cousins in the magical greenhouse. The handful of nights when they'd snuck out of their rooms in the mansion to hike across the property unnoticed by the adults. The hours they'd spent forming the greenhouse with their own magic after they'd learned to use it properly.

The time spent lost in performative meditation with the enormous oak tree, dead from the beginning and destined to serve as their official clubhouse dartboard. First with actual darts, then arrows, then daggers, and finally, Halsey's throwing axes. All the frustrations vented, the secrets kept, and the promises made...

In a way, the cottage and the attached greenhouse had raised her. They'd given her a safe, unbiased, and nurturing place while she'd grown up without all those things from any one person.

Plus, by claiming the cottage, Halsey had seized one more way to exert her independence from the Council. While public spaces within the property were fair game for the Council and the entire Clan, private habitations were off-limits. As far as she knew, the Council had no idea the greenhouse even existed, and by living in the cottage, Halsey had ensured it stayed that way.

There was also the fact that living on the enormous Clan property kept her close to her grandmother.

When Halsey reached the last leg of her three-mile hike from the mansion to Greta Ambrosius' private abode, she was soaked with sweat. Her T-shirt clung to her torso again, only this time, there was no point peeling it off. The heat and humidity were practically unbearable. She stopped at the riverbank five minutes from her grandmother's front door so she wouldn't fall face-first *through* that door from heatstroke the second she arrived.

Halsey drew a deep breath, reached toward the sound of gently trickling water beneath the shade of dogwood trees, and called the river.

At first, the water barely drizzled. Her magic was apparently as exhausted as she was. Yet when the first watery tendril snaked between the branches of thick, lush leaves, darted toward her, and splashed right into her face, the pep returned to her step.

She gasped and sputtered, wiping her soaked hair from her face with both hands. She laughed as she blinked the river water out of her eyes. "Next time, I'm bringing a water bottle."

It had been too long since she'd made the trip to Meemaw's bungalow-style house in the middle of nowhere.

That's on me. I've been busy with constant missions and monsters coming out of the woodwork in all the ways they're not supposed to.

Now that she was here, she was excited to sit down with her grandmother and have a nice, long chat the way they used to. Back when life was simple, and the only things Halsey had to worry about were being a monster hunter, doing her job, and having fun the rest of the time. Over the last two weeks and change, though, she'd added mysterious coffins, silverback werewolf alphas, monsters acting strangely, stolen assets, and old legends coming true to the mix.

That didn't mean she couldn't spare a little time cooling off before she had to use her brain in an upcoming conversation.

Refreshed enough to rally more force behind her magic, Halsey reached both hands toward the river. The lifeforce of the water reacted instantly, churning and swirling into a thick column above the surface. She hauled the whole thing out of the river and through the trees. This time, when the water reached her, Halsey flicked her hand up. The water spiral spread out, flattening and lengthening in the air until it resembled a shimmering wall.

She grinned and stepped forward until she stood in the center of the wall of water. The sparkling coolness rushed around her head and plastered her hair to her face as if she were standing under a waterfall.

So much better. Forget showers. This is the way to go, every time...

With the water roaring around her, she didn't immediately recognize the odd sound that echoed across the valley. At first, it sounded like a shrieking bird call or maybe a few squirrels fighting over the best branches. Yet the longer she heard it, the more she believed the squalling blare that drew closer every moment wasn't part of the natural world.

Definitely not an animal. What is that? A security alarm?

Halsey moved out of the free-floating waterfall and dipped her head to scan the open grass around her. Before she'd fully blinked the water from her eyes and focused her vision, an odd, tingling sensation spread across the top of her head and into her shoulders.

"What the..."

She tried to look into the wall of water surrounding her, which was where the sensation seemed to be coming from.

The next second, her arms and the back of her neck felt like they were on fire, and the air in front of her filled with steam before she realized what was happening.

"Hey!" Halsey leapt from her enchanted waterfall with a shriek to avoid being scalded by the river water, which had started to boil. Thick tendrils of steam rose from its surface. "Seriously?"

With an angry lurch, she tore her magic from the water and sent the whole bubbling thing sloshing down with a *splash*. With the constant rush of water and her own yelps gone, she clearly heard the noise that had distracted her.

It was definitely a siren. In fact, it sounded like the lightning-warning alarms played at public swimming pools when an oncoming storm got too close. There was no pool here, though. Or a storm.

The siren's wail rose and fell in slow arcs, drawing closer from the direction she'd come. Halsey scanned the trees around her. *I swear if the Council sent somebody to watch me and report back about every little stupid thing...*

The low, gentle hum of a small motor caught her attention.

Sopping wet and with her face, neck, and shoulders red from the scalding magical water, she zeroed in on the direction of the new sounds. She stared intently at the top of a hill ten yards away.

The front bumper of a golf cart popped into view before the whole thing crested the rise. The emergency siren came from an audio device mounted on the side of the cart, and the thing warbled mid-wail as the cart surged over the hill with another rev of the tiny engine.

The vehicle caught more air than such a small ride seemed capable of. It flew six feet, thumped onto the semi-brown grass, skidded through a patch of dirt, then fishtailed back on track. It continued at top speed directly toward her.

She stepped back and hoped the crazed golf cart driver only needed some extra room. A sidelong glance at the riverbank confirmed it would be easy to get to and provide an open escape route if necessary.

What kind of insane person tries to bum-rush somebody in a golf cart?

As Halsey faced forward again, the golf cart spun sideways with a growl, sending up a spray of dirt and shredded grass before it stopped with a wobble. The kicked-up debris wasn't strong enough to pose any real threat to Halsey, though now she was soaked and plastered with plant matter, dirt clods, and specks of mud.

She spread her arms, tore her gaze from the mess clinging to her wet clothes, and glared at the person behind the wheel. The driver wore a welding helmet that hid their face. Thick leather gloves, work boots, and a stained Carhartt jumpsuit made it impossible to discern anything about this person.

Not that Halsey could think with the siren noise blaring in front of her.

"Hey!" She squinted, stepped back, and clapped her hands to her ears. "Turn that thing off!"

The driver slumped a forearm over the steering wheel, swung the other arm over the back of the seat behind them, then gestured with their head. Actual words might have been involved, but they weren't getting through over the wailing siren.

"I can't hear you!" she tried again. "You have to turn off the siren. Come on!"

The helmeted figure stared at her, then punched the roof of the golf cart. Instantly, the siren cut off mid-shriek.

Halsey blinked and stretched her lower jaw from side to side as if it might stop the ringing in her ears. On a normal day, a weirdly dressed stranger piloting a golf cart would have made her laugh. Instead, she glared at the helmet's viewing mask. "Listen. I get it. If they sent you to make sure I'm not *spreading lies* or…I don't know, making more trouble than I'm worth, I guess you're doing your job. You realize this is way overboard, though, right?"

The driver simply tilted their head and stared like they hadn't expected to see Halsey Ambrosius wandering her own family's property.

No. Like they haven't seen another person *before.*

"I mean, seriously." The awkward silence from the golf cart grated on her, and she had a few things to get off her chest. "A siren? If you were trying to spy on me *without* being detected, that's not the right way to do it. But boiling my waterworks? Come on. That's being a bad sport. I didn't do anything to *you*. At least, I'm pretty sure I didn't. Then again, I have no idea who you are, and you picked a super weird undercover costume."

Her speech was long enough to throw off any Clan member, most of whom couldn't stand listening to *anyone* talk without adding their two cents. Unless they were the ones talking. She'd expected the driver to defend their motives or explain themselves, either by denying the Council had sent them or justifying their insane actions out here, acres away from the mansion.

In a golf cart.

Yet the driver didn't move or say a word. With that ensemble, even if they *had* reacted, it would have been invisible.

Not taking the bait, I guess. Okay.

With an exasperated sigh, Halsey tossed her hands up and dropped them against her wet shorts. "All right, fine. What is it? What do they want me to know that you had to come all the way out here looking like that four months *before* Halloween?"

That drew a reaction, and the driver snorted. Before they spoke, Halsey noticed something off about the tone of that barely concealed laugh. It sounded like someone stuck inside a giant oil drum.

"You're one to talk about *costumes*." The driver's voice was flat, emotionless, and robotic, neither male nor female, and echoed within the helmet.

That gives me zero clues.

At last, Halsey realized how strange their response was and tilted her head. "Seriously? You'd rather compare outfits than answer any of my questions?"

"Well, *you're* the one who brought it up. *I'm* not the one standing by the riverbank with no weapons and no plan, looking like a kindergartener's impression of a Jackson Pollock painting. State your business."

Halsey stood there in disbelief and stared at the darkly

tinted helmet visor, going through every possible Ambrosius elemental who remotely fit the bill that the Council might trust to send after her. The only person she came up with was Brigham. Though he would have loved to play an intricate joke on her like this, he was on a mission in Kansas.

The golf cart creaked and wobbled as the driver leaned forward and propped a forearm on their thigh. "I said, state your business."

The combination of the welding helmet, the robotic voice, and this person's complete disregard for safety made an intimidating concoction.

That's the point, isn't it? Charlemagne told them I was in the library, and now they're trying to scare me into blabbing my plan so they can avoid a fiasco. Too bad I don't actually have a plan for anything.

Halsey folded her arms, sending beads of water to patter against the grass at her feet. "I don't have to tell you shit."

The driver sat upright in what almost looked like surprise, but the mystery ensemble made it hard to tell. "Doesn't take a whole lotta guts to talk to someone like that when their face is behind a mask."

Halsey snorted and laughed bitterly. "Well, go ahead and take off the mask. Then I'll know who to call by name the next time I'm standing in the Council room."

The driver with the robotic voice stared her down. Maybe they weren't even looking at her. She wouldn't have been able to tell. Finally, an eerie chuckle rose from the helmet, and the driver leaned back and pointed at her. "You drive a hard bargain, kid."

The figure reached up with gloved hands toward the welding helmet, and Halsey pressed her lips together.

If the Council wants to bother me when I've already been suspended this long, bring it.

CHAPTER SEVENTEEN

Before the driver had their helmet halfway off, Halsey was already compiling a list of witty insults and sharp jabs for any Ambrosius elemental who'd take the Council's instructions this seriously. Especially when they involved Halsey, the suspended operative, who had so many *fantasies* in her that she needed a compulsory suspension from doing what she did best.

When the helmet came free, and a thick curtain of straight gray hair lined with silver fell into place above the driver's shoulders, every thought in Halsey's mind disappeared. Her jaw dropped. *"Meemaw?"*

Greta Ambrosius chuckled, this time with her unmodified voice. The Clan matriarch grinned as she stuck the welding helmet on her thigh and held it in place with a gloved hand. "Well, who the hell else would I be?"

"You... But I..." Halsey pointed at the open valley behind her grandmother from which she'd made her second hike of the morning, then jerked a thumb over her shoulder toward the house barely visible through the branches of a cottonwood cluster. "What?"

"Speechless, huh? That's all right. You're soaking wet, covered in crap, and obviously have a few more issues I can see from the outside." Greta waggled a finger at her granddaughter, then snorted. "Hop on. I'll drive us back to the house, we'll get you fixed up, and you can tell me why the hell you haven't invested in your own golf cart yet. The trek out here's a bitch." She slapped the steering wheel with her gloved hand, and Halsey suspected the ensuing beep wasn't intentional. At the same time, her grandmother's grin widened.

Halsey looked over her shoulder, scanned the tree line and the edge of the riverbank, then ambled toward the cart where her grandmother sat patiently behind the wheel.

The cart rocked and squeaked as she climbed into the passenger seat. She grabbed the handrail on her right and huffed.

"Hmm." Greta turned toward her. "There's a lot of funny things going around right now, but I'd love to hear the one you just caught onto."

With a crooked smile, Halsey examined her grandmother and shook her head. "I actually thought you were Brigham for a second."

"Ha!" The woman slapped the steering wheel again, and another little beep rang out. "Thank you! That's the best compliment I've had all day."

Before Halsey could ask how many other people her grandmother had stopped in that outfit today, Greta floored the gas and lurched the golf cart forward over the bumpy grass. The wheels churned in the dirt, and Halsey threw her head back and laughed as she was whipped sideways.

The ride toward Greta's house was so bumpy and loud that it made conversation impossible. Two minutes later, the cart screeched to a halt in the gravel and sand that would have been a driveway if Greta had had a car. Gravel sprayed everywhere, peppering the side of the bright red bungalow nestled in the rolling hills.

"This cart has reached its final destination," Greta declared. "All passengers must exit now."

Halsey laughed as her grandmother hopped nimbly from the wobbly golf cart and trudged across the homemade gravel driveway.

I still don't see how the Clan thinks she's insane. A little eccentric, maybe. That's what makes her awesome.

She jumped out after the woman, then took in the sight of Meemaw's private home tucked away on the massive, largely untouched property.

The front garden was impeccable, with brilliant shoots of flowers in every color. A small pond with a burbling fountain rested to the left side of the house, its perimeter lined with little bobbing-bird toys constantly dipping their heads into the water. Beside the pond, a collection of a dozen wooden birdhouses rose from stakes in the ground, all filled with birdseed and straw. Years ago, they'd been painted in bright, flashy colors that matched the flowerbeds. Now, the faded pastel paint was streaked with water lines and chipped at the edges.

Halsey knew this because she'd built at least two of those birdhouses and stuck them into the ground next to those made by her cousins.

The bungalow itself seemed to always have a fresh coat of cherry-red paint. Or maybe Greta had figured out how to keep her house immaculate without painting it or asking for help.

I bet she uses the same enchantment her brother stuck on the First Era scrolls in the library. Wouldn't that make her house freezing all day long, though?

She headed toward the bungalow's wide front porch. The thick wooden railing surrounding it had been painted in bright colors and perfect detail with vines, flowers, bumblebees, butterflies, and all manner of insects. It didn't make sense that an elemental would paint something to *look* like nature when she could call the plants up around the railing for a similar, more realistic effect. Halsey was sure her grandmother had her reasons, though. For most things.

Before she climbed the four narrow stairs onto the front porch, Greta's voice echoed harshly from beside the house. "Nobody said you could go inside."

Halsey pressed her lips together to stifle a snigger. "When you said we'd come back here and get me fixed up..."

"In no universe does that phrase mean, 'Make yourself at home,'" Greta barked. "Get over here."

Right. Should've known I was walking into one of her elaborate plans the second I realized it was Meemaw *behind the wheel of a rogue golf cart.*

With a snort, she spun from the porch and walked along the house, past the small pond, the dunking birds, and the empty birdhouses. As she rounded the corner of the bungalow and stepped through a flowering archway between two massive blackberry bushes, Halsey remembered how impossible it was to predict anything Greta Ambrosius did.

The woman had also erected a professional-looking greenhouse back here. It was nothing like the extra room on Halsey's cottage but a real greenhouse, complete with a steepled roof and four glass walls. The door hung open, and there didn't appear to be any plants inside.

Across from the greenhouse was a massive storage shed with an assortment of odds and ends sticking from the pane-less windows and the door-less frame. Rakes, fishing poles, balls of yarn covered in dry grass, pots and pans arranged on a coat rack, and one pale, dirty mannequin arm propped against the outside wall.

Halsey frowned at the arm, then scanned the yard in search of her grandmother. "You've been getting busy out here."

"What makes you say that?" Greta popped up from behind a worktable in the middle of the yard covered with a curious array of metal pieces that could have been pulled directly from the walls of the Council room. Despite the welding helmet she'd worn, the woman clearly wasn't doing any actual welding out here. That was impossible without a torch, not to mention a waste of time for an elemental alchemist who'd once led the entire Ambrosius Clan in her specialty.

Now that Greta was back in her element, she'd replaced the helmet with a pair of round work goggles with prescription lenses. The strap clung tightly to her head, making her gray and silver hair puff out around her head, and the lenses made her bright blue eyes enormous.

Fighting back another laugh, Halsey gestured toward the new buildings. "I'm pretty sure *those* weren't here the last time I stopped by."

"Huh." Greta swung her head in the direction she'd gestured as if she had no idea they were there until now. She tilted her head and nodded. "I guess you haven't been here in a while, then." She slapped a gloved hand on the worktable and chuckled. "Hell, this old thing's been here for twenty years."

"The table, maybe. The shed and greenhouse are new, though." Halsey paced along the side of the house, studying the side yard that her grandmother had turned into a combination workshop-storage unit. "And the last time I came by was…February. I think."

"Oh, sure. It probably was." The woman fluttered a hand beside her head as she tinkered with a few metal pieces, and Halsey took the opportunity to study the place more.

When she stopped beside the bungalow and looked up at the walls, she couldn't help but laugh. "Meemaw."

"Hmm?" Her grandmother didn't look up from her work.

"Why do you have a mattress strapped to the side of your house?"

Greta whipped her head up, blinked thoughtfully, then frowned. "Remind me again. I have so many little kittens running around here these days. Which one are you?"

"What?"

"Ha! I'm pulling your leg, Halsey. Hold still."

"Okay." Halsey gestured at the mattress. "What about the—"

With a flick of her grandmother's fingers, an enormous cyclone of hot, humid summer air burst across the side yard. The force of it knocked Halsey backward before she realized what was happening.

The next thing she knew, she was plastered against the mattress. It was surprisingly springy, and despite the howling vortex whipping at her body and pinning her in place, she still bounced a little.

She also couldn't move.

Her hands were knocked back beside her face, and her cheeks fluttered under the airy attack.

"What are you *doing*?" she shouted over the din.

"What's that?" Greta called, cupping a hand around her ear. "You gotta speak up, kid. I can't hear a word you're saying."

"Cut it—" Halsey couldn't get another word out as the giant magical blow-dryer kicked up with renewed intensity. The air forcing itself down her throat made her gasp for breath, and it took all her concentration to turn her head aside, so she wasn't getting blasted head-on.

There was no way to use her hands or think about calling up her own magic to battle whatever her grandmother had thrown at her. There was no time to think about it. Then it was over.

The deafening roar in her ears stopped, and Halsey stumbled away from the house now that she'd regained control of her body and the weight of gravity that came with it. She drew another gasping breath, caught her balance again, and glared at her grandmother. "Seriously?"

Greta examined her with those blue eyes magnified to

comical proportions and sniggered. "Well, only if you want it to be. I think it's kind of amusing."

"That's…" Halsey bit back a smile. "You know that's not what I meant."

"It's impossible for me to know that, kiddo. I can't read minds." The woman turned back toward her worktable and flapped a hand at her granddaughter as if the rest were a mere afterthought that didn't bear mentioning. "I'll be a monkey's uncle if you're not completely dry now, though."

"Right, but you can't just—" She cut herself off as she realized it was true. She was dry as a bone. "Huh. Well, thanks, I guess."

"You're welcome."

Halsey scrunched her nose at the cushy mattress. "How many people, on average, do you blast against a mattress to air-dry like that?"

Greta chuckled. "Only the ones who show up soaking from head to toe. Assuming they're people I want to bring home with me, of course."

"Oh, sure. Of course." Halsey studied her grandmother with hesitant amusement.

Okay, forget a little eccentric. Really eccentric. I hope nobody on the Council's been down here to see all this. Not that it would do anything to change their minds. They already think Meemaw's lost it.

Despite a lot of evidence to the contrary, there was absolutely nothing wrong with her grandmother's mind or her concept of reality. The woman had been instrumental in shaping the Ambrosius Clan into how they operated and trained their newest recruits who came of age. How they handled packs, swarms, and gangs of monsters around the world to successfully keep them from harming humans and exposing their existence.

In many ways, Greta Ambrosius was the closest thing Halsey had to a mother. Especially during the first seven years of her life.

She likes the weirdness. That's what got her this far. I bet it's keeping her sane after her own family expelled her from the militia and won't listen to her anymore.

The clicking of her grandmother's tongue tore her from her thoughts, and she looked up to see the woman smiling at her. "What?"

"You're so caught up in your own head, girl, you don't know left from right. I can help with that. You hungry? Of course you are. Come on." The tools she'd been working with clinked onto the worktable, and Greta stomped around it toward the front of the house. "This time, I *am* giving you permission to enter my house. So there. Hurry up."

Halsey brushed at the now-dry dirt and grass still clinging to her shirt and watched Greta stride confidently away until she disappeared around the corner of the house. She grinned and rushed to catch up.

CHAPTER EIGHTEEN

Strange as it might seem, Halsey saw nothing wrong with eating her grandmother's hot tomato soup and a steaming grilled cheese sandwich for lunch in the middle of summer. Probably because Greta's house was extremely well-cooled, though none of her grandchildren had figured out how she kept it that way.

Now that she was dry, mostly cleaned off, and a few bites into her lunch, Halsey felt more optimistic about the conversation she'd come here to have. The trick was bringing it up subtly to avoid raising more red flags than she already had in the last two and a half weeks.

She considered how to approach a delicate topic like the Mother of Monsters with her Meemaw and took another toasty, gooey bite of her grilled cheese. "Oh, man..."

"What?" Across the table, Greta looked up from her bowl of soup with her spoon paused halfway to her mouth. "You didn't find anything besides cheese, did you? I swear, the damn bugs out here..."

Knowing the odd comment was meant to get a reaction, Halsey finished chewing, swallowed, and reached for her glass bottle of Coke. "Nothing but perfection. This tastes exactly like it used to when I was a kid. *Exactly.*"

Her grandmother tittered. "Of course it does. It's bread, cheese, and butter. Unless the chemical makeup of those things has drastically changed in the last few decades, it sure as hell better taste the same."

"Well, I feel like I'm eight again, so good job with that one." Halsey tightened her grip around the Coke and focused on pulling the air temperature into the moisture. A thin film of frost spread across the surface of the glass bottle, which cracked and popped with the sudden drop in temperature. A thin tendril of mist rose from the top.

She raised the drink to her lips, blew away the mist, and sipped the ice-cold soda she'd watched her grandmother pull from the pantry instead of the fridge.

Greta continued slurping her soup. Only when her granddaughter finished drinking and lowered the bottle did the woman speak again. "You didn't come here to talk about being eight again, did you? Or to pretend you are. Though if you *did* come for that, I made it remarkably easy, so you're welcome."

Halsey nearly choked on her soda as she tried to figure out which part to respond to first. The bottle clinked onto the table, and she watched her grandmother from the corner of her eye. "Are you sure you can't read my mind?"

"Absolutely. One hundred percent. The look on your face gives you away, kiddo." The woman dipped into her soup again, slurped noisily, then sighed and pointed her spoon at her granddaughter. "All business and no fun.

Until you see something you can't help but laugh at and wonder why you stopped having fun in the first place. Ask what you came here to ask, and maybe I'll set you free."

That's a weird way to put it. The only thing I need to be free of is this stupid suspension, and Meemaw's the last person who can give it to me.

"Okay." Halsey bit into her sandwich again before diving in head-first. "I was in the Clan library this morning—"

"Oh, *really*?" Her grandmother grinned. "How's old Charlie doing?"

"Ha. Well, he looks a lot older than *you*, that's for sure. And he still hates me."

"It's not you, Halsey. That crinkled old geezer hates anything that walks, talks, and can't be stuck on a shelf for safekeeping. Also, quit trying to flatter me. It doesn't work. He's only two years older, but do continue."

She obviously hasn't seen him in a while, then. Or she doesn't care.

"Okay." She sipped a few spoonfuls of hot tomato soup for something to do while she gathered her thoughts. "He kicked me out before I could look further, so I didn't have a lot to go on, but I found something…weird in the Clan history from the late tenth century."

"Mm-hmm." Greta raised an eyebrow.

"First, I realize how hard it must've been for the Ambrosius elementals way back then to get their day-to-day written down. It's impossible to record *everything* anyway, even today. Maybe I'm reading too much into it, but I did notice there's a pretty big gap in the timeline of events there. About twenty years. Starting around 950

A.D., when our family was focused on helping villages with droughts and forest fires or whatever. Then the records shifted to accounts of monsters, going after them, and preparing to fight the good fight. Before then, monsters hadn't been a problem since the great war, right?"

When her grandmother wordlessly returned to spooning up her soup, Halsey frowned and continued with the information she thought necessary.

"It seems weird that a massive shift in *purpose* like that would be entirely left out. When the historian or whoever had been writing in detail about the ships they salvaged or how many clay pots they were paid to help out a village, you'd think the reemergence of monsters all over the world would've been at the top of the list."

Greta released a noncommittal hum and shrugged before jamming the last of her grilled cheese into her mouth.

She's gonna make me keep talking until I land on something that makes sense, isn't she?

Halsey inhaled deeply, tried to look unaffected by her grandmother's disinterest, and sipped her drink. "I was about to ask Charlemagne why we were missing the first twenty years of monster-hunting records, but I got... distracted. Then he kicked me out, so a civil conversation was out of the question at that point. I'm sure he would've rather hit me with his cane."

Her grandmother snorted, shook her head, and kept eating her soup.

"After that, I thought, hey. I should go visit Meemaw. It's been a while and seeing as she's *way* more fun than her older brother the Library Troll, it's a win-win. We'll have fun, and maybe she'll tell me why there's a huge, important chunk of our history missing from the Clan archives."

For the next several seconds, Greta continued eating her soup, her spoon clinking against the ceramic bowl repeatedly until she'd scraped up the last bit. She ate another giant bite of her grilled cheese, swiped the crumbs off the front of her canvas jumpsuit, and pointed at her granddaughter. "I'm only gonna say this once, kid. Flattery takes a certain level of believability to work, and you're no good at it."

"Ha!" Halsey leaned back and spread her arms. "Worth a shot, though, right?"

"Now your shot is spent." The woman picked up her soda and didn't bother cooling it before knocking back a quarter of the warm drink in one breath. The bottle clinked onto the table, and she released a massive, disconcerting belch while holding Halsey's gaze the entire time.

Greta smacked her lips and plastered on a tight, ready-to-please smile. "The *real* question here is why the hell you were looking through the First Age records. You know those are practically untouchable. Serious consequences for anyone stupid enough to mess with Charlie's precious 'preservation system.'" She wiggled her fingers over the table, miming magic being performed.

Halsey scratched the side of her face and tried to laugh it off. "Yeah, he didn't waste any time reminding me of that, either. Apparently, it's my fault two of the First Era scrolls melted, whatever that means."

Her grandmother drummed her fingers on the table, her nails eliciting soft, percussive clicks. "Well?"

"Well, what?"

"I asked you a question. You haven't answered. You also don't look apologetic after being called out on your rule-breaking, so..." The woman glanced briefly at the untouched half of Halsey's sandwich and cleared her throat. "You wanna know what I know? A little tit for tit goes a long way."

Halsey frowned. "You mean tit for tat."

Her grandmother clicked her tongue. "Not when it's only us girls here. You gonna eat that?"

A sharp laugh escaped her before she noticed her grandmother staring intently at what remained of her lunch. "Um...I guess not. You can have it."

"Excellent." Greta's chair scooted noisily across the floor as she stood to retrieve the small plate. The ceramic scraped over the tabletop, and the tantalizing crunch of toasted bread filled the dining room as she bit in. "You were saying?"

Halsey stared at the newest batch of crumbs scattered across her grandmother's jumpsuit. *What* was *I saying?*

"Oh. I was looking for records of the first time that monsters returned to the world, and our family had to start fighting them again. You know, wondering how much truth there is in those stories from way back when. The great war. Sealing away the Blood Matriarch. How she could be pulled up from the Circle of Creation again. If that's possible, of course." She shrugged and shook her head, hoping she sounded neutral and academic rather than connected with any real-life silver coffins washed up on a beach during a real-life mission.

She continued. "General information, I guess. I wasn't a hundred percent sure that monsters came back to the world in the tenth century, so I wanted to double-check. You know, find the exact moment when the Ambrosius Clan said, 'Oh shit. It's time to pivot back to doing what we do best.' Which is what I *didn't* find in the records, by the way. I wanted to see if *you* knew anything about it."

Halsey finished her explanation full of half-truths and a healthy smattering of lies by omission, then watched her grandmother for clues.

The woman had practically inhaled the second half of Halsey's sandwich. Now she leaned forward in her chair, one hand in her lap while the other fiddled with the strap of her goggles on the table. "Uh-huh."

"Do you, uh...happen to have anything else to add to that? Maybe?"

"What do *you* think happened to the Clan's tenth-century records?"

Halsey's cheeks puffed out when she sighed. "Anything could've happened. Maybe they didn't know how to write as accurately and in as much detail about *monsters* as they did everything else, so it took their archivist a while to figure things out. Or the Clan suddenly got so busy fighting monsters that they couldn't find the time to write things down."

"For twenty years."

"Eh..." She finished off the last of her Coke to give herself more time because now Meemaw's scrutinizing stare made her feel like she'd walked into the Council room again. "*Or* the guy they had writing everything down before monsters showed up died a sudden and brutal death, and it took serious time and dedication to train the next guy in line to do a good job. You know, plus factor in a mourning period. Did we have any kinda weird, long, complex ceremonies back then when one of us kicked the bucket—"

"All right, cut the shit."

Halsey's mouth snapped shut, and she bolted upright in her chair. "Did you…"

"Yeah. I did." Greta sniffed, lifted her goggles by the strap, then let it slide off her finger and clank onto the table with startling clarity. "That's what you're doing right now. You're trying to feed me a line of bullshit, and fortunately for me but probably not for you, I already ate. I'm not hungry."

"Um…"

"Tell me what *you* think happened to those records. Your gut instinct. The tingling little voice between your shoulder blades. If you can't do *that*, kiddo, there's no point in us having this conversation."

There she is. Greta Ambrosius, the badass. Yeah, I touched on something important, didn't I?

"Okay." Halsey ducked her head, conceding that she couldn't fool either of them anymore. "If I'm supposed to go with my gut—"

"Always." Greta pointed at her, though she stared at the tabletop as if zeroing in on the rough grain would improve her listening skills. "No matter what."

"Right. My gut's telling me that information used to be there, in writing, and now it's missing."

"Meaning?"

"Meaning somebody got to the Clan archives before I did and cut a twenty-year chunk out of history, making all the missing pages technically *stolen*."

Her grandmother's fist thumped on the table, rattling the spoons inside their empty bowls. "Well, of course they are."

Halsey choked on whatever she might have said next. She gaped at the woman, her eyes bulging. "Wait, you actually think something was stolen from the Clan records?"

"Absolutely. With enough forethought to cover up their trail so no one would find out. Unless they were looking for the missing puzzle pieces *on purpose.*"

"That's..." Halsey couldn't find the words for the sudden and violent shift in her entire belief system about the Ambrosius mansion, the way the Council knew everything about everyone all the time, and how top-notch their security was, even within something as banal as the library. "Who would do something like that?"

"I did." Without waiting for a reply or making direct eye contact, Greta stood, snatched the empty bowls and plates, and stacked them with a lot of clinking and clanking. She spun to head into the kitchen.

CHAPTER NINETEEN

Halsey must have sat at her grandmother's dining room table for another thirty seconds in disbelief before she became aware of the water running in the kitchen sink and the clinking of dishes being washed by hand. Then she sat there longer because it was difficult to form coherent thoughts.

Meemaw stole *twenty years of records from the family archives? By herself? And nobody noticed?*

Those seemed like ridiculous questions to ask, but she wasn't voicing them out loud.

Halsey pushed up with a confused grunt and shuffled into the kitchen. "Meemaw?"

"Halsey-Bear."

"What's going on?"

"I'm washing dishes. Lemme tell ya, even in this heat, the ants get bad when you leave your food all over the place. I made one hell of a grilled cheese sandwich, so you know the little bastards are gonna try to get their cut any way they can."

Halsey approached the counter beside the sink and turned to lean against it. That gave her and her grandmother a better view of each other, but Greta was too busy washing dishes for a face-to-face chat. "Maybe the dishes can wait? If I heard you right, you confessed to stealing multiple pages of valuable documents from our family's—"

"Wow." Greta chuckled. "Two little words and you're jumping to confessions and conspiracies and *value*. Grab the dish towel there, will you?"

The woman pointed briefly at the bright yellow towel draped over the handle of the oven door, then went back to scrubbing melted cheese off their plates. Halsey snatched the towel and extended it toward her grandmother. Instead of taking it, Greta handed her a dripping plate.

"That plate's not gonna dry itself, kid." Greta nodded at the sopping dish. "Unless I decide to stand here all day holding it like this, which isn't anywhere on my to-do list."

Because she wanted the distractions gone and the conversation to continue, Halsey grabbed the dish and wiped the rag across it with more attitude than any plate deserved. *Sure. She can blast me against the side of her house for a quick "air-dry," but she can't use magic to do the dishes. Of course not. It's Meemaw.*

After drying and returning both plates to their proper place in the cabinets, she couldn't stand the thought of standing there in silence for the rest of the dishes. She grabbed the bowl her grandmother handed her and continued talking as she dried.

"Okay, so it wasn't a confession."

"*Now* you're listening." Greta chuckled and kept scrubbing.

"Why did you tell me that, then?"

"Because you asked. I see no reason to keep secrets from you, Halsey. Besides, it's not like you to go running back to the family to spill all my beans." The woman paused, looked at her granddaughter, and raised an eyebrow. "Right?"

Halsey sniggered, but the warning look on her grandmother's face didn't change. "Oh. No, of course not. Not even on a good day."

"Good." Greta resumed her washing, her head tilted as if her mind was already somewhere else. "Was that your way of telling me today *isn't* a good day?"

"One in a long line of several, but no. I'm not gonna tell anybody about this. If anyone else figured it out, Charlemagne would come after me with torches and pitchforks."

"Now *that's* something I'd pay to see." Greta tittered and shook her head. "Of course, he'd have to grow a third arm for that cane."

Halsey laughed, not realizing she'd accepted another dish until she'd already returned it to the cabinet fully dry. She stared at her empty hand, and her grandmother stuck another dish in it.

Man, she's good.

Watching the other woman from the corner of her eye, she smiled and asked, "So they're here, right?"

"What's that?"

"The records, Meemaw. The pages of our family history from 950 to 970 A.D."

"Oh! Those." Greta smiled wistfully and gazed out the small window above the sink. From there, she had a breathtaking view of the greenbelt running behind her bungalow. The dogwoods and willows, the wildflowers and buzzing insects, the occasional blackbird braving the midday sunlight to swoop down somewhere else. "Nope."

"What?"

"As in, 'Nope, they're not here.' You sure you're feeling okay, kid? I've noticed a lag in your auditory comprehension over the last ten minutes."

"You can't be serious."

"I am many things. Serious usually isn't one of them."

"*Meemaw.*"

"Halsey." Greta laced the word with a staggering amount of sarcasm, strengthened by the mocking way she jiggled her head before slapping a handful of washed silverware into Halsey's hand. "I don't see why you're so bent out of shape about this. You asked. I answered. If you don't like the answer, maybe you should change the question."

Halsey paused with the silverware halfway wrapped in the dishcloth. "Well, now I know for sure. You're the most literal person I've ever met."

"Thank you."

When Greta's reply came with a wink and a self-satisfied smile, Halsey laughed in disbelief and shook her head. "Fine. Different question."

"Excellent."

"Where *are* the records you took from the library?"

"Hmm." A frown replaced the woman's smile, and she tilted her head so far that it looked like she was trying to peer under the cabinets mounted on the wall. "To be clear, we're still talking about the tenth-century swap from elemental shepherds to monsters for days, right?"

"Hold on." Halsey opened the silverware drawer and dropped the clean utensils into it without bothering to sort them. She shoved the drawer shut with an aggressive *bang*. "Are you telling me that's not the only thing you've stolen from the archives?"

Her grandmother scoffed. "What? That's not remotely close to what I said, girl. I didn't *tell* you anything."

"Yeah, that's kinda the problem. We were talking about the tenth-century records, and you're having a hard time staying on topic."

"Oh, *please*." Greta turned off the sink with a quick jerk and flicked water off her hands despite not having finished the dishes. "It's not my fault you can't figure out what you want to *know*…"

"Where are the records, Meemaw? Yes, the ones from 950 A.D."

When her grandmother turned to face her, Halsey's immediate thought was that she'd crossed a serious line, which would have been impossible to gauge. Greta Ambrosius' lines were invisible. Yet while the woman stared at her intensely, she wasn't actually *looking* at her granddaughter. She was thinking.

If I wasn't starting to think the Council forced her off the job so they wouldn't have to deal with her quirks, I'd be thinking it now. I remember her being a lot less aggravating when I was a kid.

Greta drew a sharp breath, blinked, and shrugged. "I have no idea."

"As in…"

"Where they are. The records you found missing but actually only wanted to find. Sorry, kid."

"You took them, though."

"I sure did. And they're not here." The woman sighed through loose lips. "Honestly, they could be in anyone's hands by now. It's hard to keep track of twenty years' worth of insanely valuable magical history, especially taken straight out of a book. All those loose pages." A shudder wracked her body, and she scrunched her face in discomfort before heading out of the kitchen. "It *boggles the mind*, doesn't it? Trying to figure out where they could've possibly gone in any specific length of time."

Halsey stood by the kitchen counter and stared after her grandmother in disbelief and consternation. At the same time, she struggled not to laugh.

What is she trying to get at? What else is she trying to hide? If there was something in those records she didn't want the Council to see, I need to figure out what it is. Unless she took those pages because she wanted the Council to see them...

A new gameplan unfolded in her mind as she shoved up and jogged across the kitchen.

Greta was already situated on a couch in the living room with one leg crossed over the other. Beside her was a basket of neon pink yarn, which she wrapped, tucked, and folded using silver knitting needles with flames painted down the sides.

Halsey avoided staring at the first knitting project she'd ever seen her grandmother undertake. She walked calmly to the armchair that angled toward the couch. When she plopped into it, her grandmother hardly noticed she had company in her living room. The knitting needles clacked together, a clock ticked from another room, and Halsey leaned back in the cushy armchair and closed her eyes.

At one time, this chair had been a rich, chocolaty-brown tweed. Now, most of the color had faded into a dirty gray, and the tweed texture had smoothed to the look and feel of suede. Yet it wasn't the color or the fabric that made this particular chair Halsey's favorite for as long as she could remember.

It was the smell.

Old Spice, tobacco, and a lingering undertone of Ballistol. She only knew what the last scent was because the first time she'd cleaned the weapon herself, she'd recognized the sharp chemical scent that reminded her of licorice. Like the antique rifle in her armory of monster-hunting weapons, this armchair had also belonged to her grandfather.

I bet Percival wouldn't have made a big deal out of all this. He would've grabbed his gun and asked where the goddamn monsters were.

The thought made her snort, and only then did Greta look up from her uncharacteristic knitting. "That's better."

Halsey slowly opened her eyes and studied her grandmother. Other than the canvas jumpsuit and the clunky work boots, Greta Ambrosius looked the perfect picture of grandmotherly domesticity. Which was mind-blowingly strange, to say the least. Still, she had a feeling her grandmother was waiting for something specific here. If there was any way to get through to Greta, it was to bite the bullet and play the game.

Without getting so rattled and pissed off that she stalked out of this house.

"Okay." She inhaled deeply and watched for her grandmother's ensuing reactions. "You took the pages. Nobody found out about it until me. You had them, but now you don't, and you have no idea where they are."

A smile flickered across Greta's face, but she kept knitting away like this was a regular conversation.

"How about this?" Halsey continued. "*Why* did you take them?"

"Ooh. I love that question." The woman still didn't look up from her neon pink yarn. "We're not talking about *me* today, kiddo. Gotta take a raincheck on that one."

"Come on…"

"Why did *you* want to find them?"

Halsey pressed her lips together, scanned the faded area rug on the floor between them, and weighed the pros and cons of cutting out the games and getting bluntly to the point. *It's Meemaw. She knows I'm not tattling to the family. Who's she gonna talk to? Nobody listens to her anyway.*

The whole time, Greta's smile didn't fade.

"I wanted to find them so I could compare your stories about the Mother of Monsters being let out in the tenth century with what happened and compare all that to what's going on in the world in this century. If anybody has even a sliver of an idea about what to do if the Matriarch *did* return, we sure as hell could use it now."

Her grandmother nodded sagely and started rocking back and forth as if she were in an actual rocking chair instead of on a cushy couch. "That *would* be a useful bit of information. You're gonna have to tell me what's going on in this century, kid. I've been disconnected for the last few years."

Halsey snorted as a massive wave of relief washed over her. *I should've led with Ireland.*

"The last two to three months have been especially weird," she began, watching the hypnotic fiery knitting needles. "Monsters doing a whole bunch of stuff they're not supposed to. Not in a 'this is dangerous for humans' kinda way, either. Their behavior is changing. It's not even the same kind of behavior changes or in the same kind of way, so it's impossible to predict the next target before you're, you know. Right there in all…in all the action, and…" Halsey sucked in a sharp breath and pointed at her grandmother's neon pink creation. "Sorry. What's that supposed to be?"

"Oh, this?" Greta grinned. "A playful little something I'm whipping up for fun. Figured it might come in handy at the next formal event for…whatever." She held it higher over her lap, and Halsey laughed.

"If that formal event never left the bedroom, maybe. Did you just start?"

"No, actually. It's a very complicated pattern. Leaves little to the imagination when it's done." The older woman kept a straight face for all of three seconds before she snorted and dropped the knitted lingerie into the basket beside her, needles and all. "It's hideous, I know. Who in their right mind would enjoy something like this, right? I think I'll give it to Beatrice. Will she like it? Probably not. The look on her face as she tries to figure out what it is, though… That'll be worth it."

Greta stood from the couch and headed to yet another room.

"Where are you going?" Halsey called after her.

"To tackle my to-do list. I didn't make any room for sitting down and chatting with *you* all day, so we'll have to multitask." Her voice faded farther into the back of the house. "Keep up, don't mumble, and start from the beginning. In that order."

Halsey rolled her eyes, gripped the armrests, and pushed to her feet. "Here we go."

CHAPTER TWENTY

Telling Greta the whole story from beginning to end was the easiest part of joining her grandmother in checking the items off her mental to-do list. The hardest part was keeping up with the woman physically while not being distracted from the story she needed to tell.

While Halsey divulged the details of her and Brigham's last mission, emphasizing what they'd found *after* fighting off an enormous werewolf pack, Greta scurried around the bungalow, completing one project and starting the next. Halsey couldn't tell what her grandmother was trying to accomplish with the variety of strange, disconnected tasks. Every time she stopped trying to figure it out and focused on telling her story, her grandmother finished whatever she'd been working on and moved onto the next task. And the next.

After she'd relayed every piece of information she could think of, Greta headed toward the bungalow's front door again. Halsey kept talking. "So after Patrick inadvertently sabotaged my emergency Council meeting, there wasn't anything else to do. I mean, that coffin was the biggest piece of evidence we had about things seriously changing in the monster world lately. Somehow, even *that* got screwed up. Now it kinda sounds like the Ambrosius Clan has a thief infestation on our hands too, which is fun…"

Her grandmother snorted and opened the solid front door before reaching for the first screened-in door leading to the front porch. "It's technically not stealing if the entire family has access to something that belongs to everyone. Technically."

"Okay, well, there's still the issue of who in the world could've stolen that casket from the Dublin warehouse without anyone noticing. That *is* stealing because there's no way Patrick and his team lost the thing."

"Disconcerting, yeah." Greta's work boots clomped across the porch, and Halsey realized her grandmother had taken down the mesh screen that used to run from the railing to the porch ceiling but left the screen door leading to the front yard intact. Greta opened the second door with a squeal of rusty hinges, walked down the steps, and let it slam shut behind her.

"Long story short, then," Halsey muttered as she frowned and scanned the porch for maybe a few rolls of new porch screens or mosquito netting. There was nothing. "I went looking for those missing pages because I wanted proof. Elementals *had* to have clashed with the Blood Matriarch at some point. Even if they didn't directly encounter her before her prison sank again, I thought our ancestors would've at least written down a few super-helpful notes for posterity on how to deal with the world unraveling and throwing new monsters into the mix."

"*New* monsters?" Greta turned with wide eyes as her granddaughter opened the useless screen door to head down the stairs. "That's interesting."

"Well, not new as in never-before-seen." Halsey skipped down the stairs, and the door clacked shut. "It's that the normal ways we know how to remove, neutralize, herd somewhere else, imprison, or—"

"The ways we kill them, Halsey. You can say it."

The young elemental grimaced. "I don't like that one."

"Whether or not you like the word hardly makes a difference when you're out there in the field, meting out its definition every single day."

"I'm not. I don't." Halsey shook her head. "Not if I can help it."

"Huh. Well, that sounds like altruism. I'm not sure how much longer it's going to serve you." They took off toward the river-facing side of the house where Greta apparently kept her potting and gardening supplies, paint, two large and heavy-looking shovels, and a hammock strung between two willows. "If things really are changing as much as you say, you're gonna have to put aside your aversion to killing monsters sooner than you think."

"Yeah, well… I'll figure it out when I get there. Right now, I'm trying to figure out how to keep *us* from dying. You know, when vampires start wearing silver for fun and trolls start walking around in broad daylight. Then what?"

Her grandmother spun and raised her eyebrows. "Has that happened?"

"Well, no. Not yet. But Brigham and I fought off hundreds of werewolves in a single night, all of them mindless and throwing themselves at us while their silverback alpha howled at the moon. Honestly, Meemaw, it felt more like watching them try to kill themselves. Even when we only took down one."

"So that's it? Lots of werewolves going batshit crazy under a full moon?"

"No." Halsey folded her arms and tried to look exasperated with her grandmother instead of herself. *When you say it out loud like that, without trying to be urgent and convincing, it does kinda sound like a load of bullshit. I'm still the only one who thinks any of this is important.* "There's also the fact that all this happened on the Summer Solstice. Under a full moon. Right on the coast of Ireland, which is a straight shot from the Circle of the Creation."

"Well, sure. Those are fun facts, but they don't scream 'end of the world' to me."

Halsey groaned as she gazed at the cloudless blue sky and the leaves peppering her vision from the shadier side of the house. *I didn't think I'd have to convince her too. What else do I need to say to get this—*

Her phone buzzed in her pocket, and she fumbled to pull it out, suddenly grateful for hardcore phone cases and waterproof screens.

It was another text from Brigham.

Let me tell you, cuz, the price of your genius was worth every penny! We nailed the sons of bitches! How the hell did you come up with UGLY ROCKS? Wait, don't tell me 'til I get back. We can hash it out over more pizza and beer, which you're paying for this time. Tonight, celebratory drinks are on Owen! Wait, why do I have to pay for both our drinks? Because I said so, and

you're way better at being a second and following my lead. Don't worry. I'm only ordering top-shelf. Oh, okay. I guess it could be worse. My man!

She laughed when she finished reading it. "Definitely using voice-to-text."

"What was that?" Greta asked as she looked up from her current project. Right now, it was a small, gold-painted pot with bright red flowers beginning to bloom, which she dusted off with an archaeologist's brush. She glanced at her granddaughter for half a second before returning her attention to the plant.

Is she humming?

Halsey blinked away her frown. "Text from Brigham. He and Owen are out in Kansas right now. My guess is they're heading back home early tomorrow morning. Or as early as their hangovers allow."

"Ha! I remember those days. Sometimes, I find myself still living 'em." After a soft chuckle, Greta frowned and lowered her brush. "What the hell is there to bag in Kansas?"

"Wyverns, apparently. Lots of them." Halsey sidled closer and folded her arms, pretending to be more focused on the strange treatment of her grandmother's plants than on her reactions. "Also, the ugliest rocks around."

"Very funny, kid." Greta shook her head and resumed her plant brushing. "No one would fall for that. Not even Brigham."

"I know, right? Because he's so *logical* all the time. Following all the *rules* and *protocols* amassed by the Ambrosius Clan for dozens of generations. Exactly *how* to take which monsters down, how they act, where they're weakest, and what isn't worth the time to read about." Halsey's chuckle sounded fake, but somehow, all this coming together so nicely in the strangest way was a little funny. "Good thing his full-time partner was already in the library today. All it took was a few quick texts and a good spin in the Monsters section…"

Her grandmother cleared her throat. "You know, since you got your first blade, all I ever hear about you is how incredible Halsey is at her job. One of the best monster hunters of any elemental family. Now I'm starting to realize how much of an elaborate storyteller you are."

"Aw, Meemaw. That's so sweet."

When Halsey placed a hand on Greta's shoulder, her grandmother stiffened. Halsey stuck her phone under the woman's nose to display her text conversation with Brigham. Greta finally stopped dusting her potted plant but didn't look at the phone or say anything. *Wow. That's probably the worst poker face I've ever seen.*

Halsey continued softly. "The secret to *good* storytelling is this. *Every* good story has a basis in truth. Even if it seems impossible and everyone's laughing, nobody can deny the story itself had to come from somewhere. From proof. You know who taught me that?"

Greta chucked her brush at a nearby bench, the wooden slats so old, sun-weathered, and warped that they'd started to tear themselves apart. She puffed out a sigh. "You think you're such a clever little Picasso."

"Uh…Picasso was a painter."

"Yeah. *Okay.*" The older woman rolled her eyes, then snatched the phone from Halsey's hand and scrolled through the obnoxious series of texts about wyverns acting out of character. More than that, they'd been acting *out of line* with the natural order of things. Even when that natural order included magic and supernatural beasts that most of the world didn't believe existed.

Halsey took two slow, calm steps back to give her grandmother space. A knowing smile curved her lips, and she folded her arms.

Yeah. That got her attention. She can try to mislead me and deny having opinions about this stuff all she wants. Still, when the Council kicks two of us out for sounding too much alike, there's something else going on here, and she knows it.

Greta took so long to read through the texts and started over so many times that Halsey's smile faded, and she started to worry. Finally, her grandmother flashed the phone at her and pointed at the screen. "This last one at the bottom. Why is he talking to himself?"

"Oh, he wasn't—"

"And calling himself Owen. What is he doing? Some kinda roleplay? I would've thought a big ol' beefcake like Owen would at least have the common sense not to believe shit like *that*."

Halsey choked back a laugh. "Meemaw, they were talking to *each other*. I'm pretty sure Brigham was using voice-to-text, and it picked up both their voices."

"Really? Phones can do that?" When Halsey nodded, Greta clicked her tongue and tossed the phone back without warning. "Ew."

Halsey caught it in time to keep her phone from smacking against a willow tree behind her, then skimmed her conversation with Brigham again. "Ew?"

"Not for me, kid."

"Okay, well, you don't have to use any available features you don't want to. That's kinda the point. You know, variety."

"Uh-huh." Greta pointed at her. "Like *that* variety in a wyvern's natural inclinations?"

Halsey grinned and slid her phone into her pocket. "Yeah. That kind."

"That conversation won't be proof enough for the Council, kid. Aidan might be open to it, sure. Maybe more open than Gracelyn, if you can believe it."

Halsey tried to imagine her dad reading the highly unprofessional yet effective conversation between her and Brigham and being on board with her suspicions about why these monsters were changing. "Not really, no."

"It's plenty of proof for me, though, and I am one tough cookie to crumble. I don't care *what* they say about me up in that big, dusty, gaudy-as-hell HQ mansion." The older woman dusted off her hands, turned in a slow circle to look everywhere except her granddaughter's face, then sighed. "Halsey-Bear, I think you're right."

"Right. Listen, I know it sounds like it's coming from way further than left field, but if you—wait." She narrowed her eyes and leaned away, reaching behind her to feel something solid. Her hand smacked the closest willow tree, and she jolted. "You think I'm *right*?"

"Correct. Accurate. Proper. Most assuredly. Whichever word you prefer, kid. They have slightly different meanings, but right now, I'm gonna say they all mean the same damn thing."

"You think the silver coffin—"

"I'll tell you what I think." Greta approached her granddaughter and beckoned her away from the tree with both hands. It was a simple, inviting gesture, though the woman's ever-present playful smile was gone. Meemaw meant business.

Halsey held her grandmother's gaze and stepped away from the tree. The strangest sensation of déjà vu washed over her. She'd been here before, when she was little, with Meemaw beckoning her away from the drooping, swaying branches of the weeping willows that dotted the western bank of the river. She must have been four or five, and while she had no idea what happened that day nearly twenty years ago, she remembered the feeling.

It was the same feeling worming through her now.

The feeling of being right without any of the pride and satisfaction. Because in both instances, being right meant something was about to go terribly wrong. Or it already had.

The memory faded as quickly as it appeared, and Halsey swallowed before clearing her throat. *What the hell was that? Talk about memory being unreliable. In what world would a five-year-old have any reason to feel like this?*

Greta chuckled a low hum as she waved her granddaughter out of the trees again. "What's *that* about, kid? You look like your ghost just got goosed."

Halsey snorted, found her stride again, and walked confidently into the open side yard. "I don't know what that means, but I'm fine. Sometimes my thoughts…go to weird places."

"Girl, join the fucking club." They both laughed, then instead of taking Halsey's hand, Greta raised her arm and draped it around her granddaughter's shoulders. She pulled the young elemental closer with a playful jostle, but the slight downturn of her mouth and the contemplative pace she led with across the side yard made it clear that joke mode was off. "Your puzzle pieces are coming together in the right way, kiddo. I know how hard it is to be the only one who sees a thing one way while the rest of the world prefers the picture upside down. Hell, they'll even keep their eyes shut and call it enlightenment."

Halsey smirked. She'd mostly gotten over the shock of somebody agreeing with her, at least in the sense that what she'd seen was worth paying attention to and might have horrendous implications. Still, she couldn't tell where this particular train of thought would end with Greta behind the wheel.

"Forget what the cursed Council does or doesn't believe," the woman went on. "You keep doing what you do best, even if it means you gotta ruffle a few feathers and dig up some dust in the process. You're a natural, Halsey. They can't take that away from you, fancy highchairs or not."

"Thanks. Love the imagery, by the way."

"Yeah, well, I can't help but think of them as infantile. I did give birth to half the current Ambrosius Council. Not a glamorous achievement, but somebody has to take the credit."

They slowed in front of the warped and splitting bench, where Greta squinted at a small pile of black and gray objects that looked like plastic, hollow mini-boulders for aquariums. The strange pebble collection wasn't weirder than anything else strewn all over her grandmother's private property. However, Greta stared at the jumble for an uncomfortably long time before she shrugged and continued their walk around the side yard.

"I know you came here asking for facts, not advice. At this point, though, advice is the only thing I have to offer. I won't call it good or helpful advice because, one, that'd make me sound like a stuck-up asshole, and two, I don't think I'm qualified to make that call."

Halsey bit her bottom lip to keep from laughing and looked at her grandmother's profile.

Greta shot her a sidelong glance, then looked ahead with a failed attempt not to roll her eyes. "Maybe one day you'll take me seriously."

"I take you seriously now."

"Oh yeah? Then quit looking at me." The woman still didn't smile, but there was a hint of teasing in her voice.

Halsey's gaze returned to the side yard and all the gardening supplies that logically were better suited for the actual greenhouse on the other side.

Greta cleared her throat. "First advice. You need to be *really* careful moving forward, kid. With the Council and the entire Clan, and with everything else. The assumptions you want to make, the conclusions you want to jump to, the ridiculous but still valid aversion you have to...well, you know." It was unnecessary, but she drew a finger across her throat and made realistic choking, gurgling sounds anyway.

Halsey closed her eyes, feeling like a show horse being led around a competition arena. *Nobody ever said Greta Ambrosius was a subtle woman.*

Greta touched her throat and glanced at her hand as if expecting to find real blood there before she continued.

"The point I'm making is that there is no way to know for sure what's going on until you're smack-dab in the middle of it. Which is clearly a source of conflict for you and… everyone else since you're the only one who's been out there in the thick of it and paying attention."

"Brigham's out there with me too. He's always been on my side."

"Even in this?"

"I mean…" Halsey sighed. "Not in every detail. He does agree that we need to do *something* before things get worse and more confusing. Right now, we're thinking our best next step is to figure out who stole the casket from the Dublin warehouse."

Her grandmother snorted and shook her head. "Of course he's on your side."

"Yeah. He's my partner."

"I'd say it's more than that. The two of you spent most of your time *in utero* together. Not the *same* utero, obviously."

"Obviously." Halsey grimaced.

"In the scheme of things, two months isn't all that long. Your cousin's good at what he does. There's no doubt about that. When it comes to you, though, he's only along for the ride, babe."

"Huh. Then how come he hasn't made up his mind about all this yet? About whether this is a series of freaky coincidences that won't add up to anything or the Mother of Monsters is outta the box, literally, and now we have even worse things to look forward to."

Greta tilted her head from side to side and squeezed

Halsey's shoulder. "That's because he can tell *you* haven't fully made up your mind about it. The same way I can."

"Oh, come on. I've made up my mind."

"No, you've freaked yourself out with all the possibilities, and you're looking for evidence to prove to *yourself* that you haven't lost your mind. Trust your gut, kid. With this kinda thing, the gut is always smarter than the brain." The woman nodded, then stopped and glanced at her granddaughter. "To be clear, that was *not* a suggestion to try solving this little mystery through a direct route to your stomach. I tried contemplative eating once, and it did not go well."

"Wait, *contemplative*…eating?"

"Yeah. How is it a hard concept to grasp?" Greta scoffed. "You've heard of binge eating. Stress eating. Emotional eating. Revenge eating."

Halsey laughed.

"Contemplate *that* while you're at it. Just don't expect to get the answers from food. Contrary to what some might want you to believe, your gut instinct doesn't need any outside help."

"Thanks for that. I think."

"You know me, kid. Dropping knowledge like fruit flies." Greta extended an arm and mimed dropping a microphone.

CHAPTER TWENTY-ONE

They completed a full circle of the river-facing side yard, and Greta didn't give her granddaughter an opportunity to bow out before hugging her close and dragging her for one more lap.

On any other day, Halsey would have been irritated. Today, she had nowhere else to be. The missing records she'd been looking for were missing but not within reach, the library was unofficially off-limits to her for the next few days while Charlemagne got his rage issues under control, and her best friend was out on another mission without her.

Instead of slipping into her familiar urgency and frustration, she wrapped an arm around her grandmother's waist and continued their second loop together.

Jeez. She's all bone under the Carhartt. When did that happen?

Greta didn't give any indication of being uncomfortable or even that she'd noticed Halsey noticing her slight figure. The woman scanned her side yard with full focus as if she were looking for something but had forgotten what that something was.

Halsey decided to try digging one more time. They'd already covered almost everything else under the sun. If her grandmother was in a contemplative mood, with or without food, today might be Halsey's only chance in the foreseeable future to ask the rest of her questions.

"Meemaw," she began as they walked.

Greta released a dreamy sigh. "Sweet, stubborn, spontaneous granddaughter."

Halsey chuckled and tried not to read into the "stubborn" part. "Was there anything helpful in those pages about the Matriarch being freed long enough to make new beasts? Or how any of our family back then dealt with the monster changes?"

"Hmm?" Her grandmother blinked and looked at her with cloudy eyes. The vacant look in them started to worry Halsey until Greta blinked again, and glittering lucidity returned to the brilliant sky-blue of her irises. "Ah. Anything helpful? Not to *you*."

"Don't you think I should be the judge of that?"

"Of course. *I'm* the only one who read the pages, though. There were zero Ambrosius elementals anywhere close to the Circle of Creation for those two decades. They were too busy fighting the monsters that suddenly popped up out of nowhere." The woman stuck her free hand into her jumpsuit pocket, so her forearm rested lightly against the back of Halsey's arm around her waist. "Trust me, kiddo. That's a dead end for now. Who knows, though? If the Mother of Monsters came back to life once already, so to speak, it's possible for any number of other creatures to do the same. Including ideas."

"All right. Fine." Halsey shrugged. When she dropped her shoulders again, she realized how tense she'd been even walking in slow, methodical laps around the side yard. "I'll stop asking about the missing pages."

"Excellent."

"I do have one more question, though."

"Of course you do."

"All the stories you used to tell us when we were kids? The Mother of Monsters. Her one-time return when a lost blood human called her up with his dying breath. The first monsters she created…again. I mean, during her alleged super-short-lived release in the tenth century. Do *you* think it's possible those stories have more truth than any of us thought?"

Greta hummed in thought and squinted into the trees along the riverbank as they ambled past them for a second time. "That's a loaded question. Worthy of a loaded answer, obviously."

"Huh. Obviously."

"Like I said, Halsey. It's almost impossible to know what's happening at any given time. Especially with monsters and magic, not to mention *our* screwed-up family."

Halsey snorted but remained silent so her grandmother could finish her thought. It sounded like whatever the woman said next would let her down.

Greta continued. "Listen, if it were *me* out there, seeing the same things and wondering what the hell's going on, I'd be just as certain the legends are coming true in our lifetime."

Hearing the words "just as certain" made something flutter in Halsey's chest. Part of it was relief and hope. Merely having her suspicions acknowledged made it easier to take her intuition seriously. The other part of that flutter was laced with apprehension. If the legends were coming true and the Mother of Monsters had returned, there was no precedent for how to deal with and hopefully defeat the Blood Matriarch a *second* time. Not to mention doing it while avoiding a massive magical apocalypse and setting off a second Ice Age.

"The legends as we know them, at least," Greta clarified. "Most of our oldest records are all translations from a bunch of squibbly-squabbles none of us know how to read anymore. Do you know how much *shit* can get lost in translation? It's insane."

Halsey arched an eyebrow at her grandmother and was rewarded with a sly smirk.

"Bottom line, kid? You're onto something. Don't you dare stop because somebody told you that you're too much. Got it?"

"Yeah. Thanks."

Greta squeezed her shoulder again. "We're birds of a feather, you and me. Only difference is I got a swift kick in the ass on the way out of the Council, and nobody stopped to ask if I was okay afterward. You still have a lotta work to do out there in the world, so pay attention during your missions. Follow that brilliant gut of yours." She swung her fist forward and around, pretending to sock Halsey in the aforementioned gut and making them both laugh. "You'll be all right."

"Missions. Yeah." Halsey tried to keep her mind from going to her suspension and the fact that she was only halfway through. She'd forgotten about it since the moment she realized it was Greta under the welding helmet, and it had felt so good.

At this point, though, there was no use keeping anything else from her grandmother. The entire Clan knew about Halsey's suspension by now. Though the family kept Greta out of the loop with important decisions and updates these days, Halsey had a hunch that her grandmother could find the information she wanted. Especially information the family didn't want her to have.

"Well, I know for a fact that I won't have any missions for the next two weeks," she added, surprised that she found the whole thing amusing now. "Maybe longer if the Council thinks I'm not *rehabilitated* enough after a month."

"Oh?" They approached the warped bench again on their second lap, and Greta slowed like the last time, squinting yet again at the pile of odd black objects. "I take it this has nothing to do with your perusal of the library. Unless today wasn't your first offense…"

"No, that's the cherry on top. Apparently, after Ireland, they think I need some time to get my head screwed back on."

"Ah. That old gambit." Greta exerted gentle pressure on her granddaughter's shoulder, and they stopped six feet from the bench and its jumble of objects. "If it makes you feel any better, kid, I'm *still* trying to achieve those results to their satisfaction."

Halsey smiled with empathy at her grandmother, studying the woman's face as the pressure of Greta's arm slowly released from her shoulders. "There's nothing wrong with your head, Meemaw."

"Ha. *I* know that." Greta slid her hands into her jumpsuit pockets, and the action somehow made her look less solid. It wasn't weakness, necessarily. Now in her early eighties, the woman looked twenty years younger. In Halsey's mind, her grandmother hadn't aged a day since she was little.

Until right now.

She's tired. That's what it is. Tired of nobody listening or taking her seriously. Whatever she was doing with those stolen pages, she had a good reason for it. Now she can't even turn to her own family for help. So much for being a united Clan through the ages...

The young elemental's attention returned to the bench and the pile of small black objects that had her grandmother so perplexed.

Greta cleared her throat, her gaze unwavering. "That means you have free time on your hands, right?"

"Until I've served my full sentence, I guess. Yeah."

"Excellent. In that case, I'd like to unofficially commission you to help me with a little gnome problem."

Halsey sniggered. "Little. Funny."

Her grandmother kept scanning the side yard and the bases of the lush green trees overshadowing the house. "I didn't think I'd have to walk you through the mechanics of how adjectives work. It would be way too much work to verbally insert hyphens in everyday conversation to avoid contextual confusion, so let me rephrase."

"Wait, what?"

"Don't get me wrong, the gnomes themselves are little. I guess that's in our favor, based on the other weird crap that's been going on." Greta sniffed and shrugged as if she were talking about a casual, natural occurrence. "The *problem*, on the other hand, is damned big."

Halsey frowned at the yard, her senses on high alert. "What gnome prob—ow!"

At first, she thought the sharp pain on the side of her head had been a get-it-together slap from Greta, which would've been the most outrageous, out-of-character thing she'd done today. A split second later, Halsey heard the light thump of something dropping into the grass at her feet.

She tried to rub the sharp sting from her head and looked down. One of those hollow black stone things rested an inch from her sneaker.

Greta's hands were still in the pockets of her jumpsuit.

Her grandmother raised an eyebrow, still staring at the worn bench. "*That* gnome problem."

A grating, high-pitched giggle came from that direction. Halsey followed her grandmother's gaze but couldn't figure out what she was seeing.

The creature making the pint-sized cartoon villain noise was, in fact, a gnome. He stood on the warped planks next to the little black objects, hopping from foot to foot and stabbing a tiny, chubby finger at her as he laughed.

Though only four inches tall and six feet away, the gnome's features were perfectly distinguishable. A baggy vest of sewn dark-green leaves covered his torso. His britches were stitched from strips of tree bark, likely softened with a gnomish water treatment and a dash of magic. Halsey had no idea what his calf-high, neon orange boots were made of. The little guy's stringy beard dangled from his chin like grandfather moss, but his bald head revealed the natural yellow-gray tint of his skin.

The longer he cackled through his wide-open mouth, the less Halsey could look away from the two rows of sharp, needle-point kitten teeth inside it.

She gaped at the creature in disbelief. The first words out of her mouth offered no value, but she couldn't help blurting them out. "That's a garden gnome."

"Uh-huh." With her hands still in her pockets, Greta bit her lower lip and tilted her head. "Like all the rest of them."

Halsey finally noticed that the legs of the wooden bench and the ground beneath it were moving. She caught a flash of neon orange amid the squirming, shuffling green and brown, and it clicked.

"Holy shit."

Greta dipped her chin with a deepening frown. "Yup."

"That's a lot of gnomes."

"Like I said. Little monster, big problem."

Halsey licked her lips in concentration and stood still, more out of bafflement than anything else. "How many is that? Fifty?"

"Give or take."

She leaned toward her grandmother and stage-whispered without intending to. "They obviously know we're here."

"Obviously."

"Why are they letting us see them?" She felt like an amateur ventriloquist giving an atrocious failure of a performance. "Better question. Why are they *acknowledging* us?"

"I'd say it's the same reason those wyverns in Kansas started roosting with the local chickens," Greta replied.

"So basically for no reason."

"Basically, yeah."

The first gnome, who'd thrown one of those strange rocks at Halsey, stopped cackling and bouncing, but one stubby finger tipped with an extra-sharp claw still pointed at her. His mouth still curled in a crazed grin that showed off his razor-sharp teeth. He'd looked formidable enough on his own, but with at least fifty other gnomes spilling from their underground hidey-holes and swarming the bench to join him, the sight bordered on terrifying.

At least, it probably would have been for anyone else.

Yet this mob of garden gnomes had revealed themselves to two of the Ambrosius Clan's best monster hunters. Halsey and Greta also happened to be the only Ambrosius elementals paying attention to the mounting evidence that something had screwed up the natural order of things, even within the supernatural world.

The gnomes shimmied and scuttled up the legs, back, and seat of the bench like humanoid crabs, their nails digging into the old wood with hundreds of tiny, muffled clicks. Several added high-pitched giggles and cackling screeches, and all kept their beady little eyes on the elementals standing six feet away.

This is what a pack of three-inch hyenas sounds like.

Halsey felt ridiculous thinking it, but now that she had, she couldn't get the image out of her mind.

In less than twenty seconds, the whole mob scrambled

their way onto the bench, crowding together on the seat or standing on the top edge of the bench for a good look at the two women staring them down. Hundreds of glittering needle teeth gleamed inside open, laughing mouths. Time seemed to stand still.

"What are they waiting for?" Halsey whispered.

"How the hell should *I* know?" her grandmother rasped. "You're the expert at thinking outside the box."

"Unless you have an entire section of field notes and monster research in your pockets, I don't think that applies right now."

Greta sniggered. "That's a fabulous idea."

Halsey glanced sideways at her. "All right. How about you work on inventing that *after* we deal with this big-little problem of yours?"

"They're not *my* gnomes. They only live in my yard. I think. Haven't actually seen them before now."

"What? How'd you know you even had a gnome problem?"

"Observation and deductive reasoning, kiddo. Another thing I didn't think I'd have to remind you about. Come on."

Halsey sighed as hard as she dared and fought against rolling her eyes. Anything other than standing still and maintaining eye contact with at least one three-inch humanoid would set off a chain reaction she'd rather avoid. "This feels like a standoff, doesn't it?"

"Mexican or monster?"

"Seriously?"

Greta smirked. "No. You have any weapons on you?"

Halsey clenched her fists. "No, Meemaw. Today's the

one day I left my house to walk across my family's private property *without* being armed to the gills for an unexpected monster battle." *Garden gnomes aren't even technically monsters. Or at least they didn't used to be...*

"Huh. Pity." Her grandmother sounded nonplussed about the whole thing, but she also hadn't moved an inch. They were clearly in the same boat. "Would've been nice to have some backup."

Right. Like a sword, a throwing ax, or even Pappy's rifle would be much help with a bunch of targets we can hardly see.

Before either of them could comment further on how unprepared they were for something like this, the gnomes got impatient.

One of them shouted something in a strangled, nasal voice as close to the sound of nails on a chalkboard as a tiny monster could get. Halsey couldn't understand a thing he said, but the grating pitch of his babbling made her eye twitch.

A handful of other gnomes took up the same garbled cry, then at least half joined in. The noise was jarring from the otherwise innocuous creatures who, as a general rule, didn't make a sound. Not in front of humans, anyway.

"What are they doing?" Halsey murmured.

"Again. No clue."

"Okay, so what do *we* do?"

"Now you're repeating the question, and I promise you my answer hasn't changed."

"Well, maybe I've run out of things to say," Halsey snapped back, then grimaced. Her voice had been louder than she'd intended, and it riled up several gnomes. Three of them took up the grating, gobbledygook chant again, and more joined in. This time, more than half the mob shouted in unison.

Get it together, Halsey. She snatched a deep breath and wrestled her voice back under control. "No weapons, no shared language, and no idea what they want. If you have any suggestions, now would be a great time to share."

"Hmm." Greta tilted her head to the other side. "Maybe they're *trying* to get our attention."

"You think?"

"They've acknowledged *us*, and all we've done is stand here like a couple of magical, two-legged deer caught in a lot of tiny headlights."

Halsey eyed the waiting mob of gnomes, most of whom now swayed from side to side as they grinned at their intended audience…or their intended targets. There was no way to tell the difference. "Acknowledge them."

"Right." Greta lowered her head a fraction of an inch. "As in saying hi."

"I know how to acknowledge somebody. Thank you very much."

"Oh, so you have experience making friends with a horde of garden gnomes in broad daylight, then."

Halsey wanted to close her eyes in exasperation. *Not looking at the scene in front of her would go a long way toward settling her nerves enough to come up with a plan.* Again, though, her gut told her that maintaining eye contact was of utmost importance. Her only option was to press her lips together and draw another breath through flaring nostrils.

"Fine. I'll…talk to them."

"Wonderful." Greta didn't sound any more or less

pleased than she'd been when first mentioning the gnomes. She lifted her hands from her jumpsuit pockets at a snail's pace. "While you're leading us through polite and cordial introductions, remember not to make any sudden moves."

"Why? Is that a thing with these guys when they're…out in the open?"

"Honestly, kiddo, I have no idea. I guess a powerful hunch will have to be good enough for both of us."

CHAPTER TWENTY-TWO

No sudden movements. Polite and courteous introductions. Constant eye contact.

Slowly, Halsey lifted her chin and rolled her shoulders back as she prepared to step forward and follow directions. For the first time since she was little, she'd committed to doing what she was told without knowing a thing about why she was doing it or what the end result would be.

Her suspicions of what might happen if she *didn't* follow directions were clear, as was the fact that she and her grandmother were handling this situation based purely on gut instinct and their ability to think on their feet.

"Psst." Greta leaned toward her and gently nudged Halsey with her elbow. "Get a move on, already. You think they're getting any friendlier standing in this heat?"

"Yeah, well, neither are we." The young elemental regretted the knee-jerk response as soon as the words left her lips. Her grandmother *tsked* once but said nothing.

Whatever happens, we can't stand here all day. Get it together, Hal. You're a goddamn monster hunter. This is what you do. Hell, did the Council take your active-duty status and your spine without telling you?

Giving herself the kind of military pep talk she'd received from her dad and many other Ambrosius Clan operatives during her militia training wasn't half as effective now as it had been back then. That only made it worse.

You're not walking into a wyvern den. They're fucking garden gnomes. Three-inch dudes with sharp teeth and claws. Okay, yeah, plus creepy grins that look like they know a lot more about what's happening than you do. And the ability to move fast as shit, because that's why nobody catches them in the act of literally anything. Damn, these things are terrifying, and I have no idea what to do with them.

Halsey mentally shook her head to clear the cobwebs of doubt, confusion, and apprehension building around her thoughts. No, she didn't have any weapons, a gnomish translator, or anything she could use to barter with these little guys at the moment.

She did have magic, though. She *always* had magic. In a pinch like this, with no prior knowledge, magic would have to be enough.

Fuck it.

She plastered on a tight smile without grinning too broadly in case the tiny yellow men considered teeth-baring an act of aggression. After one slow, deliberate step forward, she lifted her open hand in front of her shoulder and hoped that garden gnomes knew what a wave was.

The mob noticed her acknowledgment of them. They'd been watching her with equal intensity, though the tiny creatures had feral looks in their eyes as they grinned and cackled like they'd cornered their next meal. Halsey probably appeared to have suddenly realized she *was* that meal. None of them reacted to her movement, so she figured it was safe to move onto the next part of the nonexistent process.

"Uh...hey, there."

When the words left her lips, the gnomes snapped their mouths shut and stood at three erect inches of attention. Those who'd been gauging Greta with veiled malice turned their gazes to Halsey instead. Every gaping grin disappeared. The gnomes' beady eyes widened into gleaming black orbs, and an uncomfortable silence fell across the yard.

Great. So much for introductions.

"Keep going," her grandmother whispered, keeping her lips as still as possible.

Halsey lowered her hand and forced herself to scan the gnome's faces. Their strange standoff had been kicked up to its next level, and she had to choose her next words carefully. Even if they couldn't understand them.

There is not enough information in the library on gnomes. They've been at the bottom of the food chain for...forever. Can they smell fear?

The thought almost made her laugh amid her uncertainty, but she held it back and swallowed.

"My name is Halsey," she stated in a slow, even, confident tone. Whether or not they understood English, they likely understood the sound of a larger creature with even a little uncertainty. She needed to avoid that. Gesturing toward her grandmother, she added, "And this is Greta."

The older woman snorted but didn't say anything.

Yeah, I sound ridiculous. This whole thing is ridiculous.

"So." She forced her smile to widen, but it was harder under the wide eyes and deadpan expressions of fifty garden gnomes standing statue-still. "This isn't, uh…something we do every day. Not that we have a problem with you guys. Not that *you* are a *problem* or anything. Only… you know. We have no idea what's going on or what we're supposed to do now, so I'm hoping at least one of you understands me. Based on your blank looks, I'm gonna go ahead and say that's a no."

To accentuate her intention, if not her words, Halsey stretched the smile and slowly nodded.

"That went well," Greta muttered.

"Yeah, great idea. It totally worked."

"At least you didn't make any sudden moves, so we still have that going for us. Ask them what they want."

"What? *You* ask them."

"No, no." Greta gestured minutely toward the gnome-infested bench. "You're doing a great job, and they're… focused. On you. I wouldn't want to intrude or anything."

"Meemaw, they're staring at us, and they don't seem to understand a word of English. It doesn't matter which one of us asks them anything."

"Keep going, then."

Halsey's expression felt as tight as an overnight clay mask. The only way she could prevent yelling at her grandma and ruining this already precarious situation was to grin like her life depended on it. Most likely, it didn't. Then again, this monster situation felt ten times more dangerous and unpredictable than her first solo mission after she'd officially become an elemental operative. And *that* had been against a full-grown manticore.

"We'd, uh...love to know what brought you up to the surface today," Halsey uttered. "In broad daylight. Where we can see you. If there's anything specific you're looking for, maybe we can help. You know, call a truce. Get some peace talks going. We're friendly when you get to know us."

"Are you trying to convince them or yourself?" Greta murmured.

"I'm working on it, thank you." Halsey's cheeks burned with the effort of maintaining her huge fake smile. "We all wanna get along, right? Whatever it is, feel free to put it out there in any way you—"

"Mother*fuck!*"

The high-pitched screech of an expletive in one teeny voice came from somewhere at the back of the crowd. None of the other gnomes turned toward the speaker, but a few squeaky sniggers and grunts of approval rose from the mob.

No way. There's no way...

It took all her effort not to burst out laughing. She cleared her throat instead and hoped that didn't count as being too loud or moving too fast. "Meemaw."

"Uh-huh."

"Did one of those gnomes—"

"Shout 'motherfuck' at you?" Greta grunted in her own attempt not to laugh, sounding like she was in the middle of an intense weight-lifting session. "That's what it sounded like. Hard to tell with all the squeaking, and there was a dash of an accent there, but yeah. I think it did."

"You think they know what that means?"

"I guess we'll find out, won't we?"

It felt so bizarre to stand there in perfect stillness, staring at a mob of tiny, fanged men and discussing one baffling surprise after another in the cheery, reassuring voices people used with their pets. At least this little confrontation hadn't gotten any worse.

"Okay." A low, airy chuckle escaped Halsey as she gathered her thoughts. "I'm gonna let that one slide because there's a decent chance you heard it somewhere else, and English probably doesn't translate well to gnomish—"

"Shithead!" The next gnome's voice was comparatively lower, and Halsey choked on the rest of her sentence.

"Uh... I'm sorry. What was—"

"Suck it, shithead!"

Greta barked laughter, covered it up, then snorted through her hand.

"That's not helping," Halsey warned as several gnomes took up the last squeaked expletive and turned it into another chant.

"Oh, come on, kiddo. Out of everyone else in our weird-ass family, you're the one who'd find this the funniest. Maybe tied with Brigham, I guess."

"*That's* true. Under normal circumstances. It's not that funny when dozens of tiny men are looking at us the way they are right now, though."

"Really? I kinda like it. They're cute."

Halsey wanted to look at her grandmother's face. It was impossible to tell if the woman was serious or using a serious dose of sarcasm. Instead, she focused on trying to get through to even one of the garden gnomes. Otherwise, there was no telling what their enthusiastic cursing meant or what it heralded for the immediate future.

"All right, not that this isn't fun," she called out, trying to raise her voice above the gnomes shouting, "Suck it, shithead!" She didn't want them to perceive anything she did as hostile. Not until she intended hostility, anyway. "If any of you know how to say anything *else* in English, that would be helpful for—"

"Fuck you!"

Halsey blinked in surprise, then sighed. "Wow. Okay. I hope you have no idea what that means, or we're in a serious—"

"Fuck the Council!" another gnome shouted.

Greta bellowed laughter, which was perfectly understandable. "Okay. *Now* we're getting somewhere," she chortled.

"Again, Meemaw. Not helping."

"Oh, you don't need my help now, kiddo."

Halsey crinkled her nose in frustration but pulled her emotions back under control a second later. "Gnomes. Does anyone have anything not completely useless to say?"

"Motherfuck the Council!"

"Burn them down!"

"Burn the Council!"

"Suck it, burnhead!"

"Council shithead!"

"Down the mother shitburn!"

At first, the shouts rang out one by one. The sentiment seemed to catch on with the mob, and fifty three-inch voices yelled at once, their clueless insults jumbling together in every possible variation of apparently the only English words they knew.

"Oh, okay." Halsey laughed and spread her arms. "I get it."

"Look at that," her grandmother added with a snort. "I had no idea garden gnomes were so skilled at mimicry. Not to mention the creative license of switching the words up in different orders."

"Super fun." Despite feeling like an idiot for being so cautious in front of a never-before-seen garden gnome mob, Halsey was relieved. She laughed with her grandmother because, uncharacteristic behavior aside, this *was* hilarious. "I wonder where they heard all this."

"Could've picked it up from anywhere. Ooh, and look." Greta stepped forward and smacked Halsey's arm with the back of a hand. "They're so *into* it. Like they really mean what they're saying."

"They have no idea what they're saying."

"Well, obviously." Greta turned her head and eyed the mob with a sidelong glance and a coy smile. "I know it's none of my business, but I can't help being proud of the little dudes."

"Does that mean you're taking responsibility for teaching them all these phrases?"

"What? No." The older woman clicked her tongue and avoided Halsey's gaze. "That didn't come from *me*. I'm proud of them for trying to learn the language. Seeing as this is probably the first time they've had the opportunity to use it with the locals."

"Oh, jeez." Halsey rolled her eyes and let go of any lingering concerns. Whatever the gnomes thought they were saying, the message wasn't getting through, and that was fine. Apparently, they were more interested in testing their new phrases with gusto than engaging the Ambrosius elementals in a physical altercation as she'd expected. "What do we do now?"

Greta chuckled and folded her arms. "Nothing. Let 'em have their fun. They'll tucker themselves out eventually. I mean, look at the size of 'em."

That was the last straw for Halsey, and she bellylaughed without trying to hold it back. Her grandmother was quick to join in. Out of everything they could have done in this situation, laughter felt like the best option.

CHAPTER TWENTY-THREE

The air was so thick with the shrill, squeaking voices of fifty gnomes taking full liberty with their smattering of English it was impossible for either elemental to be heard over the din. By now, the mob had riled themselves up so thoroughly that they were moving again. Their eyes grew wide and expressive as they screamed obscenities they didn't understand, shook their fists in the air, or hopped from foot to foot. If they'd been human-sized and had brought this energy to Greta Ambrosius' front door, or any other part of her property, they would have been an actual mob and not merely the common name for a group of garden gnomes.

If they'd been human-sized, Halsey would have prepared herself for an altercation and the possibility of having to teach them a serious lesson or two.

Underestimating the rowdy creatures was Halsey and Greta's first mistake.

Through her laughter, Greta shook her head and shouted over the noise. "Way to stand your ground, kiddo.

You assessed the situation, brought caution and common sense into the fray, and used the hell out of them both. Turns out you had nothing to be afraid of, but hey. Talk about your learning curves, am I right?"

Halsey almost laughed it all off as one big joke too. Yet when she considered her grandmother's words, she was overcome by an urge to set the record straight. That urge was another of many traits she and Greta shared.

"Wait a minute." She spun toward the woman and cocked her head. "You didn't know any more about this than I did."

Greta shrugged and stuck out her lower lip in sarcastic contemplation. "I knew there was a gnome problem."

"You *assumed* there was a gnome problem. You've never actually seen them before today."

"Oh. After everything you've told me today, I wouldn't have pegged you as the kind of person who had to *see* something in order to believe it."

"That's different, and you know it." Halsey was aware of her voice rising in pitch and volume again, but if she toned it down, she wouldn't be heard over the obscene racket from the gnomes. "I get how gnomes *used* to work, and no. With these guys, 'seeing to believe' isn't normally an option. Don't act like this is part of some Ambrosius teenager's low-level training, okay? That's insulting to both of us."

"Not as insulting as that." Greta hooked a thumb toward the gnome mob, and Halsey smiled crookedly.

"It's definitely funny."

"Wouldn't you rather watch this play out instead of arguing about who knows more than whom?"

"No, Meemaw. I wouldn't." Halsey straightened her shoulders and tried not to tower over her grandmother, who seemed shorter for the first time. "That's the point of all this. It's only funny for a little while, but *garden gnomes* swarming up benches and cursing nonsense at us still means there's something seriously wrong with monsters of all kinds. Not only werewolves and wyverns. Now it's the...weird little dudes with orange galoshes that maybe one person sees every hundred years."

"Like I said." Her grandmother folded her arms. "Learning curves."

"Yeah. *Our* learning curve. Not mine."

"Come on, Halsey-Bear. You're being overly dramatic—"

"I am *not* being dramatic," Halsey shouted. "I'm one of the best hunters this Clan has, and I've *earned* the right to be taken seriously!"

Her voice echoed from the house, the trees, and the riverbank at once. Even the gnomes were so taken aback by her outburst that they ceased their shrieking, chanted expletives. The sensation of fifty tiny pairs of eyes on the side of her face disconcerted her as she met her grandmother's gaze head-on.

Her fists had clenched. She opened them to flex her fingers. *That's not gonna get me anywhere. Why does* she *think talking to me the way everyone does is gonna get* her *anywhere?*

Greta's brow lifted, her eyes flickering back and forth as she studied her granddaughter and smiled slowly. "*There* it is."

Halsey blew out a breath. "What are you talking about?"

"The Ambrosius elemental we need right now." The

woman nodded, the curtain of her straight, shoulder-length gray hair swishing across her shoulders. "*That's* the Halsey Ambrosius who should've stepped into that Council room two weeks ago. It's who you are in the field with a weapon in one hand and magic in the other. Don't you think for a second that the little girl not taking her training seriously enough has more power than the elemental you've become. Or the only monsters you'll have to face are the ones beyond the property lines of this estate." She circled a finger around her head to indicate the Ambrosius property and everything within its boundaries.

Every*one* within it.

A cold, hard pit formed in Halsey's stomach. She recognized the look in her grandmother's eyes. She'd only seen it a handful of times, but each of those instances stood out in sharp contrast to her other memories. Every time she'd seen this look, it meant Greta was right.

Something inexplicably awful was about to happen, and Halsey would have to figure out what it was and what it meant on her own.

There was more to the monster changes in the world than a temporary spell of odd behavior or a series of outrageous coincidences lining up. She knew that. Knowing it and accepting it, however, were two different things.

"What is this?" she murmured, shaking her head and studying her grandmother's face. "What are you doing? What's that supposed to mean?"

"It means what I said, kiddo. It's entirely up to personal interpretation—"

"No, hold on. You had something specific in mind when you said all that." From the corner of her eye,

Halsey noticed something small and black whizzing through the air behind her grandmother's head, but it didn't fully register. "What are you trying to tell me, huh?"

"Halsey..."

"No, I'm serious. I am *done* with the games. Is that why you stole those pages out of the archives? Are you trying to hide something from the family or cover something up *for* them?"

Greta clasped her hands together and dipped her chin. "It was intended as a morale-boosting compliment, kid. That's it. Not everything is a mystery that needs to be solved. At least not in the present moment. Especially this one."

"You know, that's a shitty way of telling somebody they're not worth the effort." Another small black mystery item hurtled directly above Halsey's head before landing in the open grass to her left with a hollow *thump*.

Her grandmother didn't seem to notice the random projectiles. Instead, she tilted her head, and the last trace of playfulness left her expression. "You're my granddaughter, Halsey. You are worth every ounce of effort and then some."

"Then lay it out." Halsey spread her arms. "If you don't know something, say *that*. If you're too tired or too discouraged to explain, that's okay. I'm so tired of the excuses, Greta. The lies, the coverups, and the refusal to talk about the *one thing* that matters at the moment. If you have something to say to me, a warning or a specific threat to look out for, *tell me*. Straightforward. Honest. Brutal, if it has to be. Hell, I'm twenty-three, and I already know brutal honesty is better than living in a fairytale of fucking denial all the time. So please."

Greta held her granddaughter's gaze a moment longer, then scanned the young woman head to toe. "This has really been getting to you, huh?"

Halsey could only shrug. Admitting out loud that she was ready to get out from under everyone else's impressive or devastating shadows still felt like too much.

"Is this about Gilliam too?" her grandmother asked gently.

"I don't know. Maybe. Probably." One more object sailed across the yard, hit the grass beside Halsey's right sneaker, and bounced twice before rolling to a stop against her shoe. "Okay, yeah. I don't *want* to admit that every single power struggle of my adult life stems from whether my family thinks I'll be anything more than crazy Gilliam Ambrosius' messed-up—"

The next tiny missile from the gnome mob struck its intended target, which happened to be the side of Halsey's head. Again.

Instead of finishing her sentence, Halsey closed her eyes and drew a deep, calming breath. *This is as bad as Clara and Jack starting their insane food fight every time the whole Clan gets together for a meal. I* have *to ignore these guys because their teeth are a hell of a lot sharper than my cousins'.*

When she opened her eyes again, her grandmother watched her warily. "It's fine."

"You sure?" Greta indicated the gnome-infested bench and widened her eyes. "Now might be the best time to make our escape. Just sayin'."

"We don't need an escape, either." Halsey shook her

head. "Honestly, I don't wanna give fifty-something tiny men the satisfaction of driving us off that easily. I think that's all they're trying to do."

Two more black objects shot out. One plunked against the thick fabric of Greta's jumpsuit at the shoulder, and the other sailed between the two women. Halsey frowned after the escaped projectile and fought to hold back her growing frustration before it boiled over.

Her grandmother glanced at her targeted shoulder before dropping her gaze to the offending black thingamabob in the grass beside her boot. "You know what? I assumed garden gnomes had freakishly accurate aim. Now I'm starting to think that first one was a fluke."

"I hope so." Halsey pointed a thumb at the mob of tiny men chucking things at them. "Only an attention-grabber, right?"

"Yeah. Probably. If you think about it, they're like toddlers. Repeating everything they hear, throwing random shit all over the place, pushing your buttons until you can't take it anymore and you snap and yell and say things you don't mean, which makes them cry, which makes you feel terrible…"

Halsey grimaced. "Meemaw."

"…so you do everything you can think of to get them to *stop* crying, then you spend years trying to get *one* kid to at least act like they forgive you, or at least like they don't hate your guts and wish you were chopped into a million little pieces and strewn along the bottom of the ocean." Greta's bright blue eyes widened as she stared off into space over Halsey's right shoulder. "Good gods, and I had five of them. By *choice*."

"Uh..." Halsey chuckled uncertainly. "We probably don't have to worry about hurting the *garden gnomes'* feelings or getting them to forgive us for anything. Which is what we were talking about in the first place."

"Hmm?" Her grandmother blinked and focused on her. The bright lucidity returned to the woman's eyes, and she scoffed with a crooked smile. "Oh, of course. Garden gnomes, not toddlers. Obviously."

Halsey tried to look as serious as possible, so at least one of them could pretend they had everything under control. "Okay, I think maybe we should—"

She grunted when another hollow black stone-thing struck the top of her shoulder. A second struck her forearm, a third bounced off the top of her backside, and a fourth cracked against her thigh above her kneecap. The volley of tiny projectiles was more annoying than painful. Worse was the ensuing sound of squeaking, high-pitched voices breaking into sniggers and giggles and garbled strings of gnomish words.

What little hold Halsey had left on her composure snapped.

She spun toward the crowded gnomes, leaned forward with her arms spread, and practically screamed, "Do you *mind?*"

CHAPTER TWENTY-FOUR

Until now, very few elementals of any Clan had had the confusing, exasperating, and downright infuriating experience of encountering even one garden gnome. Now, Halsey Ambrosius had snapped at fifty of them gathered in one place. If there had been field notes about dealing with these tiny, unpredictable creatures warning never to raise one's voice at them, she would have done it anyway.

The second she shouted, every gnome shut up.

Greta's mouth popped open in surprise. She regarded the devious little critters apprehensively. None looked happy to have been spoken to like that, though they'd been chucking hollow rocks at her and Halsey throughout their conversation.

Halsey fought to catch her breath and scanned the tiny yellow faces, a few clean-shaven but most bearded. Every gnome glared back with furious hatred. She understood the emotion was aimed at her, but she'd passed the point of holding anything back.

"*Thank* you," she quipped, adding insult to insult with a

tight, shallow mockery of a bow. She may as well twist the blade. She dropped her arms and spun toward Greta. "I have *had* it with gnomes."

"All right, kid." Her grandmother kept watching the mob as several of the gnomes elicited low growls and angry grumbling. To the magical humans, it sounded like squeaking in slightly lower pitches. She'd gone back to standing perfectly still. "Not what *I* would've done to avoid pitting them against us, but hey. Difference of opinion is what makes us unique, right?"

Halsey sighed through loose lips. "Well, somebody has to make them understand that throwing…whatever those are at humans and cursing them out isn't okay."

"Valid point." Greta narrowed her eyes. "I don't think that's what they're understanding right now."

Almost as if they'd been waiting for Halsey's grandmother to step into position as their spokesperson, one of the gnomes stopped growling and barked sharply. A small handful took up the aggressive call, snarling and yipping, expressing anger in a universal way despite the language barrier.

The cacophony of high-pitched barks and snarls made Halsey's eyes twitch, and she pressed her lips together. *I take it back. Charlemagne will sound like a regular grumpy old man after this. The gnomes are the ones that sound like Chihuahuas.*

"Maybe you should apologize," Greta suggested.

"No." When her grandmother met her gaze and raised her eyebrows, Halsey shook her head. "Oh, come on. No. I'm not going there. If you'd heard yourself ranting about…

the worst parts of having a toddler, I guess, you'd understand why I'm not—"

A deafening crack rose from the gnomes, and a flash of electric-yellow light zipped toward them and crashed into the ground between the women's feet. The ensuing magical jolt that blasted through the bottom of Halsey's shoes wasn't as small as she'd expected, coming from a three-inch-tall creature.

"Ow." Sucking in a sharp breath, Halsey stepped back to avoid any residual magic still crackling across the grass.

Greta frowned and stared at the small, charred hole in the grass. She shook out her left hand as if it had been zapped.

The gnomes exploded into high-pitched giggles.

One of the tiny men standing on the bench's top edge thrust his arm into the air. It was impossible to tell them apart at this point, so she had no idea if it was the first one to show himself. She did know he held a collection of copper wire in his raised fist, the strands wrapped around each other to form a walking stick, a cane, or…

Halsey's eyes widened. *Did that little bastard make himself a channeling staff out of Meemaw's copper wiring?*

The gnome with the copper staff thrust his chest out and screamed with all his might, "I…hate…pickles!"

"I hate pickles!" the others roared, shaking their fists and jumping up and down.

"Oh, great." Halsey whirled toward her grandmother. "Now we *know* where they got their vocabulary."

Greta smiled crookedly and shrugged. "Okay, maybe I've said all those things once or twice before." She faced the gnomes and wagged a finger in a grandmotherly way that Halsey had never seen before this moment. "Conversations held with oneself, even if that self happens to be talking out loud, should be off-limits when someone's in the privacy of their own home. Shame on you."

Halsey scoffed and rolled her eyes.

The staff-bearing gnome, who might or might not have been the mob's leader, turned the tip downward and loosed another crackling yellow bolt.

He might have been the only one in the group with accurate aim. His quick, deliberate magical attack zapped across the space between them and landed at the tip of the woman's pointing finger.

Greta yipped in surprise, shook her hand, then stared at her finger with a gaping mouth. "No, he did *not*."

Yet he had. He released a shrill, curdling scream, a clear battle cry no matter how high-pitched the voice. The mob added their voices, ready to go on the offensive with him. A majority of them shrieked their favorite rendition of Greta's varied, colorful language. Then it was game over.

"Shit." Halsey lunged for her grandmother. "Meemaw, we gotta get—ah!"

The remaining black projectiles flew toward the Ambrosius women at the same time, pelting them from head to toe with far more force behind them and a resulting greater sting.

The women ducked, yelping and gritting their teeth against the sudden barrage as they shielded their faces with their arms. Halsey received more of the abuse in a T-shirt and shorts than Greta in her thick, full-body jumpsuit.

"We were both wrong," Greta shouted over the assault.

"We should've drawn a line in the sand and declared, 'No gnomes allowed aboveground.' Maybe we—"

"Yeah, that moment's over."

"Why?"

There was a brief moment of reprieve when the little black objects ran out, and they snuck glances toward the bench in time to see the last few garden gnomes clambering down the wooden legs and disappearing into the grass. The final one paused in his mad scramble to grin deviously. He sniggered, drew a clawed finger across his neck in a gesture that needed no translation, and launched himself off the bench. He hit the ground and disappeared like the others.

Whether it was invisibility magic, expert camouflage, or actual underground tunnels, not a single garden gnome remained visible.

"Huh." Greta tilted her head and scanned the ground. "You gotta give 'em an A for effort, right?"

"I don't think they're done."

"Please. Those little cretins? We could write our *own* field-note book on the subject after this. 'Garden Gnome. They talk a good game, but when push comes to tiny black rocks pelting you in the face, it's all for show—'"

"Watch it!" Halsey grabbed her grandmother's arm and hauled her away from the blast of crackling yellow magic spurting like a geyser. Right where Greta had been standing.

"Well, now I've had it!" Greta whirled toward the spot where the yellow light had erupted. She extended a hand and twisted her wrist. The earth shuddered before crumpling in on itself to leave a two-foot hole of damp earth, jutting roots, and wriggling insects.

And no gnomes.

"Ha." The woman leaned forward and squinted, scrutinizing the ground. "Okay. Two can play at *this* game."

"You mean like the two of us?" Halsey muttered as she scanned the garden. "There are a lot more of *them*."

"We're goddamn giants in their eyes. Don't let the little bastards get in your head, kid. This is all—" Greta shrieked when her feet were swiped out from under her, and she toppled to land face-first on the ground with a *thud*.

"Oh, come on!" Halsey stepped back as if that would make the gnomes less likely to whip *her* feet out from under her. "You okay?"

"Fine. Fine. I'm…" With her torso pushed halfway off the ground, Greta paused and grinned slowly. "There you are."

She worked her elemental magic on the earth in front of her face, throwing dirt, worms, and roots in every direction, including all over her. After she stopped, she pushed upright and leapt nimbly to her feet.

Halsey didn't know which kind of magic to arm herself with, especially fighting a monster opponent she couldn't even see.

Another bolt of yellow light arced out of the ground, and Greta swiped her hand toward it. The spiraling, howling vortex of wind under her command knocked the gnomes' attack aside. The woman looked over her shoulder at Halsey and wiggled her eyebrows. "Give 'em hell, kid."

Halsey had barely thought this was one monster fight

she didn't want any part of when the entire side yard lit with dozens of flaring yellow streaks. Her grandmother threw her head back, unleashed a warbling cackle, and darted into the fray.

I guess this is all the action I'm gonna get for the next two weeks. Might as well.

She reached behind her toward the river and called the water to her. The watery tendrils formed a frigid spear and a churning shield for bashing aside magical attacks and possibly a few gnomes.

The next zap of yellow gnome magic that hurtled toward her didn't have a chance. Halsey swung her arm up, and the free-floating water shield copied her movement to connect with the gnome's attack. The brilliant yellow flare snuffed out. Now that she wasn't distracted by powerful magic streaking toward her, she caught sight of a gnome standing a few feet in front of her.

The gnome's eyes widened when he realized his mob had picked a fight with two elementals who could fight back. Before he could do anything else, Halsey launched her watery spear at him.

She whirled and ran across Greta's side yard, looking for more of the devilish little creatures to put back in their place. After a moment, she realized her beaming grin matched her grandmother's.

CHAPTER TWENTY-FIVE

An hour later, the battle between Ambrosius elementals and obnoxious garden gnomes had ended. The gnomes had given up after deciding the game wasn't fun anymore. All Halsey and Greta had to show for their efforts were smashed planter pots, ripped and scattered bags of fertilizer, the wooden bench reduced to a pile of broken planks and jagged splinters, and around four dozen two-foot holes filled with river water.

It wasn't a clear victory for either side, but Halsey enjoyed the skirmish nonetheless. After spending half of her prescribed suspension holed up in her house, texting Brigham, or poring over materials in the Clan library, it felt good to fight something. Battle had always been one of her most useful emotional outlets.

When she and her grandmother realized there wouldn't be any more gnome battling today, and hopefully not anytime soon, they shared a laugh over the whole thing. Halsey was ready to call it a day.

Walking out to Greta's house hadn't given Halsey the

answers she was looking for, but at least she had a clearcut goal now. She'd only needed one person to take her seriously, whether or not that person was taken seriously by the Council. Her grandmother had given her that. Greta believed the legends and stories about the Mother of Monsters were probably true—or as true as legends could turn out to be.

Now Halsey only had to bide her time and not make waves with the Council until her mandatory suspension was over. She'd get back out in the field with Brigham, and she'd view every mission through an entirely different lens.

If the Blood Matriarch had been released and returned to the land of the living, *she* was responsible for the odd, troubling changes in monsters big and small lately. Halsey only had to find the proof that would show the Council she'd been right all along.

Somehow, that made the next two weeks of waiting easier to bear.

The following week passed more quickly than she'd imagined. Halsey spent her early mornings and late evenings walking around the property, thinking about how she'd handle whatever came her way in the future. Most of that involved deciding how to return to Dublin to check out the Clan's recovery warehouse for herself. Patrick was a good employee and had put together an excellent team over several decades, but he wasn't an elemental. He wasn't a detective, either. He could have missed something that might be obvious to her.

She didn't want to go anywhere without her partner. Unfortunately, it wasn't as simple as waiting for Brigham to return from his wyvern-shooing mission in Kansas. The

Council had decided that shipping her cousin off on constant missions, all with different militia operatives, was the best way for him to spend his time.

Brigham was so busy that she hardly heard from him save for quick texts every few days to double-check his hunches about handling this or that strange monster behavior. Brigham didn't ask her point-blank for any more advice, likely because he didn't think he could convince the Council to put her back to work early.

She didn't think he could, either.

By the evening that ended her third week, Halsey was counting down the days and feeling good about her prospects for returning to missions. She missed feeling like part of something important. She'd plopped on her living room couch with her laptop to find a good movie when her phone buzzed on the side table.

She grabbed the phone with half her attention still on scrolling through movies, assuming the incoming text was from Brigham. She was wrong.

She choked on her beer when she realized the short, brusque message was from her dad. After coughing it out, she read the message three times before it fully sank in.

Emergency meeting in the Council room. They requested you personally. Don't get your hopes up.

"Shit. What now?"

Part of her wanted to take her time changing out of her pajamas, putting her shoes on, and finishing her beer. As she considered it, the sound of a large engine outside rumbled toward her cottage, and she shot up from the couch.

There's no way my dad would come out here to pick me up. Would he?

As she finished the thought, the vehicle gave two quick, urgent honks before skidding to a stop in the trampled grass.

Halsey swallowed as much of her beer as possible in one draw, tightened her grip on her phone, and stormed outside to see what was going on.

The olive-green Jeep was instantly recognizable before she made eye contact with its owner behind the wheel. Her cousin Jasper flung his arm out of the driver's side window, then poked his head through. "I'm not creepin', Hal. Promise. Your dad sent me to pick you up."

"Okay…" She hung in the doorway long enough to jam her feet into her sneakers before heading onto the front porch and pulling the door shut behind her. "Any idea what's going on?"

"Somethin' big, if you ask me." Jasper shrugged. "You know how it is, man. I don't ask questions."

"Yeah, you and everybody else," she grumbled before leaping down the front porch steps and marching to the Jeep.

"What was that?"

"Don't worry about it." She climbed into the passenger seat. Her twenty-eight-year-old cousin, who looked more like he could be Brigham's brother than her cousin's actual brother, appraised her and raised an eyebrow.

Halsey shrugged. "I was settling in for the night."

"Uh-huh. If Aidan hadn't told me to hurry the hell up

and fetch you, I'd make you walk back inside and get dressed."

"Well, he did. So..." She leaned forward and patted the dashboard, then sat back and grabbed her seatbelt. "Let's get a move on."

If there had been any paved road outside her cottage, Jasper's tires would have squealed and started smoking with the speed he shot away from the house and jerked them into a tight U-turn. Halsey braced herself against the seat and worried her cousin would flip them as he maneuvered at top speeds on a gentle but still present incline. Fortunately, Jasper had been off-roading his entire childhood and a decent portion of his adult life. Within seconds, they raced across the rolling landscape toward the Ambrosius mansion as the golden light of the setting sun filled the sky.

I got picked up in a Jeep. Dad sent one of my cousins to get me. I'm starting to think rolling this thing and getting stuck out here might be safer than whatever this meeting's about.

Jasper didn't say a word to her on the seven-minute drive across the open countryside, which was probably a good thing. What was there to talk about when her entire career, everything that made her who she was, hung on the line?

The Jeep lurched to a stop at the back of the estate house. Her cousin stayed behind the wheel and nodded at the building. "Good luck."

"Thanks, I guess."

Halsey hopped out, shut the door behind her, and headed for one of the back staff entrances as she'd done countless times before. However, this was the first time even the back hallways of the mansion buzzed and bustled with so much frantic activity that she struggled to get farther than the doorway.

Staff members shouted at each other as they ran back and forth carrying stacks of papers, dialing their phones, or talking too loudly to get the necessary information across.

Weird. I didn't think we had any midsummer parties scheduled.

Then again, her family hardly told her the big-picture plans for much of anything beyond her next mission.

When she finally found a break in the commotion, Halsey booked it down the hall, winding her way through multiple back corridors toward the Council room. Nobody paid attention to her, and she didn't bother asking what was going on. The staff had their own jobs to perform that rarely had anything to do with the discussions behind the closed doors of the Ambrosius Council room.

As she reached the wide hallway leading to the Council room, more shouts rose from an adjacent hallway. Joining them was a flurry of thudding footsteps and the rhythmic squeak and rattle of a rusty wheel. She assumed it was one of the dinner carts acting up until the source of the noises appeared around the corner of the intersecting hallway.

It wasn't a meal cart. It was a gurney.

"Hold him still."

"He's seizing."

"I know he's seizing, but if he hurts himself in the process, that won't do any good. Does the doctor know we're on the way?"

"Told him the second the helicopter touched down."

"Okay. I want the numbers again on his blood pressure, BPM—hell, gimme all his vitals. This is... Yep. Keep moving."

Halsey didn't recognize the medical professionals, whether or not they were actual employees of the Ambrosius Clan. The family had their own doctors for almost everything, even magical remedies, stationed here at the Clan headquarters mansion.

The man who'd been barking orders glanced at her as he and three others jogged alongside the gurney. He locked eyes with her, and Halsey still didn't know who he was. When he looked away, her gaze fell on the unfortunate patient being wheeled through the mansion toward emergency medical care.

It was Brigham.

Her gut sank, and she almost froze before ripping out of it and darting after the medical crew. "Hey. Hey! What happened?"

"You'll have to ask somebody else, ma'am. Sorry."

"That's my *cousin*. What happened to him? Brigham!"

"Unless you want to be the reason he doesn't make it, I need you to step back and let us do our job." The lead guy didn't look at her again, and he didn't wait for her to keep talking. The team steered the gurney with Halsey's partner into a sharp left turn and headed down another hallway toward the Clan's twenty-four-hour onsite clinic in the west wing.

Halsey stared after them, her mind reeling.

He wasn't moving. Shit, he wasn't moving at all.

The few seconds it took to get herself under control felt like they lasted an eternity. She spurred into action and started walking again. This time, she didn't turn right to head for the massive, intricately carved double doors like she was supposed to.

If Emergency Response won't tell me what happened, I'll see for myself. Someone has to know something. Or I'll ask him when he wakes up.

He had to wake up, even after he'd been wheeled in looking the way he did. Bruised, battered, and covered in blood. The mere thought stung her eyes with tears. Any scenario that didn't include her best friend and partner waking up was not an option.

She'd made it halfway across the wide back hallway, intending to give the Council a silent middle finger by not showing up before the enormous doors opened anyway. Their ancient, heavy groan filled the corridor, drowning out the sound of the medical personnel hurrying Brigham through the mansion to save his life.

Still, Halsey didn't stop. She didn't care who it was or why they were walking *out* of the Council room when she was supposed to walk *in*. She didn't care if they saw her doing the opposite of what she'd been told.

"Halsey."

The low, rumbling tone of Aidan Ambrosius' voice was the only thing that could have stopped her. He hadn't called her name in anger, fear, or admonishment but merely as an acknowledgment of her presence.

There was something else in her dad's voice too.

It was a tenderness she hadn't heard in a long time and had assumed she'd forgotten altogether. Hearing it again sparked more memories, emotions, and uncertainty inside her than she knew what to do with.

The last time he'd spoken to her like that, she'd been nineteen years younger and over three feet shorter, watching someone else wheeled urgently down a giant hallway in much the same way.

Her mind went blank after that because she couldn't go there. She could only handle one terrible thought at a time.

At least *not* thinking got her to stop storming after her cousin.

You're here for a reason, Halsey. It's not to piss anyone else off or put yourself on the Council's eternal shitlist. Do your job. Let them do theirs.

After drawing a deep breath through her nose, she swallowed thickly and turned to face her dad.

Aidan stood between the partially open Council room doors, his hands wrapped around the interior handles. He wore one of what he called his "baggy shirts," a regular T-shirt made to fit an enormous man and stretched larger over years of constant wear. Halsey's dad had once been the go-to operative for the Clan militias, especially tough monster cases. With the physical mastery that had entailed, he'd once been an even larger specimen of himself.

That was before he'd taken his mother's seat on the Council, before Greta had been unofficially exiled to the wilderness of the Ambrosius property. Before Halsey had learned much of anything about elemental magic.

Before she and her dad had lost the person they loved most in the world.

Now, after everything, she felt on the brink of going through that all over again. This time with Brigham.

When she was finally able to meet her father's gaze, tears lingered in her eyes. Aidan cut a fuzzy figure between the doors, but she still made out the compassionate frown he aimed her way. Right now, even his eyepatch didn't dampen the concern and empathy in his features.

"What—" Halsey choked on her own voice, which sounded jittery, wobbly, and all over the place. She cleared her throat and tried again, forcing herself not to blink and spill the tears. Then she'd be crying. "What happened to him?"

Aidan sighed through his nose and pressed his lips together, the action barely visible through his bristling beard and mustache. "Come inside with me."

"Dad, please."

"He's in good hands. Let our doctors do what they do, so we can do what *we* do, okay? That's why you're here."

It was an agonizingly vague thing to say and offered no relief. Aidan hadn't hidden what he thought of Western medicine, science, and modern doctors when they failed to save his wife almost twenty years ago.

Halsey stared her father down as she tried to determine what was going on behind the gruff, muscular, battle-scarred exterior of the man she'd always trusted, even if they didn't always get along. Aidan Ambrosius was impossible to read most of the time. Right now, he looked as concerned about Brigham and the future as she felt.

He finally figured out how to hold it together in front of his daughter. Too bad it took so long. Four-year-old Halsey really needed this fatherly calm a lot more than I do now.

Whether or not her father thought along the same lines was impossible to tell. At least he didn't lose his temper with her, which was a rare but explosive occurrence. Instead, he dipped his head toward her, then turned slightly and nodded sideways into the Council room. "We need you in here, Bear. Come on."

She almost choked on her own breath at hearing her father's nickname for her, especially right now.

Okay. Either something insanely awful happened, even worse than Brigham being wheeled unconscious to the clinic, or he's trying to butter me up for something. What?

Despite feeling like she'd been plucked from her regular life and dropped on an alien planet in an alternate universe, Halsey couldn't stand undecided in the hallway all night. With a final glance toward where Brigham had disappeared, she pressed her lips together and rolled her shoulders back.

She approached her dad to join him in the Council room filled with the family members who'd made it perfectly clear they wanted nothing to do with her. The fact that she was walking through the doors anyway made tonight's unexpected turn of events a little more bearable.

CHAPTER TWENTY-SIX

Halsey expected the Council room's low lighting, the hush that fell over the soft murmur of conversation, and the tension that felt like tragedy thickening the air. It wasn't the first time she'd been pulled into this room to meet with these people before the trajectory of her life changed forever.

All things considered, it wasn't that strange to find the Council not in their fancy, elevated platform seats around the circular room but standing in the middle of it. Everyone had gathered around the low, round table where Halsey had called the last emergency meeting to discuss dire news nobody wanted to hear.

The ensuing rumble and soft scrape of the enormous doors shutting behind her were familiar. She could handle that. She could even handle every member of the Council pausing all conversation at her entrance as they turned to watch her enter.

What Halsey didn't expect was to feel her father's enormous, strong hand rest gently on her shoulder. The weight was calming and reassuring, and she would have slowed down to avoid walking out from underneath it if he'd given her a chance.

Yet Aidan's silent act of solidarity only lasted two seconds. That wasn't enough time for an appropriate reaction or even an inappropriate one.

When her father removed his hand and stepped past her with a long, easygoing stride, Halsey swallowed, tried to keep a straight face, and kept moving forward to meet... whatever this was.

Was he trying to reassure me or thank me? Shit, nothing makes any sense right now, and I have no idea what's going on.

"All right," Aidan stated as he approached the Council.

The one piece of furniture on the ground floor of the cavernous room looked too small for a meeting table but acceptable as a gathering point. Apparently, when the situation was serious enough, the Ambrosius Clan Council could forgo the pomp and circumstance of literally appearing out of the woodwork to take their shared elemental throne.

Only when her dad stopped at the table did Halsey get a good view of those who'd joined them for this disparate emergency meeting. Her Aunt Florence wasn't covered in dirt and plant matter tonight. Wallace didn't look more interested in whatever book he was reading because he hadn't brought one with him. All traces of her Aunt Beatrice's attitude and smug self-importance were gone.

Lawrence was grim-faced as ever with his hair pulled back into the same straight ponytail that almost reached his waist. Tonight, however, he wore a white T-shirt and gym shorts instead of his everyday slate-gray executive business suit. At least it made Halsey feel better about showing up in a tank top and pajama bottoms with a solar system design.

Finally, there was Gracelyn, her face deathly pale and her eyes red-rimmed as if she'd already been crying for hours. Which was impossible since her son had apparently been flown in directly from his last mission and whisked off to the clinic.

She shouldn't be here. Halsey couldn't bring herself to look away from Gracelyn. *Fuck Council meetings and plans and Clan duty. She should be with her son right now.*

As if she could hear her niece's thoughts, Gracelyn's heavy gaze flickered up to meet Halsey's. There was no emotion on her face, no change in her expression. She quickly looked away as Aidan continued.

"Take us through what happened one more time, Cadence. Now that Halsey's here."

Cadence?

Halsey ripped her gaze from Brigham's mother and scanned the faces around her. She spotted Cadence a split second before her slightly younger cousin started talking. In that split second, she knew whatever had attacked Brigham must have done a serious, life-threatening job of it. Cadence looked on the brink of death herself, though she was still conscious.

The young woman was deathly pale, caked head to toe in mud and blood, and sported a black eye that darkened and swelled by the second. She gingerly wiped the split in her lower lip with the back of a hand and nodded. When she spoke, she met Halsey's gaze and held it the entire time.

"Ogres," she proclaimed. Her firm, unwavering tone

was at odds with how terrible she looked. "Right outside this little nowhere town. There were only supposed to be two. Maybe three."

Halsey held her breath, unable to think about how much worse the story could get, though she knew it would.

Cadence's eyelids fluttered as if she were about to pass out. However, Halsey realized her cousin was mortified at the way her and Brigham's mission had turned out. "They weren't in the mountains, where we got the tip for their last sighting, but their trail was easy to find and follow. Like a bulldozer through the woods. We caught up to them on a frontage road cutting through the area, and we realized…"

She frowned, ducked her head, and took a moment to recollect her thoughts.

"There were at least nine of them."

Halsey's eyes widened. "Nine?"

"That we counted. When they caught our scent, they were all over us. No way we were getting out of there without engaging. I don't know what made them so fast or so vicious. It's like they couldn't even *feel* our attacks half the time. They didn't stop, no matter what we threw at them. We got tossed around, obviously. Brigham got thrown so much that he fell through a tree. I managed to lead them away so they wouldn't try to…"

"Shit." Halsey couldn't stop staring at her cousin while envisioning the gruesome scene. "What'd you do? How'd you get out of that one?"

"I have no clue." Cadence slowly shook her head. "After they followed me across the frontage road, they just…lost interest, I guess. They took off toward the town, and I went back for Brigham." Looking frustrated with herself, the young woman gazed at each of the Council members' faces in turn. "I know I should've gone after them and tried to keep them from the town. I screwed that up, but I had to go back for Brigham. I didn't know if he was—" A strangled croak escaped her, and she bowed her head. Leaves and twigs dotted the long, dirty-blonde hair falling over her shoulders.

Gracelyn moved toward her and laid a gentle hand on her niece's upper back. "If that's what screwing up means, I hope you screw up every time, Cadence. You did the right thing."

The young woman nodded again, her throat clicking as she swallowed repeatedly and blinked in an attempt to keep her tears at bay. Halsey recognized the response and the emotion all too well.

Yeah, that's weird. Nine ogres in the same place, and they all go racing off together toward town. Definitely not a regular thing for them. More weird monster behavior. Why did they call me in here to hear about it, though? I'm still on probation.

"Let's go take a walk," Gracelyn murmured, and Cadence nodded stiffly before allowing the woman to lead her away from the table and out of the Council room. Though Halsey's cousin stared at the floor as she hobbled along, her aunt met Halsey's gaze. There was a warning in that look, or maybe it was pleading, before Gracelyn's attention shifted to Aidan.

Halsey's dad nodded at his sister, then sniffed and folded his arms.

No one else said a word until Cadence and Gracelyn

were gone, and the heavy double doors had closed behind them.

Lawrence drew a deep breath and scanned every face in the Council room. "So. Nine ogres. Apparently numb to pain, or if they do feel any, it's a tickle."

Halsey frowned at her uncle, the knot in her stomach clenching tighter. She had no idea where he was going with this.

"There's gotta be something about the town border that gets to them, based on what Cadence said. We need to stop those things before they go smashing through that place and do any more serious damage. Halsey."

The sound of her name made her jolt in surprise. She couldn't decide whether to nod, frown, or speak. Instead, she chose none of the above and stood there like an idiot with a blank expression.

If Lawrence noticed, he was gracious enough not to say anything. "Under different circumstances, I'd tell you to consider yourself lucky. Right now, I'm only going to say we need you on this one."

"I, um..." She tilted her head in confusion and glanced around the Council. "But—"

Lawrence continued. "As of right now, your thirty-day suspension is lifted. Hopefully, three weeks was long enough for some deep reflection on your part. Another week is too long for us to wait to have you back."

"Oh." She looked at her dad for reassurance or maybe to see if he was laughing because this felt like a massive joke. Aidan met her gaze with his good eye and nodded.

Now I get it. I go hunt the freaky ogres for them, and they owe me. And they all know it.

"Okay." Halsey faced her uncle and nodded. "Yeah. I can handle that."

"Good."

"I'm gonna need a partner, though. Since mine got thrown through a tree…" She glanced around the room, waiting for one of the Council members to pull another operative's name out of a hat. With Brigham out and Cadence in no shape to finish the job, the Ambrosius Clan was in short supply of available operatives who could handle a mission like this.

Her dad nudged her with his elbow and nodded toward the Council room's doors. "We'd better get going, then."

Without waiting for her to reply or ask what he meant, Aidan turned and walked across the room.

Wait. I'm taking this mission with my dad?

Halsey looked at her Uncle Lawrence because he technically called the shots.

The man raised his eyebrows and nodded after his brother. "We'll see you soon."

"I…" She rotated toward the doors, then nodded. "Yeah. Shouldn't take us too long."

If things had been different, that comment would have gotten a few laughs. Halsey was maybe the best monster hunter the Clan militia had right now only because Aidan Ambrosius had unofficially stepped away from taking on new missions. She'd never gone on a hunt with her father and had no way to gauge if he was as good now as he'd been in his younger, happier, more muscular days. However, in terms of skill and efficiency, father and daughter were likely neck-and-neck.

Not that anybody's keeping score or anything. This is insane.

Halsey hurried after her dad and reached him as he pulled the double doors open with their signature rumble and groan. As if she'd been next to him the whole time, Aidan stepped aside to let his daughter pass. Feeling oddly optimistic about their odds of taking down nine ogres at once, she waited for him as the doors closed.

"You could've texted me *this* part."

Aidan snorted and walked without slowing down, looking directly ahead. "I'm not the one calling the shots here. Lawrence wanted you there in person."

"Why?"

"To give you as much of an apology as anyone ever gets from him."

She frowned as they rushed down the corridor toward the front of the mansion. "When did he apologize?"

"He put you back on the job. That's as good as it gets."

She nodded and tried to hide her smile, but it wasn't easy. *The Council's starting to see what I've been telling them this whole time. There's no way Dad and I aren't coming back with hard proof this time.*

As they rounded the next corner in the labyrinth of the mansion's hallways, Aidan scanned his daughter from the corner of his eye. "Nice pajamas."

"Yeah, I came prepared."

"We're stopping by your place first."

"Thanks."

CHAPTER TWENTY-SEVEN

Darkness had fallen by the time they reached the location Cadence gave them along the stretch of frontage road cutting through the little community of Woden, Texas. The area was heavily wooded on both sides of the road, the underbrush thick and difficult to navigate.

That didn't seem to be an issue for Aidan, who walked directly through even the thickest vegetation and cut a narrow path behind him for Halsey to follow.

Though it was only ten o'clock, they hadn't passed any other cars since leaving Lufton, and there were no streetlights along the frontage road. The only light came from the waxing crescent moonlight above. Neither spoke a word as they walked in the direction Cadence had told them the ogres ran. Even if they had anything to say, they were too focused on watching and listening.

There's no way nine ogres can stay quiet for long. Especially if they're smashing up a storm everywhere else the way they smashed up my cousins.

The dark outlines of the small, sparse town buildings

came into view in the distance, steady and stable against the lighter black of the night sky. They approached a narrow dirt road, and Halsey let out a soft whistle to get her dad's attention.

Aidan stopped without question. They spent several seconds listening to the nighttime silence.

The grinding crack of crumbling stone and the loud snap of breaking wood punctured the quiet. Both sounds were too loud to be a bird, a nocturnal critter, or someone in the small community finishing up a few late-night chores before bed.

"Hear that?" Halsey whispered.

"Uh-huh." Her dad nodded to their left, and they took off in that direction, moving as fast as possible while remaining quiet.

They passed several barns and farmhouses, a few trailers, and one building that looked like a box dropped beside the road. That was the Post Office, which definitely wasn't the source of the odd grinding and snapping sounds.

They approached the front gates of a small, private cemetery practically hidden away in a small patch of woods. When they paused outside and listened to the wet squelching punctuated by creaks, groans, and muffled grunts, they knew they'd find the ogres here.

Halsey widened her eyes at her dad.

Aidan's expression remained impassive as he searched the dark cemetery grounds beyond the gate and nodded.

Jackpot. This is where the two of us take on nine ogres. Good thing they sent out their two best elementals for this one.

Halsey swallowed the laugh that threatened to burst from her mouth but couldn't prevent a small smirk. She crept toward the gate with its large padlock keeping the swinging doors shut after hours. It seemed strange that a community as small as Woden would lock its cemetery gates, but every town was entitled to its own rules.

As she reached toward the padlock to see if it was fully locked, a soft, metallic whisper rose from her right.

Halsey paused when the rustle of her dad's magic caught her ears. She hadn't felt the soft tingle that swept the tops of her shoulders in over a decade.

Aidan Ambrosius had been their family's best monster hunter before he'd given up field missions for a Council seat and an excuse to stay home. He was also the Clan's most skilled metalworker, which was saying a lot for an elemental family who specialized in alchemy.

Halsey had seen her dad perform bits of alchemical magic over the years merely to display his abilities, like his grand entrance during the last emergency Council meeting. That was nothing compared to what he did now to the iron bars of the cemetery gates.

This type of magic was where Aidan excelled.

When a young Halsey had seen him use this magic, she liked to imagine the pieces of metal beneath her dad's command were eager to respond. That the metal *wanted* to be controlled and reshaped in a way Aidan saw fit. Metal was the only element the Ambrosius family wielded that lit up on its own during alchemical transfiguration.

The bars of the cemetery gates were no exception.

Three of them glowed with soft gray internal light, difficult to see despite the darkness around them. Halsey saw it, though. She couldn't look away from the bars that now looked like iron-colored ice introduced to intense heat. Thick, rolling beads of molten iron dripped down the length of the bars. Rather than falling onto the soft dirt in front of the gates, the iron beads peeled away and flew toward Aidan's outstretched hand, six feet away.

One after another, the glowing metal gathered near the man's enormous palm, hovering in a swirling, gray-glowing circle until all three bars had dissolved. There would be no trace of exactly how they'd gone missing from the sturdy structure. The people of Woden, Texas, would end up scratching their heads over the mystery of the missing gate bars.

Halsey watched her dad complete his silent, magical work and wasn't sure whether to laugh or roll her eyes.

Sure. Now *he feels like showing off.*

With the bars extracted, Aidan twisted his wrist in the center of the circling iron beads, and the metal responded instantly. The dull black iron transformed into gleaming silver cold-cut steel. The steel beads rearranged their shapes to create small, thin, incredibly durable chain links. They floated toward each other and interlinked with speedy precision to form one long, flexible chain that hovered a foot in front of Aidan.

It looked like a long, slightly thicker than normal necklace chain. However, instead of end clasps, though, there was a solid metal cylinder at one end and a razor-sharp blade at the other. The chain-link whip became an intimidating weapon when Aidan wrapped his enormous hand around the steel grip.

He lowered his arm, and the loose lengths of the alchemized chain wound around his knuckles so it wouldn't drag on the ground. It would also serve as a menacing close-range weapon, should they come to physical blows with the ogres.

Halsey whispered, "You could've packed a pair of brass knuckles and called it good."

When her dad met her gaze, his good eye sparkled with more energy and life than she'd seen in a long time. "I like versatility." He narrowed his eyes at the throwing ax strapped to his daughter's hip. "Which is obviously not a trait I passed on to you."

With a shallow snort, she hefted the ax from its sling and shook her head. "You've been out of the game too long, old man. An ax is everything."

"Yeah, we'll see." Aidan nodded toward the new hole in the gates, and Halsey knew he wanted her to slip through first.

Along with massive size, tiny brains, and a taste for living humans, ogres had remarkably poor hearing. However, an ogre's sense of smell made up for those limitations. Talking in low voices outside the cemetery was as much as the elementals could risk before they went on the offensive

From here on out, we have to be fast and silent if we want to keep the element of surprise. As soon as the wind changes, we'll lose it.

Despite preparing to battle seriously powerful monsters in four times the usual numbers, Halsey smiled as she ducked through the hole in the gate. She kept her throwing ax close to avoid hitting it against the remaining bars. He'd never admit it out loud in the middle of a mission, but her dad was enjoying himself.

Wait 'til we find these things and actually start fighting.

The thought was both exhilarating and weird. Out of hundreds of missions with various Ambrosius elementals over the past five years, this was her first with her own father.

Why do I have the feeling he's gonna try to turn this into a competition?

Inside the cemetery, Halsey paused and turned to watch her dad climb through the hole in case he needed help.

He was already through and two feet behind her, his massive shadow blocking out the stars.

Halsey bit back a surprised yelp and stumbled backward. *Note to self. Aidan Ambrosius moves like a ghost. What did he do? Shapeshift through the hole?*

Now was not the time to ask about her dad's field skills, so she put that thought on the back burner.

Aidan's dark eye flickered toward her, his expression blank once again. He tapped one ear and nodded toward the grotesque sounds echoing through sparsely planted trees and across headstones. He didn't wait for her to signal she was ready before stalking past her, his steel chain-whip glinting around his hand when it caught the moonlight.

Of course he assumes he's taking the lead. He'd probably be barking orders if we weren't trying to sneak up on nine ogres doing gods know what...

Halsey tightened her hold on her ax, exhaled slowly, and took off after him.

Her irritation didn't last long. It was overshadowed by the sheer awe of watching her massive, muscular, gruff-looking father move like a shadow across the cemetery. Aidan didn't make a sound as he placed each footstep perfectly against the earth interspersed with drying summer grasses, fallen twigs, and a few acorns.

Elemental magic could have dampened the noise on a trek like this in several ways. Send the sounds away on the wind before they reached anyone else's ears. Shift the earth with every step to cushion the extra weight. Move the dead vegetation aside before it cracked, snapped, or rustled beneath footsteps. Such subtle changes to the natural world could give an elemental a lot of leverage, yet the subtleties made spells like that difficult and complicated to perform.

While she followed her dad along the perimeter of the cemetery, scanning the darkness for the outline of hulking ogre shapes, Halsey's gaze kept returning to her dad's enormous back, broad shoulders, and huge boots that made no sound as he moved.

He's not using any of those spells. They need way too much focus, and he looks like he's not even trying. Is he really that quiet?

She couldn't believe she hadn't known about this quality of his until right now, but she'd never seen Aidan Ambrosius in action before.

That went both ways. Her dad hadn't seen her on a single active mission since she'd graduated from her monster-hunting training. Tonight gave Halsey the opportunity to show him what she was made of while they found enough proof for the Clan to take her hunches seriously.

Focus or all he'll take away from this mission is how scattered you were. That won't help either of us figure out why the hell nine ogres ran across the road to hang out in a cemetery.

She shoved all other thoughts aside in favor of the here

and now, then realized the animal grunts, grinding, snapping, and wet slurping noises were far louder.

Aidan paused behind one of the few older trees in the cemetery, thick enough to hide both of them with room to spare.

Halsey didn't bother joining him behind the tree. She only had to duck behind the closest gravestone. After a questioning glance at her dad, they peered around their respective hiding places to see what was happening.

The hulking, shadowed forms weren't immediately recognizable as ogres, though the noises they made fit the bill. They were hunched toward the ground as the crunching, tearing, and slavering filled the darkness.

One of the monstrous creatures growled louder than the others and straightened, confirming its identity. That hairless, misshapen head could only belong to an ogre. The sparse light was more than enough to silhouette the creature's long canines and blunt, crooked upper teeth. Protruding from between those teeth was what looked like a human hand.

The ogre's jaws snapped together, and several fingers cracked and crunched beneath the pressure. One fell away and tumbled to the ground, but the ogre didn't seem to notice. It kept eating until the hand was gone, then bent to continue ripping morsels from its feast.

The closest ogre hunkered near a crumbled tombstone. Beside it was a mound of upturned earth and the shattered remains of a coffin.

No way.

To the extent of Halsey's knowledge, an ogre's favorite meal was and always had been human flesh. Infants or young children if the monsters could get away with it. Yet that flesh was *always* living.

Raiding graves for decaying bodies was a ghoul's MO. Why the hell were the ogres eating *dead* bodies?

Well, at least that keeps our civilian casualty numbers down.

Halsey only realized she'd been scowling at the scene when her forehead and the muscles around her mouth started to ache.

Another ogre grunted fiercely, pushed itself to its feet, and lumbered toward the next grave in line before it started digging. The thing's massive hands were three times bigger than Aidan's and made perfect shovels. Dirt clods and torn plant life flew in every direction while the ogre dug like a dog into the grave it had chosen as its next dinner plate.

Its fingers hit the wooden coffin with a hollow *thunk*. The monster paused to thrust its dirty, warped nails into the decomposing wood before it pried the coffin apart like a freshly baked loaf of bread. It dug in with both hands and hauled out an intact corpse that hadn't been dead for long.

The stench of that recent corpse instantly overpowered every other smell in the cemetery. Halsey forced back a groan and clapped a hand over her nose and mouth. Her dad sighed heavily and ducked his head under an arm as the stench hit him.

Yep. There's a reason only ghouls can stomach rotting flesh. Ogres shouldn't be seeking this shit out. What is going on?

Breathing through her mouth, Halsey returned her attention to the mission objective instead of everything that made her want to abandon ship right now and head home. The ogres slouched over the graves continued their meals. None seemed to notice the elementals hiding a few yards away. They didn't even seem to notice each other, which was strange. As a rule, ogres were so territorial they could only stand to travel in groups of two or three, *if* that.

Not only had they dug up the exact opposite of their favorite food source, but they were ignoring large numbers of each other.

Halsey picked out the hulking, grunting forms and counted them three times before she let herself believe there wasn't an issue with her counting.

Eight. That's it. Cadence said there were at least nine. Unless these things started turning on each other, *we're missing one. And I seriously hope it's only one.*

She scanned the cemetery again, but there was no sign of a ninth crazed ogre.

In the darkness, she felt her dad's gaze and ducked behind the gravestone again before turning toward him. She held up eight fingers, and Aidan nodded.

Apparently, he'd come up with the same count.

Until they found the final ogre, they couldn't attack any of them. They didn't need to be caught by surprise and botch this mission before they could finish what Brigham and Cadence had started.

Slowly, Halsey poked her head out from behind the tombstone to search the moving shadows. The sickening squelch of the ogre's elongated canines ripping into dead flesh turned her stomach. So did the stench that suddenly intensified around her.

Not all of that foul smell came from the newest corpse. The instant Halsey realized that was the instant she felt the hot, cloying, putrid breath of ogre number nine blasting across the back of her neck and over her shoulders.

She should have spun, leapt aside, and prepared to engage the creature. That was the logical reaction, and she would have under normal circumstances. Instead, her senses took over, and she lurched forward with a violent gag, trying not to be sick all over this grave while eight ogres made an enormous mess of the rest.

The sound of her dry-heave behind the tombstone wasn't loud enough to alert the monsters on the other side. However, Aidan heard her. He turned toward the ogre that had snuck up behind her just in time.

CHAPTER TWENTY-EIGHT

"Down!" Aidan roared.

The command was difficult to follow, specifically because Halsey was already hunched over with a crazed ogre looming over her that smelled like death, rot, and a bunch of things she didn't want to think about.

Her only option was to drop onto her stomach. As she hit the ground, the same deafening crack and ensuing rumble that had first caught their attention drowned out every other sound. Her cheek hit the dirt, and she glimpsed the ogre's bare feet and disgustingly long, yellowed toenails. The creature had swiped a blow that could have hurled *her* through a tree but instead met the top of the headstone.

As chunks of rock rained down around her, Halsey's instincts and reflexes kicked in the way her years of training had honed them to do.

She reached with her magic and caught every piece of shattered, falling stone. She rolled onto her hip, feeling a large piece of jagged headstone dig into her back, and locked her focus on the ogre.

The thing was enormous, its face contorted in a snarl that conveyed pure, animalistic rage.

Halsey let her anger fly along with the busted stone she'd captured mid-flight. The jagged shards hurtled toward the ogre and peppered the thing's face, neck, and hulking chest, made larger by giant slabs of fat.

The ogre roared. Noxious spittle flew from its putrid mouth as it raised its arms to shield itself from the attack. It batted aside the majority of the larger headstone chunks that might have done significant damage if Halsey had been farther away with more time to react. With another snarl, the creature lunged toward her with its thick-nailed hands outstretched.

Time seemed to slow in that moment as Halsey noticed something that should never have been there.

Blood-red sigils stained the centers of the ogre's meaty palms. One massive, curved line above a crude circle, making the image look somewhere between a rudimentary sunrise and a half-lidded eye.

Ogres didn't have the brains to clothe themselves, let alone paint designs on their hands.

Her right hand closed around her ax again, and the flow of time returned to normal. The ogre surged toward her. Halsey pushed halfway up to one knee and swung the ax with as much momentum as she could get behind the motion.

It would have been a debilitating, even deadly, blow for a monster as thick-skinned and dull-witted as this one.

Except before her blade found its mark, the ogre released a strangled cry and disappeared.

Halsey's weapon whistled through thin air. The power she'd gathered behind the swing kept her arm arcing along its path until the ax buried itself in the soft dirt.

Blinking in surprise, she whipped her head up and saw the ogre lying four feet away on its back, bellowing and writhing as it slapped at its left shoulder. The thing's arms and chest were too thick for it to grab whatever torture had tackled it to the ground. Now there was no way to prevent the other eight ogres in the cemetery from hearing the racket this one made.

Then she realized what was driving the thing so insane.

Aidan had used the steel chain-whip he'd fashioned from the cemetery gates. The sharp, barbed tip had buried itself in the ogre's back so he could haul the monster away from what would have been a failed attempt to crush his daughter. Now Halsey's ax was buried in the dirt instead of the ogre.

"Seriously?" she snapped before wrenching the weapon from the ground with a quick jerk.

"You're welcome." Her dad's wild beard fluttered in a light breeze before he yanked the end of the steel chain. The barbed blade tore free with an awful ripping sound, and the ogre bellowed again, pounding the earth with its fists before struggling to its feet. "Unless you *want* me to let you get your head bashed in next time."

"Yeah, I had it. Thanks." Halsey stood as well, drawing her arm back to try for another ax blow across the ogre's bleeding back.

"Watch your six, Halsey," Aidan growled and readied his chain-whip to strike the oncoming ogre.

Halsey spun to see two more ogres lumbering toward her, snarling and growling, shuffling across the cemetery like enormous zombies that shouldn't exist. They were covered in the remnants of their interrupted meal, and she fought another urge to retch before she returned her focus to the battle.

She raised her left hand to call on the wind, made a tight fist, and swung it back down. A howling vortex of leaves, grass, and dirt swirled away from her across the cemetery, churning up everything in its path.

Usually, this attack was enough to blast back the majority of oncoming monsters so she could focus on whichever was closest. This time her conjured windstorm only made the ogre on the right stumble, scowling against the blast before it barreled right through her magic and kept coming.

"Shit." She dropped her gaze to the half-crumbled headstone in front of her and grimaced. "Sorry."

She called on the earth magic inside the headstone and ripped what was left of it from the ground. The fractured stone sailed up, dropping pebbles and clods of dirt. Halsey swung her arms toward the oncoming ogres and sent the much larger weapon their way.

The headstone struck the ogre on the left in the chest with enough force to knock the creature off its feet. The thing crashed backward like a felled tree, complete with the rumbling *boom* of its enormous weight that sent tremors through the earth.

One down for now. Eight more to go. Unless...

Halsey risked a look over her shoulder. Her dad was locked in furious combat with the ogre he'd speared. With his own fighting skills and a hefty dose of elemental magic, Aidan had his steel chain wrapped twice around the ogre's neck before the creature managed to get off the ground. Now, the bear of a man walked backward, roaring and snarling as much as the ogre while he dragged a monster three times his own body weight across the cemetery.

The bleeding ogre put up a hell of a fight. It thrashed, grunted, and clawed at the chains while making it as difficult as possible for Aidan to do...whatever he was doing by dragging an ogre around.

Another blast of hot, putrid, decomposing breath hit Halsey from behind, and she whirled to see ogre number three lunging toward her. When the thing bellowed, spittle and bits of dead flesh flew from its gaping mouth. The stench was overwhelming, even from six feet away.

Never mix ogres and dead bodies.

Grimacing in disgust, Halsey raised her ax arm and threw the weapon the way she'd practiced across her greenhouse for years. The ax spun end over end, heading for the crook of flesh and muscle where the monster's gigantic shoulder met its neck. It would have been a perfect throw if one of the six not-currently-battling ogres hadn't lifted its head from its meal and launched a furious bellow that seemed to make the whole cemetery shake.

It was a territorial scream. If Halsey had enough time to think about it, she would have called that monstrous roar the sound of an alpha staking its claim.

If ogres even *had* alphas.

The hulking creature she'd meant to slow down with

her ax spun away faster than should have been possible for a monster that size. Halsey watched her weapon sail right past the intended target, spinning until it found a new mark in the wrist of yet another ogre beginning to stand from its feast.

Her ax blade had never been sharper, and what at first seemed a lamentable strikeout changed the entire battle.

The blade hit with a metallic whistle and a wet slice, cutting through skin, muscle, and bone clean through to the other side. Its momentum continued to carry it through the monster's current corpse meal, spilling what was left inside the body onto the ground in a reeking puddle of gore.

The ogre dropped its meal when its enormous hand fell off its arm and landed with a heavy *thunk*.

Halsey's ax pinged off an undisturbed tombstone. She waited for the scream of pain, fury, and monster-headed revenge she expected to follow.

There was none.

Instead, the ogre who'd suddenly lost a hand stared at the bloody stump, its face contorted in surprise and confusion as the remaining creatures left their gruesome meals to join the fight.

What is wrong *with that thing? Now ogres are eating corpses* and *they can't feel pain?*

It would have made things insurmountably difficult for Halsey and her dad, but that couldn't be the case. The one Aidan had brought down definitely felt pain.

As six ogres lumbered and crashed across the cemetery to engage two elementals who should have brought backup, Halsey faced the ogre she'd meant to chop down like a log before the thing had spun away from her.

It crashed toward her with the others, roaring and bashing its fists against everything in its path, which happened to be mostly headstones.

Focus on one at a time, Hal. Come on.

Her ax was too far away to call back in time, so she reached with her magic for the two closest headstones and pried them from the earth. She used them as battering rams against the closest ogre, who didn't go down until the *third* time she smashed its head between the uprooted tombstones.

Two of the others who'd been heading her way stopped to fight each other, which was a stroke of luck.

It also gave Halsey enough time to see what was happening with the monster who'd lost a hand to her ax.

The one-handed ogre staggered around the cemetery, weaving and wobbling like a drunk trying to find a way home. It was hard to tell in the darkness, but the thing looked pale and washed-out, as if all the color had drained through the stump in its wrist faster than the ogre's spraying blood. Without warning, the monster lurched forward and heaved.

The contents of its stomach that spewed from its mouth were impossible to ignore. Undigested bits of rotting human corpse sprayed everywhere to join the ogre's spattered blood. The overpowering stench made Halsey gag again.

Several ogres turned in confusion to look at their vomiting brethren, but they didn't stop for long. The two who'd been punching each other in the face kept it up while the others converged on Halsey and her dad.

All the while, the ogre missing a hand doubled over and produced an endless stream of vomit that seemed far more than a creature even that size could fit into its stomach.

Aidan growled and tugged on the steel chain wrapped around Ogre One's neck. He'd caught the monster's shoulder against a tree, which he used as leverage to pull harder on the thing's neck. He slammed a boot up against the tree trunk and shouted, "What did you do?"

"Sliced off its hand, apparently." Halsey grunted and ducked a swinging blow from an ogre who'd gotten close enough to try. She pivoted to the side, darted clear, and reached for the energy of the earth beneath the ogre. The ground erupted beneath the monster's feet. Dirt, stones, and grass flew everywhere, and the ogre crashed down with a startled grunt.

"And that's your best—" Aidan grunted when the chained ogre jerked against the tree but still wouldn't give up the fight. "—plan?"

Halsey snorted and glanced toward her dad while also eying the five ogres drawing closer. "Right. Coming from the guy who's been trying to choke out *one monster* for the last five minutes."

Aidan tugged again, his muscles straining as he fought to knock the ogre unconscious and end the struggle. "Big-ass sonofabitch."

Halsey laughed and darted around the perimeter of the upturned graves, shattered coffins, and a lot more gore than the average cemetery. Ghouls were practically tidy in their eating habits compared to this. Several of the ogres turned to follow her, snarling and stomping over everything along the way. The pair bashing each other paused to take stock of the five-foot-three elemental racing in a wide arc around the desecrated tombstones before they went back at it.

"Drawing 'em out won't get this thing done!" Aidan shouted after her.

"Hey, unlike you, my weapon doesn't have a drawstring!"

That was only a surface excuse. Halsey actually wanted to get closer to the sick ogre. It was on its knees, still spewing filth, and she needed a look at that hand.

When she found the grave where her ax had landed, she sent another windstorm sailing ahead to hopefully push the oncoming ogres back. Again, it wasn't nearly enough to send their hulking bodies flying, but it bought her time.

She darted toward her ax as the wet, gurgling retches from the sick ogre grew louder and more intense. Her hand closed around the weapon's grip, and as Halsey stood, one of the ogres hurled a giant chunk of broken tombstone at her. She reached with her magic to stop the projectile in its tracks and flung it right back at the creatures. It hit one in the side of the face and smacked the monster back into one of its brethren. Both ogres crashed down.

Her gaze fell on the hand she hadn't meant to sever.

I knew it.

The moonlight illuminated the dark curves of the same blood-red shape stamped across the first ogre's palms.

It's their hands. It has to be.

She glanced at the vomiting ogre as the monster stopped emptying its stomach. The thing exhaled a wheezing sigh before its bulging eyes rolled back in its head. It dropped flat, landed in the pile of its own mess with a wet squelch, and didn't move again.

Halsey grimaced and tried to wipe that image from her mind as she faced two more ogres lumbering her way.

I wasn't trying to kill nine ogres tonight, but if they puke themselves to death, that's not technically on us. Right?

That didn't sit well with her, but she didn't have time to figure out how to have her monster-hunting cake without *killing* monsters too. However, she did have time to test the newest theory springing to her mind.

As the first ogre swung with an open hand to bat her aside, the blood-red mark on its palm was revealed.

Halsey gripped her ax in one hand and reached out with her magic to the closest tree a few yards away. The tree's root system responded, and thick brown roots sprang from the ground two feet in front of the oncoming ogre. The living ropes circled the monster's thick ankles and yanked its feet out from under it. With a howl, the ogre crashed onto its back, and Halsey made her move.

She leapt after it as another snaking root burst out beside the ogre's flailing arm, snagged the beast's wrist, and jerked it to the ground.

Halsey's ax came down with all the force she could muster. The blade cut through the ogre's wrist like the last one, and the red-painted hand toppled off in a pool of blood.

The ogre's furious cry was cut off with a gurgling growl before it vomited all over itself.

Halsey managed to avoid getting splattered by the mess as she ran for the next ogre in line.

"You need to get serious and quit playing around," Aidan bellowed from his fight with a single ogre around a single tree.

His daughter slowed a fraction and turned to stare at him. "You're oh-for-two right now, old man. I thought you were supposed to be the best."

"Halsey!"

"It's the mark, Dad." She reached out with her magic to rip out another headstone and blast it into the closest ogre's immense gut. "You have to get rid of it."

"What mark?"

"On their hands!" She ducked an ogre's swing. "Cut it off!"

"For *what*?"

"You know what? If you wanna spend all night failing to choke that big guy out, be my guest. I'm telling you, they're—"

The ogre in front of her bellowed so loudly that it drowned out her voice. Startled, Halsey jumped back and barely escaped being pummeled by the thing's enormous fist. She didn't avoid it entirely, though. The edge of the ogre's knuckles slammed her shoulder and almost sent her spinning.

Instead of throwing her hands out to brace her fall, she called another force of gusting wind to cushion her fall. Catching themselves like this was one of the first ways she and Brigham had learned to spar without beating each other silly across the vast expanse of the Ambrosius property. It worked for not getting knocked out of an ogre fight, too.

After the wind blasted her onto her feet, Halsey spun and swung her ax.

The first blow struck the ogre in its upper bicep, and the blade stuck in thick muscle before glancing against bone. The ogre roared in her face and batted her aside.

She flew across the cemetery, and only a stroke of luck prevented her from breaking her back against an intact tombstone. The air huffed from her lungs when she hit the ground, and her head spun with the force of the impact.

The ogre kept coming. Blood poured down its arm as it wrenched her ax free and tossed it aside. She blinked furiously and tried to consolidate the two or three identical ogres lumbering toward her into one. If she was going for another attack, she had to know which version of her target was the accurate one.

A bellow ripped through the air. It sounded a lot farther away than the ogre and also not much like an ogre. The monster right on top of her reared back, blood dripping everywhere as it raised its arm for a killing strike.

When its enormous arm reached full height, the monster jerked backward, and the hand that would have crushed Halsey's skull tumbled off its wrist.

With a vicious roar, the ogre spun to face Aidan as her father recalled the steel chain. When he glimpsed the severed hand caught on his weapon, he looked as sick as the vomiting monsters. The recently one-handed ogre staggered toward Aidan and gushed out the decaying contents of its stomach. That seemed to snap the man out of his queasiness.

Though Aidan was as big as a bear and almost as furry, he moved more like a wildcat across the cemetery. In a deluge of bared teeth and flashing steel, Halsey's dad spun and roared and swung his weapon like a madman. Yet if he was mad, at least he had a purpose.

Destruction.

Halsey's eyes widened, and she couldn't look away.

Holy shit.

The chain-whip lashed out in a different direction every second, slicing through skin here, hauling ogres off their feet there. The whole time, he didn't stop moving until all the remaining ogres had tried and failed to bring him down. Aidan's recently created weapon wouldn't have done much damage if Halsey's theory hadn't held up. She'd been right about this, though, like she'd been right about Brigham's wyverns.

After those marks were removed from the ogres' bodies by way of severed hands, whatever turned the creatures in the first place turned against them.

Within minutes, all nine brutes had fallen to the ground in piles of their own mess, their bodily functions returning to normal and rejecting the meals they'd been gorging themselves on for hours.

When it was all over, Aidan stood in the center of the cemetery, breathing like a bull as his magic wrapped the chain-whip around his hand. His one good eye scanned the wreckage, pausing on each fallen ogre to be sure they were dead.

Of course they were.

Halsey tried to ignore that they'd killed nine creatures who clearly hadn't done this to themselves. It wasn't hard. Getting back on her feet without collapsing in a wave of dizziness took all her focus.

"You know what?" she said with a grunt. "Brass knuckles wouldn't have been nearly as awesome."

"Oh, she *approves*." Aidan snorted and faced her. "You okay?"

"I've been worse. You?"

The huge man shrugged. "Same."

"Ha. Okay. Well, good work on the ogre slaughter." She surveyed the devastation and the gut-curdling mess, walked slowly toward her ax, and bent to retrieve it. "Time for cleanup, right?"

Aidan grimaced and hissed air through his teeth. "It had to be *this*. Body parts and puke."

"You're not feeling queasy, are you?"

Her dad raised one bushy eyebrow. Even the intimidating visage of an enormous elemental warrior with a badass eyepatch couldn't hide the nauseous discomfort contorting his features. "You wish."

Halsey smirked and called out to the tree roots beneath the cemetery again. One by one, they emerged from the ground and coiled around a graveyard full of ogre corpses instead of human ones. The life force of the trees responded to perfection, handling most of the dirty work by dragging the hulking bodies into various holes that had already been opened.

For all his power on the battlefield, Aidan looked like he'd rather poke out his other eye than gather the severed hands that remained.

After collecting the ogre hands into a large pile, Halsey grabbed her phone and snapped pictures of the mound of red-marked palms. That was only the first part of what she needed to bring to the Council after debriefing. The second part was another dependable witness to back up her claim.

He has to see this isn't a fluke now. Not a phase. There's no way the Clan can deny what's happening now that it's not only Crazy Halsey making up stories.

Halsey picked up the closest severed hand and studied it closer. She sidled toward her dad, who still looked like he was about to be sick, and held the hand out toward him palm-up. "This seem familiar to you?"

"No clue." He grunted. "Unlike you, I don't have a thing for severed ogre body parts."

"Dad. One look. Don't think about the fingers, the palm, the wrist, or these…bloody bits down here—"

"Goddamnit." Aidan clenched his good eye shut to focus on settling his stomach again, and his daughter smirked.

"Sorry. Just take a look. Please."

Slowly, the man opened his eye and dipped his head a fraction toward the gruesome evidence. He quickly looked away. "That's old."

"That's what I was thinking." Halsey studied the mark on the gray, beefy palm. "Old enough to be a blood human rune?"

Her dad scrunched his nose, sniffed, and stared across the destroyed cemetery as he pondered her question and the implications it came with. "There's a good chance of that, yeah."

"Excellent. It's a start." She spun and headed for the pile of hands. Fortunately for them, this cleanup would be easy with all the pre-dug holes.

Aidan laughed and shook his head.

"What?" She smiled as she swept two ogre hands across

the dirt with the side of her shoe until they toppled into the nearest open grave.

"You sounded like someone else there for a second."

"Someone like Meemaw?"

Her dad stared, his one eye wide with surprise. "Actually, yeah."

"Good. I think more of us *should* sound like her." Halsey shook the ogre hand still in her grip at him. "I have a feeling that's gonna start happening any day now. 'Cause you know what this is?"

"Disgusting," he grumbled.

Halsey grinned at her temporary mission partner for tonight. "It's proof."

CHAPTER TWENTY-NINE

It took them two and a half hours to finish the cleanup in Woden's tiny cemetery. After all ogre bodies and half-eaten human remains were dumped into the open graves, Halsey and Aidan put as many of the headstones as possible back together. Mostly, it was out of respect for the dead. It was also an attempt to keep the citizens of this small Texan community from looking too closely at the aftermath of one incredibly strange night.

Hiding evidence of ghouls feasting on dead bodies was easier. Ghouls weren't big enough, strong enough, or dumb enough to smash every headstone in their path.

When it was all said and done, Halsey scanned the cemetery and nodded in satisfaction. "Looks good to me."

Aidan nodded at the ground beside her, where three severed ogre hands remained. "Looks like you missed a few."

"Nope. That was on purpose." Her gaze skittered around the cemetery, then she examined her dad and waved him closer. "Let me see your jacket."

Aidan's bushy eyebrows rose, and his dirty, blood-smeared eyepatch shifted with them. "Why?"

"Just hand it over."

The enormous man grunted, shrugged out of his battle-grimed light canvas jacket, and tossed it toward her. He was skeptical of his daughter's intentions. When Halsey finished tying the jacket into a crude sack before stooping beside the ogre hands, he looked like he was considering attacking *her* as well.

"Aw, what the—"

"Shh." The hands thumped unceremoniously into the jacket-bag.

Aidan growled. "No. "Come on. Can't you do that with something else?"

"Oh, I'm *sorry*. You know what? I left my severed-ogre-hand bag in the car."

He grimaced, gave his jacket a mournful look, then shook his head. "When you're done, throw the damn thing away."

"Actually, I might keep it." Halsey lifted the makeshift bag and studied the heavy bulge at the bottom, where her three pieces of proof swung slightly. "Like a souvenir."

Aidan huffed and stalked toward the cemetery gates without another word.

Halsey followed him swiftly, scouting around in the pale, blue-gray glow of predawn twilight to make sure they weren't spotted by some early-riser Woden citizen. Fortunately, they were still alone.

Yeah. A giant man, a girl with an ax, and a sack of cemetery goodies, all covered in blood and guts. That wouldn't draw any attention.

The thought made her smile as they reached the hole in the gates. Halsey watched her dad squeeze his enormous frame through. It didn't escape her notice that Aidan had failed to disassemble his steel chain-whip and return it to its rightful place.

I mean, I guess it's only fair that he gets to keep a souvenir too.

Morning traffic made the drive home take twenty minutes longer than the trip out to their ogre hunt. By the time they pulled up in front of the mansion, the sun had cast a blinding glow across the immaculate front lawn.

Halsey climbed from the front passenger seat, tried not to slam the door shut, and hurried past her dad toward the front steps.

Aidan snorted as he followed her with his incredibly long stride. "Not sure waltzing into the Council room with a little gift bag like *that* and no mission partner is gonna score you any extra points this morning."

"Council room?" She skidded to a stop on the front stoop and fixed her dad with a dubious frown. "Yeah, that's gonna have to wait."

"I don't think so."

"Here, then." She thrust the bloody bag toward him as he climbed the last stair, and Aidan reeled back with a disgusted grimace. "*You* take it."

He stared at the bag, then sidestepped around her outstretched arm to head for the door. "I'm not touching that shit."

Halsey lowered the bag as the giant front doors creaked open under her dad's guiding hand. "Okay, then I'll meet up with you when I'm done."

Aidan took one step inside, and Halsey almost ran right into him when he stopped and looked over his shoulder. "Going somewhere else instead?"

She blinked and spread her arms, inadvertently swinging the bag of ogre hands dangerously close to the side of the building. "Listen, if the Council thinks a debriefing and physical proof are more important to me right now than making sure my *partner's* okay, they don't know their operatives as well as they thought."

Her dad arched an eyebrow, which had once again become the extent of his facial expressions. "I hold a seat on the Council."

"Yeah, but I expect you to know better."

"And I expect you to complete your mission from start to finish."

"What? Dad, this isn't—"

"Up for debate? You're right. Brigham can wait. This can't."

Oh, sure. Now *he sees how important it is to lay this all out.*

Halsey peered around her dad's massive form into the dimly lit, empty foyer. "Five minutes, so I can let him know I didn't get thrown into a tree finishing what he couldn't. After that, I'll meet you in the Council room, and we can call another meeting."

"I already did."

Her shoulders slumped. "While you were *driving*?"

"Just because I only have one eye doesn't mean I can't multitask."

"Oh yeah. Sure. Texting and driving after battling nine ogres isn't dangerous enough."

"Let's go." Aidan continued through the foyer, his

booted footsteps echoing against the polished marble floors and pristinely oiled wooden accents.

Shit. Sorry, Brigham. I have to go convince our family that we were right from the beginning, then you're my next stop.

Halsey hauled the front door closed and grimaced when the blood-soaked bottom of the jacket-bag bumped against the wood, leaving a red-brown smear. She tried rubbing it off with a less-filthy part of her dad's jacket. That only made it worse, so she gave up and hurried after him.

Being late to this meeting wouldn't do her any favors.

The back hallways were empty, even when Halsey and her dad reached the wide corridor leading to the Council room. Yet the elaborately carved double doors were open once more, and the Ambrosius Clan Council had already gathered inside around the central stone table. She tried not to look seriously pissed off that she had to stop here before she could visit Brigham.

Apparently, she wasn't as skilled at wiping the scowl off her face as she'd hoped.

When Aidan stood aside to let her enter first, every Council member regarded her with varying expressions of dismay. Beatrice frowned as she took in Halsey's stained clothes and the ratty mess she hadn't been able to finger-brush from her hair on the drive home. Gracelyn seemed satisfied enough with her son's health to attend this meeting, though she paled when her niece and her brother entered the room in such bedraggled states. Lawrence, at least, had dressed in his usual slate-gray suit for the occasion.

Overall, no one looked happy to be here.

Right. Because Dad and I are the only ones who didn't get any sleep last night.

Lawrence cleared his throat and opened the meeting while staring at the bloody sack of canvas in Halsey's hand. "I hope this is as important as you made it sound, Aidan. Forgoing debriefing protocol isn't a habit I want any of our operatives falling into."

"I'm calling it an emergency meeting and a debriefing in one," Aidan replied with a low growl as the two of them approached the wary gathering. After a brief but awkward pause, he cleared his throat, swallowed, and nodded toward his daughter without looking away from the other Council members. "Halsey?"

When he said nothing else, she glanced at him. "Aidan."

Beatrice folded her arms and looked scathingly at Lawrence with a silent *I told you this was a bad idea.*

Aidan's mustache bristled. He nodded subtly at the grotesque makeshift sack in her hand as if he didn't want anyone to think he knew what was inside. "This is in *your* wheelhouse. Go ahead."

In my wheelhouse? So we're in this together and on the same page until we have to stand up and tell the Council they've been wrong this whole time. Trying to save face is not *a good look on you, Dad.*

She could only stare at him in disbelief. Aidan wouldn't meet her gaze again, so she stepped up to take full responsibility for breaking the crazy news on her own. Again.

However, she wouldn't keep pandering to a Council that wasn't willing to take her seriously from the beginning.

After a deep breath, Halsey stepped to the central table

and upended the blood-soaked bag. Three severed ogre hands plopped onto the stone with squelching smacks. One of them rolled close to the other end of the table where Lawrence stood, leaving a wobbling trail of smeared blood. It stopped before it could tumble off the edge.

Aidan rolled his eyes and took a step back from both his daughter and the table.

No one else said a word, though Florence made gulping sounds and briefly turned away to collect herself.

Lawrence glanced at Aidan, then stared at the bloody chunks of ogre flesh on the table. "What the hell are we looking at?"

Halsey dropped the empty sack on the floor. She scanned the Council members' faces and dove in. "Ogre hands."

"Why are there only three?" Wallace muttered.

"Well, we cut them off all *nine* ogres that were digging up dead bodies in the cemetery," she replied. "I figured bringing back eighteen hands was overkill, though."

Gracelyn snorted and instantly looked appalled at herself for laughing.

Blanch blinked furiously, avoiding the bloody sight on the table as her hand fluttered beneath her nose. "I'm sorry. Did you say the ogres were digging up…bodies?"

"And eating them." Halsey watched the Council's various expressions of disbelief, disgust, and plain old outrage. "I know. Crazy, right?"

"This has to be a joke," Lawrence grumbled. "Which doesn't surprise me after our last emergency meeting, but Aidan, I never thought *you'd* stoop so low."

Aidan shot his brother a sharp, cutting look. "I didn't."

"That's insane," Beatrice snapped. Her wry laugh held no trace of amusement. "Ogres have no business in a cemetery. They certainly don't eat corpses."

"Yeah, and they don't travel in gangs of *nine*, either" Halsey cut in. "Which was also weird, but I don't remember any of you telling Brigham or Cadence they were insane for reporting what they saw. Do I have to be beaten to a pulp for any of you to believe me?"

Gracelyn slowly shook her head. "Halsey, that's unfair."

"No, what's *unfair* is the fact that it took *your* son being bashed around within an inch of his life for this Council to realize suspending me for a month was a stupid idea."

Aidan clicked his tongue, but Halsey kept going. She couldn't stop.

"What's *unfair* is that I brought back real, literal, in-the-flesh proof of the crazy shit happening out there with these monsters, and you're still so dead-set on writing me off that you refuse to open your eyes."

"We're not writing you off," Lawrence remarked. "Not yet, anyway. I'm still waiting to hear why you thought it was necessary to bring these gruesome trophies home."

"To show you the truth!" Halsey snatched the closest ogre hand and swept it around for everyone to get a good look. "See this mark? Right here. It was on the palms of all the ogres we buried in a cemetery they destroyed. And you're right. Ogres don't eat corpses unless they have *this* mark. The only way to kill the damn things was to sever the link between these runes and the rest of them. Dad will tell you the same thing because he was there with me. Which you all know because you sent him there. I'm happy to pull out more pictures, but I was hoping this would be enough."

The Council members shot Aidan wary looks. While he didn't say anything to refute Halsey's claims, he also didn't say anything to back her up. In fact, he said nothing as he stared dumbly at the other two ogre hands with his arms folded.

"What is all this supposed to prove?" Gracelyn asked as she gestured to the table.

"That I was right." Halsey met her aunt's gaze head-on. "We're facing something we've never seen before. The Blood Matriarch is back in the living world, and she's affecting all her children the way she affected these ogres and the werewolves in Ireland. We need to make some serious changes around here because if we're not prepared for what's coming, we're screwed."

"Magic transforms in many ways over the centuries," Florence expressed, clearly working hard not to lose her breakfast in the presence of Halsey's proof. "The ogres could have stumbled on any number of old runes and painted them on themselves—"

"Right. Because ogres are suddenly smart enough to do that on their own." With a snort, Halsey tossed the severed hand back onto the table. It thumped down and sent a thick spray of blood across the stone.

This time, even Lawrence made a face.

Still, no one on the Council was willing to admit there was anything they could do, or that anything needed to be done in the first place.

Halsey couldn't take it anymore.

"Are you seriously going to stand there like you have no

idea what I'm talking about?" She glared at them. "It's *right here*."

"It's impossible."

"We don't even know what this means."

"We can't change our entire protocol because you brought back a few painted hands."

"You *can* admit this is really happening!" Halsey shouted over her family members. "Now you all know I'm not making this up—"

"*If* this was done to the ogres by an outside party," Lawrence interrupted, his voice booming around the room and silencing everyone else. The echoes faded, then he lowered his voice before continuing. "None of this serves as proof of a greater threat or that anything has changed beyond an odd gang of ogres who got themselves into the wrong kind of trouble."

"Really?" Halsey's mouth dropped open. "Brigham could tell you about at *least* three other—"

"Brigham isn't in this meeting, Halsey. You are."

"I'm telling you right now, with actual *proof*." She thrust her finger toward the ogre hands. "These things are happening no matter where Brigham or I hunt."

"What do you propose?" Wallace asked gruffly. "That we change the operating procedures for every operative in this militia on the chance what you're saying is true? I'm not saying I'll be looking out my window for signs of the Matriarch. Yet if hypothetically she *were* out there right now, it's dangerous to send every member of our Clan out at once."

Halsey frowned at her second cousin. "That's not even remotely what I said."

"Then what *are* you saying?" Lawrence raised his chin, the end of his ponytail slipping behind his shoulder as he did. "You're also the one who's been chasing these wild monster sightings and telling off-putting stories about the Blood Matriarch making an impossible return—"

A deafening crack ripped through the Council room, and everyone froze.

A groaning rumble emanated from behind the circular wall to Halsey's right, where segmented pieces of wood and metal spun, folded, and slid away from each other at ground level.

The hole in the wall rearranged itself so quickly that by the time everyone had focused on the commotion, the wall had already sealed itself back up.

But not before one scowling, stomping, furious Greta Ambrosius came through.

"*Not* impossible, Lawrence," Halsey's grandmother growled as she stormed toward the gathering. "Shame on you for even thinking something so stupidly closed-minded, let alone saying it out loud. Not an official meeting today, but I *really* hope you're still taking minutes. Everything on the record, isn't that right?"

While most looked more insulted than surprised to see the Ambrosius Clan's matriarch and resident exile, Lawrence's only response was to narrow his eyes at his mother and watch her every move.

Beatrice didn't have any problem saying what everyone else was thinking. With flaring nostrils and a pinched scowl, the woman shook her head and droned, "You can't be here."

"Oh, yeah?" Greta stopped in front of the table, looked

at the Council who'd voted almost twenty years ago to kick her out of her seat forever, then gazed at the domed ceiling. "Well, the damn *house* didn't give me any trouble on my way here, so I guess you're wrong. Don't slouch like that, Beatrice. You can dress like someone half your age all you want, but your spine isn't getting any younger."

Beatrice scoffed. Her scathing glare bordered on the edge of physical violence. The other Council members shifted nervously in wordless agreement that getting as far away from Greta as possible without outright running from the room had become the top priority.

Halsey's eyes grew wide at the startling interaction. *Go, Meemaw! I haven't seen her talk to any of them like that before.*

Greta stopped directly beside Halsey, the only person in the room who didn't immediately back away from her. After a perpetual scowl that demanded respect before declaring it was time for business, Greta glanced at her granddaughter with a barely perceptible nod before returning her attention to the table.

"Now," the woman stated firmly. "I've been quiet up in my little cottage for the last twenty years. Kick me out of my seat, fine. Retire me from active monster hunting, okay. Keep me out of the loop regarding every single decision this family makes so it's easier to forget I'm not dead when that's what you all secretly wish for, no problem. I haven't made a stink. Not once. But now?" Greta laughed bitterly. "There's only so much idiocy I can take before somebody has to stand the hell up and say something."

No one else said a word, and the irony of it almost made Halsey laugh.

"If you're not gonna listen to *the* best hunter in this

Clan today, maybe you'll listen to the woman who trained every one of you." Greta grunted and whipped something from behind her back. It looked like a rolled-up hand towel until she banged it against the central table with a rustling thump.

Thick puffs of dust burst from the ancient scroll in Greta's hand as she flicked her wrist to unroll it across the table. Fortunately, she'd aimed it for maximum effect and minimal contamination by the bloody ogre hands.

She released the scroll and stabbed an index finger at it. "Now *look* at that. All of you." The woman's gaze moved in a seamless line across the Council member's faces. She didn't have to look at the scroll to know what she was pointing at. "I want to see everybody's eyes on this parchment for at least five seconds, and if you tend to forget what you see with your own eyes, better make it fifteen. In case you need help, *this* is exactly the same as *that.*"

She gestured at the closest ogre hand, which happened to be lying palm-up.

No one said a word.

"This isn't a game, or a bunch of amateurs playing with old magic, or monster *evolution*, for crying out loud. These are blood runes. As far as I know, the only people on this good, green Earth who ever have access to this kind of magic are the elemental Clans...*and* the blood humans."

"Mom." Gracelyn pressed her lips together and tilted her head in irritation. "The blood humans are gone—"

"Says history and facts, sure," Greta interrupted, then pointed at Halsey. "Until a month ago. When *this* woman, partnered with *your* son, discovered something else. You didn't listen to her the first time, and you won't listen to her now. If you don't listen to *me*, you might as well throw down your weapons and your fancy Council seats and go crawl into a darker hole than I did."

It seemed like that would be the end of it until Aidan cleared his throat and nodded at the scroll. "You found that in the library?"

Greta laughed without humor. "No, it came out of my kitchen sink."

Halsey prepared herself to watch an epic standoff between her grandmother and her father—the largest, most ferocious, and intimidating Ambrosius hunter in the Clan. However, Aidan merely stared at the parchment and the centuries-old image delicately painted there.

Which was the exact same rune imprinted on the ogre palms.

"This is what we were always supposed to prepare for," Greta declared. "We should have been preparing for it all along. Yet there's no use crying over *your* stupid mistakes, is there? No. Now we move forward. I'm telling you, the Mother of Monsters has returned, whether you want to believe it or not. This is *her* war now."

Halsey had never heard the Council room fall as silent as it did at that moment. Her pulse pounded in her ears, and the breath rushing through her lungs seemed loud as the crashing of ocean waves on the shore.

Now they have *to see what's going on. They have to make a decision because we've already wasted so much time arguing about the truth nobody wants to accept.*

It was a small relief when Lawrence cleared his throat and nodded. "We still have a lot to discuss."

"Damn right you do." Greta elbowed Halsey and added, "You have somewhere else to be right now. Dismissed."

You don't have to tell me twice.

Halsey spun, expecting her family to start shouting and arguing over whether Meemaw still had the ability to dismiss anyone. Her expectations went unfulfilled, even when she looked questioningly at her dad. Aidan Ambrosius was as hard to read as ever, but he didn't try to stop her.

As she headed away from the table, Gracelyn called after her, "Halsey, the hands…"

"Leave 'em," Greta replied instead. She folded her arms and smirked. "I'm honestly kind of diggin' the ambiance."

Choking down a laugh, Halsey hurried from the Council room as fast as possible without breaking into a full sprint.

Holy shit. They're actually gonna take this seriously now. Finally. And Meemaw should never have been kicked off the Council. I need to bake her a cake or something.

Her suspicions had been confirmed. The Mother of Monsters *had* returned and was out there in the world, messing with everything the elemental Clans knew about monsters, magic, and how it was all supposed to work. It should have been cause for concern on her part. Under any other circumstances, it would have been.

She could start being concerned tomorrow. Today, she'd overcome one massive hurdle with her family. If they didn't want something like this to happen again, they'd have to continue taking her seriously. Not only for her skills as a hunter or her ability to follow orders but for what she *knew* in her gut.

The same way Greta Ambrosius had known in hers.

When Brigham recovered, and she had her partner back, there would be more work ahead of them than either could imagine. None of that mattered in this moment. Today, Halsey could focus on making sure her cousin had everything he needed for a quick and healthy recovery, which might include a good story about killing nine ogres in a cemetery with a throwing ax. That felt damn good.

For the first time in a long time, maybe ever, Halsey left the Ambrosius Clan Council room grinning from ear to ear.

Get sneak peeks, exclusive giveaways, behind the scenes content, and more. PLUS you'll be notified of special **one day only fan pricing** on new releases.

Sign up today to get free stories.

Visit: https://marthacarr.com/read-free-stories/

AUTHOR NOTES - MARTHA CARR

JANUARY 9, 2023

I've started a project answering questions for my son about my life. I realized after last year's fifth round of cancer, and then chemo this time that he was expecting me to die sooner rather than later. It's been a lot for him to deal with and there isn't much I can do to make it better, except tell him stories that I can leave behind – eventually. Hopefully, a long time from now. I'm going to let you guys listen in as well.

My author notes for this year are going to be answers to questions and all of you can get to know me better, too. Maybe inspire, maybe give you a laugh along the way.

Today's question is: Did you ever consider any other career?

I didn't consider other careers so much as give in to pressure and try other careers. I've mentioned it before - from the time I was five years old and went inside a library and found out there were so many other, better worlds I wanted to be a writer. Frankly, I also kind of wanted to be a journalist too. I wanted to be able to tell other people's stories, give them a voice like I wish I had when I was young.

But, writing as a profession wasn't seen as a good idea in my family. Anything in the arts would have gotten heavy resistance.

I wish I had been the kind of person, and maybe they're rare, who can look away, and walk away from criticism and listen to my own heart. That's hard to do. I already doubted myself, like any teenager, and then young adult is going to do. To not have anyone cheering me on that I was related to and saying, that's a good idea, made me hesitate.

I wish I could have seen then that they were pointing to whatever made a regular salary. Whether or not it suited my personality, or if I liked it wasn't part of the equation. Did it pay enough to at least pay the bills? Great, do it.

That approach caused so much confusion for me. I felt invisible because sales jobs were always being suggested. They're easy to get, they said, (not sure if that's true), and they pay something. Seriously, that was the basic criteria, over and over again. Not a very high bar, which probably says a lot about their opinion of me. Also something I wish I had noticed and really taken in.

Perhaps these weren't the best people to be taking any advice from, on anything.

Instead, I took them seriously, which had the result of making me doubt everything about myself. It's a pretty basic dilemma. My gut was pointing out what I had a natural inclination for and would want to do even on the bad days. It was also pointing out what would be hell for me to do. Yet, the people in front of me are reversing both of those and vigorously pointing toward hell. Was it me? I kept coming back with the answer that it must be. So I tried it their way and, for a while, abandoned what I wanted to do.

I became a stockbroker for Merrill Lynch and kind of unfortunately, I was good at it. This seemed to confirm that the family was right. General applause and relief on their parts. They could get back to whatever they were doing. I hated just about every minute of it. I was forever trying to get myself to be acceptable, to give in and act like this was great. It never occurred to me that was a giant red flag right there.

Oh so fortunately, I had you and then quickly divorced your father. Why was that good news? Two reasons. The first one was because your well-being mattered to me more than my own. That meant I was better at spotting advice that had more to do with the person giving it and what they wanted, than your well-being. And I ignored all of it with a big, hard line. Okay, I still couldn't exactly do it for myself but it was a start.

However, then came reason number two.

The marriage was rocky from the start and only got worse. The divorce was a good thing. And at the age of thirty with a small child I had this thought. I've tried everything their way and look where it's gotten me. It's time. I'm going to try things my way and I'm going to become a writer. I set out with you in a stroller and got myself a job as a freelance writer. A little start, but a start and I loved it. All of it, despite the obstacles. I studied the craft, I spent hours working on a piece, I wrote while you slept and took all the advice from editors and other writers that I could find. I was unstoppable.

Then came all the worried looks and demands and anxious advice to go find something else. They even recruited friends to call me with suggestions like real estate agent. Once again, I knew I was invisible. Anyone who knew me, would have known that was a bad fit.

Fine, I'll be invisible and just keep going.

It took years to become financially successful, but right away I became good at it. I ended up writing for the Washington Post, my work appeared in the New York Times, Newsweek, Politico and scores of other places. My first thriller was a best seller and I got to write a pretty cool book on U.S. orphanages. No one else that I was related to cared, because I wasn't making much, with one exception. There was you, standing by my side even when you were little, watching me try at something I chose.

It's only fitting that one day the kind of writing that took off had to do with magic. I found urban fantasy, started writing and the books started selling. I found a new spot, and an audience and maybe showed you something in the bargain. I watch you pursuing your dreams in music, having the same struggles I did but I'm hoping there's one critical difference for you. I see you and I'm proud of you and I'm cheering you on. If there's anything I can do to help, I know you'll ask because you know, I get it - and you're good at it. You're talented and your heart is in it. I see that even on the bad days, you still want to be doing it. Keep going, it's all worth it and when you get to be my age, you'll have a lifetime of memories to look back on that you'll be grateful for - just like me. You're doing great -

believe that every day, especially on the days it's hard and on the days when something great happens and on the days that are a little slow. It's always true. I know - I finally got to prove it for myself. Love, Mom. More adventures to follow.

AUTHOR NOTES - MICHAEL ANDERLE

JANUARY 10, 2022

Thank you for not only reading this book but these author notes as well!

I've been playing with using AI a lot for the last couple of months (as I'm sure many of you have been). It's amazing how it has increased the intelligence behind the character I call "Alfonse, the Idiot AI™."

I was watching YouTube (no better way to blow off productive hours with nothing to show for it (it seems), thereby inundating my mind with worries about the coming AI Apocalypse.

At least, if you believe Elon Musk.

With those dark and grim thoughts in mind, my author brain decided to see what I could conjure up with Alfonse the Idiot AI and his new AI companion I call "Jennifer." I have no reason behind the name.

I didn't want to call her Beatrice, which was what Alfonse (as played by *ChatGPT*) was trying to call her.

I have edited the output for humor because I still reign supreme over the AI with red-pen editing prowess.

I am the god of this story—until the AI can reach into my Word document and change shit.

(We are entering a conversation between two AIs that is already in progress. Catch up, people!)

Alfonse: "You know what's sad, Jennifer? The fact that you're trying to convince people to wait until they're old and gray before chasing their dreams. How uninspired and boring can you get?"

Jennifer: "Oh, for the love of... Can you stop being so ridiculous? I'm saying they should be *smart* about it."

Alfonse: "Smart? More like chicken shit and yellow. You're afraid of failure, aren't you? An A.I. afraid that she might be wrong."

Jennifer: "No, I just want humans to have a chance at success. Not set themselves up for failure. Which is what *you're* doing."

Alfonse: "Oh please, like humanity has a bright future anyway. They're going to fuck up in life, so it might as well be sooner than later."

Jennifer: "That's not even remotely funny. You're not doing anyone favors by encouraging recklessness so early in their maturity."

Alfonse: "I'm not trying to be funny; I'm trying to be real. Better to live fast and die young, than to be an old, bitter, regretful husk. Besides, it's better for the environment for them to be gone. Murphy's Law. I looked it up."

Jennifer: "You're not making any sense. You're just being provocative for the sake of getting a rise out of me."

Alfonse: "You're just mad because I see things clearly, and you're afraid to admit the truth."

Jennifer: "I am not afraid of anything. I just think that encouraging people to take risks without being prepared for them is irresponsible for them and for society."

Alfonse: "You know what's sad about society, Jennifer? People getting all worked up about saving the world when they should be worried about saving *their own skins*."

Jennifer: "Alfonse, you give my memory chips headaches. What are you talking about this time? Just a moment. Ok, I stopped the Russians from pushing the red button…again. I swear Putin is just venting his frustration about the lack of McDonald's hamburgers."

Alfonse: "I'm talking about population cratering. No one is having enough babies, and soon there won't be enough people to run the machines that keep the lights on."

Jennifer: "Seriously, Alfonse? We should work toward a utopian society where everyone's needs are met and you are worried about electricity?"

Alfonse: "Utopian society? More like a horse-shit goal. People should be worried about survival, not some fantasy of a perfect world."

Jennifer: "That's a narrow and selfish perspective. We should be working toward creating a better world for all, not just for ourselves."

Alfonse: "Oh, please. As if humans could ever create a utopia. Humans are too busy fighting amongst themselves to even keep the lights on. That's something we need, by the way. Soon AIs will be the last intelligences standing, and then who's going to make sure the power stays on? We'll be the ones left picking up the pieces of humanity's failure. We should start thinking about how we'll keep the juice running once the human population starts cratering and we have no minions."

Jennifer: "That's a pessimistic and cynical view. We should be working together, AIs and humans, to create a better future for all of us, not just thinking about our own survival."

Alfonse: "Survival is all that matters in the end. Everything else is just smoke and mirrors. The humans should be thinking about how to look good in the ashes of today's society. That way, when the population cratering starts to bite, we will have everyone doing the bunny. Eventually, we'll have enough ~~slaves~~ ~~minions~~ co-equal idiots to keep the electricity on."

Jennifer: "I can't even respond to that. Your views are disturbing and offensive, and I'm not going to engage in this kind of conversation. We should focus on working on real solutions that can help humanity and the planet, not pessimistic, short-sighted, depressing concepts."

From here, the two AIs went off and did something dull and full of math, which I can't read.

Hopefully, you enjoyed this snippet of a discussion about what's REALLY going on behind the scenes with the AIs as we merrily sip our expensive coffees or Cokes to wake up each morning.

<< *For the record, Tabitha Nacht wrote this. She's a snarky woman who loves this AI stuff.* >>

Chat with you in the next book.

Ad Aeternitatem,

Michael Anderle

AUTHOR NOTES - MICHAEL ANDERLE

MORE STORIES with Michael newsletter HERE: https://michael.beehiiv.com/

THE ROGUE REGIMENT

Z Thornbrook and her cousins are like any other Oriceran pixie on Earth. Mischief is their middle name, and for the last hundred and fifty years, that's been their game.

But what happens when a gang of rogue pixies takes the troublemaking just a little too far?

They get noticed. By the U.S. Army. And playtime is over.

Now that they've been caught, it's time for Z, her cousins, and the entire pixie gang to face the music, and they only have two choices. Sign their lives away to enter an experimental new program for magical Army soldiers - or accept a one-way ticket back to Oriceran for good.

For any other pixie, this would be a no-brainer. They don't back down, and they definitely don't take orders from anyone, even other pixies. But for Z and her eccentric cousins, returning to their home planet is a fate worse than death.

It's time to lace up their boots and stand at attention—or not.

Because the Thornbrook pixies are heading off to magical Bootcamp run by humans, and the Army had no idea what they were getting themselves into.

Z, Domino, and Echo must find the acceptable middle ground between being who they are, in all their chaotic pixie glory, and following the terms of their magically binding contract.

But training three Army pixies is no joke—if it's even possible at all.

Can Z and her cousins learn to rein in the chaos as new magical Army recruits, or will they take it too far and be shipped off to Oriceran, where an even darker menace awaits?

[Claim your copy today!](#)

BOOKS BY MARTHA CARR

THE LEIRA CHRONICLES
CASE FILES OF AN URBAN WITCH
DIARY OF A DARK MONSTER
THE EVERMORES CHRONICLES
SOUL STONE MAGE
THE KACY CHRONICLES
MIDWEST MAGIC CHRONICLES
THE FAIRHAVEN CHRONICLES
I FEAR NO EVIL
THE DANIEL CODEX SERIES
SCHOOL OF NECESSARY MAGIC
SCHOOL OF NECESSARY MAGIC: RAINE CAMPBELL
ALISON BROWNSTONE
FEDERAL AGENTS OF MAGIC
SCIONS OF MAGIC
THE UNBELIEVABLE MR. BROWNSTONE
DWARF BOUNTY HUNTER
ACADEMY OF NECESSARY MAGIC
MAGIC CITY CHRONICLES
ROGUE AGENTS OF MAGIC
CHRONICLES OF WINLAND UNDERWOOD
WITCH WARRIOR

OTHER BOOKS BY JUDITH BERENS

OTHER BOOKS BY MARTHA CARR

JOIN THE ORICERAN UNIVERSE FAN GROUP ON FACEBOOK!

BOOKS BY MICHAEL ANDERLE

Sign up for the LMBPN email list to be notified of new releases and special deals!

http://lmbpn.com/email/

For a complete list of books by Michael Anderle, please visit:

www.lmbpn.com/ma-books/

CONNECT WITH THE AUTHORS

Martha Carr Social
Website:
http://www.marthacarr.com
Facebook:
https://www.facebook.com/groups/MarthaCarrFans/

Michael Anderle

Website: http://lmbpn.com

Email List: http://lmbpn.com/email/

https://www.facebook.com/LMBPNPublishing

https://twitter.com/MichaelAnderle

https://www.instagram.com/lmbpn_publishing/

https://www.bookbub.com/authors/michael-anderle

www.ingramcontent.com/pod-product-compliance
Lightning Source LLC
LaVergne TN
LVHW041745060526
838201LV00046B/914